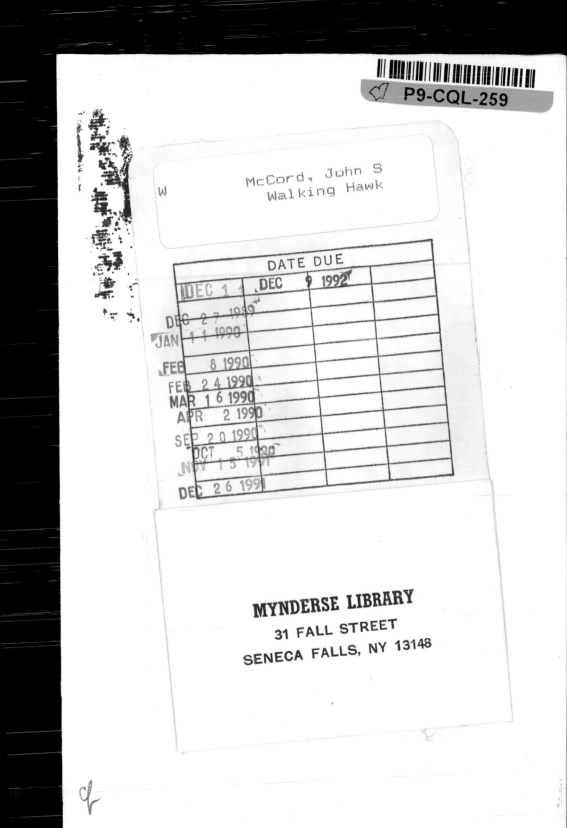

MYNDERSE LIBRARY

31 FALL STREET

SENECA FALLS, NY 13148

WALKING HAWK

WALKING HAWK

JOHN S. McCORD

A DOUBLE D WESTERN
DOUBLEDAY
NEW YORK LONDON TORONTO SYDNEY AUCKLAND

A Double D Western
Published by Bantam Doubleday Dell Publishing Group, Inc.
666 Fifth Avenue, New York, New York 10103

A Double D Western and the portrayal of the letters DD are trademarks
of Doubleday, a division of Bantam Doubleday Dell Publishing Group, Inc.

Library of Congress Cataloging-in-Publication Data

McCord, John S.
Walking Hawk/John S. McCord.— 1st ed.
p.   cm.—(A Double D Western)
I. Title.
PS3563.C34439W35   1989
813'.54—dc20   89-32039
CIP

ISBN 0-385-26263-9
Copyright © 1989 by John S. McCord
All Rights Reserved
Printed in the United States of America
November 1989
First Edition
OG

*To Joan, who tended to everything else
while I was timing my labor pains with this*

*And to the DFW Writers' Workshop,
artfully concealed in Bedford, Texas*

WALKING HAWK

I

He watched the scene below, his body relaxed in the saddle. The sound of gunfire had briefly echoed and rattled through the quiet of the early morning, but the fight was over now. There were only two wagons, and the warriors had already emptied the contents of one onto the ground and were now moving toward the other. He could hear the derisive, wild cries and laughter as one of the war party wrapped a dress around his greased body and minced around, cruelly mimicking the walk of white women.

He didn't think there had been trouble with Indians in these parts for years, but Dan Walker wasn't certain. He had been riding alone for weeks, and he had only a vague idea about where he was. He hadn't ridden this way since he was a child, but the thinly settled Montana Territory of 1885 was slow to change.

The Indian half of him was filled with contempt for the white men who had been so stupidly unaware and careless. Their bodies were sprawled in plain sight, both of them, limp in that peculiar, awkward manner that meant death. Dan was in a perfect position to see everything. His horses stood on a small wooded knoll only fifty yards from the wagons. The chopped ground under his animals indicated that this was the spot where the Indians had waited to launch their surprise attack.

Dan felt his lips curl in a harsh sneer. It was none of his affair. Men without sense deserved no help from him or anybody else. A man could get into a lot of painful trouble trying to help someone that stupid. Dan had been riding long and hard to leave his last load of trouble behind; he wasn't looking for a new one. Besides, it was too late—nobody could help dead men.

Only an involuntary flick of eyelids indicated his surprise when a series of shots sent all four of the Indians dodging and rolling for cover. One brave lay squirming on the ground while the other three bounded back to their feet and leaped into the second wagon. They dragged a small figure, kicking and screaming, out from under the wagon cover. A big warrior's fist silenced the screaming and stopped the struggle.

The warrior held the already limp little figure with one hand. As his arm rose to strike a second time, Dan's bullet caught the Indian full in the chest. He staggered back and then stood woodenly, looking down and clutching at the wound with both hands. Dan operated the lever of the Winchester with the fluid ease of long practice. The echoes of the roll of shots gradually faded away. The other two braves had reacted instantly, but they had no chance to avoid such deadly short-range fire. The big brave still stood on trembling legs, dazedly holding his chest. Dan shot him again.

Dan felt the sneer deepen on his face. He didn't remember drawing the saddle gun from its buckskin sheath, didn't remember deciding to intervene. "What the hell, that's just a kid down there. That makes things different," he mumbled to himself. He could hear the sheepish tone of his own voice. Then he thought, Four can't be all. I bought myself grief again, as sure as Hell's too hot.

His hands worked as if they had their own eyes, shoving shells into the repeater while his gaze remained on the downed Indians. Then, just as the small figure started to move and try to sit up, Dan carefully and coldly shot twice more into each of the sprawled warriors. He reloaded again and searched all around with narrowed, suspicious eyes. His lips moved with the words as he thought, A cautious man is a smart man. A cautious man would ride back through those woods and get clean away from here fast. A smart man wouldn't ride out on that open ground. He growled to himself as he urged his horses from the woods toward the wagons. *Dan, you're a disappointment to me.*

His big red horse at an easy lope and the gray packhorse following, he snared the reins of the best of the Indian horses before easing over to the wagons. His head turning in smooth arcs, scanning the area, he dropped the reins in front of the kid. Without looking at him, Dan said, "Mount up."

"But all my stuff is in the wagons. I can't just leave everything. What about my men?"

Dan didn't lower his eyes from his inspection of the surrounding terrain or allow a flicker of expression to cross his face. The kid looked big enough to have good sense. If he didn't, then a lot of talk would change nothing. Those Indians had to be part of a larger party. This was no time to stand around debating with an idiot child. Dan said, "Adios," and started back to the cover of the woods.

"Wait for me. I'm coming." The voice was high, strained with anger.

Dan didn't slow his pace or look back. That's better. His lips only formed the unspoken words. The kid was a little slow in the head, but he wasn't a drooling lunatic.

He kept climbing. He just felt better to be high up when there was trouble coming after him. But he was disgusted with both himself and the kid. He'd let that boy draw him into something that was none of his business. It irritated him so much that he didn't keep a cool head. He should have taken time for a closer look at those Indians. It always helped to know who you were up against. Forgot to break up their weapons, too. Serve me right, he thought, if I get myself shot with a gun I should've busted on a wagon wheel.

The sky was falling down on them, dark, gray, mean-looking. Night was coming on fast. An early blizzard, a "squaw winter," was almost blasting him off the trail. The wind was sharp enough to shave with, loaded with icy rain mixed with sleet. This was bad and looking to get worse. Dan was fully aware of the deadly challenge such sudden, unexpected storms presented to a mountain man.

The dangers involved in getting caught up this high were ugly to think about, but he was going still higher. He was running into the teeth of a brutal wind to get away from Indians who might not even be after him. And he was burdened with a tenderfoot kid about to fall off his horse. Right now all Dan wanted to do was avoid leaving a trail and find a place to get warm.

He was running for the high mountains again. Dan figured that no man alive could find him if he was in high country. He had been driving the horses hard, jumping out of the saddle and running beside Big Red whenever there was room on the trail. He was going to make the kid run, too, but one look told him it was no use. Soft! The kid was struggling just to stay on his horse. Now Dan was worn out himself, just plain used up.

Snow started blowing straight across his line of vision. Dan walked up a trail along a narrow ridge. He had a feeling; a little voice somewhere said, "You've been here. Look around, this is familiar country." Coming over a crest, Dan looked down into a narrow valley, mountains rising steeply on both sides. Did he know this place?

Cold, oh God, how the cold was draining away his strength. The wind found him any way he turned. Gave that dumb, blue-faced kid his sheepskin, and now he was the one turning blue under an old blanket. Meddling, simple-minded meddling, had gotten him into this bind. Saddled with this kid, he couldn't make speed. He should have been holed up in a warm place by now, not out in a wind that was cutting out his heart and sucking his breath away.

He remembered when he was starting to get too big for his britches, reaching out toward manhood. Suddenly, that giant with the bush of red beard reached out and grabbed him, picked him up like he was a bundle of sticks, and carried him over to the huge rocking chair in front of the fireplace. Struggle was useless against that enormous man with muscles as hard as rock; he was trapped in his father's lap, as helpless as if he were four years old again.

That rumbling, laughing voice said, "Getting to be a big man, are you? Well, son, just remember that being manly means doing the manly thing all the time, no exceptions. It means doing what you feel is right in your heart. If you don't, your heart will be weak and unhappy, and it will fail you when you need it most. When the going gets hard, you'll fall down and cry while the men with happy hearts keep going."

Suddenly, Dan's head snapped up. What was he doing? He couldn't stand here and dream in the teeth of a killer wind. Get down into that valley, that was it. Get down there where the wind was broken by the sharp mountains on each side. Find a place to build a fire.

The trail sloped downward at last. Dan turned back. He was going to say, "Hang on, young'un, just a little more and we'll have a chance." The Indian pony was there, but the kid was gone!

There was something familiar about the valley ahead. Was there a narrow cave at the edge of that cliff? When had he seen this lonesome, high valley? Suddenly, like waking again from a dream, he realized that he was standing alone on the high trail. The horses had gone on. Why was he standing here? He had been walking to rest his horse and to try to get warm. He'd forgotten something—that slow kid. Not a word from him during the whole ride. A fighter, even if he was little. That kid had gotten himself an Indian. He'd done better than the two grown men with him had. Where was that boy?

There he was. Dan hadn't gone twenty steps before the small shape was visible on the trail, with a dark mark in the snow where he had slid after falling off the horse. Dan bent stiffly, grabbed, caught something, and started dragging the kid along. He started laughing. "Dumb tenderfoot. Fell off the damn horse on a downslope. Come on, kid. Down we go." Laughing like a fool, he slipped, rammed against the cliff, and spun down on the seat of his pants.

Wearily, he wiped his face and looked, astonished, at the bloodstains on his hands. "Must've banged my head." The words sounded slurred to his ears, but the words in his head were clear and harsh: "You're dying. Make a fire, quick."

He looked back up the trail. Hell, the kid was right there, not four or five steps away. Dan struggled back up to the small form. He reached down, but his hand wouldn't work, couldn't get a grip on the kid's coat. Hands didn't work. Got to get him up.

Using his numb hands like scoops, he got the kid against his chest, holding him in his arms. Damn! Heavy as hell and as limp as a wet rag. Now, go down. Walk. Walk will make warm.

The gray shied and spun around when Dan staggered against its rump. The horses had stopped beside a wall of rock, protected from the wind. Suddenly, Dan's mind was clear again. There was a cave, just around the bend. He tried to throw the kid across the saddle. The little limp body kept sliding off. Not far now.

He kept falling down, and the rocky trail kept banging new sore places all over him. It didn't seem so cold anymore. Like a sharp pin, an inner voice jabbed him, "When it's cold but doesn't feel cold, you're dying." Something inside Dan rose up in anger. He mumbled, "I'm not going to die like this. By God, somebody'll have to kill me."

That old cave was right there in front of him now. He half-staggered, half-crawled in with the horses following. Wood, stacked along the side of the cave, beckoned like a dream of warm fires. In the center of the cave, a pile of kindling and dry grass waited. Dan crouched, trying to dig out his flint and steel. His hands wouldn't do anything. They were numb, as if he were dead already.

The horses started and wheeled, eyes wide and white, when Dan started his weird dance. "Oh, ha, ha, ha. Whoa, ha, ha, ha." Dan spun around like a demented drunk, crashing against the walls, staggering against the nervous horses, his hands in his armpits under his coat, shouting and chanting to imaginary drums in a frantic effort to warm himself.

At last, he dropped to his knees and tried again. His hands were still numb, but they worked. Sparks flew and tinder ignited. He had a fire! "Come here, you dumb kid!" he shouted as the fire rose, warming the cave. Dan reeled over to the prostrate form and dragged it closer to the blaze. With tingling hands he pulled off boots and rubbed the small feet, but he kept pitching forward on his face. Blood from the cuts on his forehead kept running into his eyes while he massaged the limp little hands. "Ain't gonna lose no fingers," he sang with a hoarse, dull voice. "Ain't gonna lose no toes."

Snow and ice began melting from the kid's clothing and running onto the rock floor. Dan curled the little body half around the fire. Then, grinding his teeth with the effort, he crawled to the wall of the cave. He walked up the wall with his hands till he was on his feet, then tottered over to his big red horse. He fought the knot until it finally released his bedroll, then fumbled with it till it dropped to the rock floor. Trying to bend to pick it up, he fell again. Anger came to him like an inner fire. "Damn! I gotta quit that fallin' down. That hurts."

Again on his feet, and working better with the spreading warmth in the cave from the horses and the fire, he jerked the saddle off of Big Red and the pack from the gray. He slipped the bridles from all three horses and rubbed them down with his only dry shirt. Then he weaved his way back to the fire and shouted, "Off with'em, kid. Off with those wet clothes."

He sat next to the motionless form, pulled it to a sitting position beside him, and stripped off the heavy, wet sheepskin. The boy's hat, smashed down tight over his ears, finally slipped off, revealing a mane of blond hair. Blinking eyes that wouldn't focus, Dan mumbled, "Need a haircut, dumb kid." He started to rip open the wet shirt, looked down, then looked up into wide blue eyes, and said, "Aw . . . aw, hell, . . . dumb kid." Dan's head rolled back, and his wind-scoured eyes closed. He had never felt so beaten down. He just needed a minute or two to catch his breath. Damn, it felt good to be warm.

He opened his eyes slowly. He felt that he had slept too long. Old habit ruled him; he looked around as much as he could without moving his head, just like his Iroquois mother had taught him. Everything was quiet; he could hear the soft crackle of the fire. He shifted gently, as if stirring in his sleep, his eyes narrow slits as he looked around.

He was under a blanket. He didn't recall covering himself. He held the trigger down so his pistol wouldn't click when he cocked it. He jerked to a sitting position and flipped the blanket away. The sudden movement hurt him so much that a sharp grunt of pain escaped his lips before he could cut it off. The cold had crept into his battered body from the rock floor despite the fire and the blanket.

Dan hurt all over, like he had been stomped by a herd of cattle. His face stung like it had been rubbed with sand. The skin on his hands and feet felt tight and dry.

Something or somebody had taken away the kid's body, added wood to the fire, and covered Dan with a blanket. A chill raced up his back, and he felt like he couldn't breathe. His mother's stories of the spirits in the high mountains held him rigid. He could see his gun barrel jumping in time with his pounding heart.

A soft sound of movement jerked him around, gun moving back and forth as he searched for a target. Then he saw a long dark shape outlined on the lighter color of the stone floor in the shadows. Slowly, keeping his gun trained on that vague shape, he got to his feet.

A trembling voice came from the shadows. "What're you doing?"

It was the kid's voice. Dan could feel the muscles in his legs jerking out of control. His knees were trying to buckle under him, and he could hear his own sobbing breath. "Come out! Come on out in the light!"

"All right. I'm coming. What's wrong? You're not going to shoot me for using your bedroll, are you? I was cold. I put a blanket over you." The shadow moved slowly, stood up, and walked into the light.

Dan moved forward, the gun barrel lowering. He stretched out a long arm and touched the warm face. The words burst out of him. "You're alive!"

"Why, of course I am, thanks to you. Why are you acting so surprised?"

Dan felt as weak as water. He backed away and sank down on the blanket. "I thought you were dead, you dumb kid. I saw all that dried blood on your shirt and your eyes all fixed lookin'. I just figured I broke my back getting you away, and you up and died on me."

Head bowed, the kid said in a low voice, "That's Jed's blood. Jed was hit bad. He fell against me when he shoved me back down into the wagon. He was trying to hide me."

"You ain't hurt then? Not at all?"

"Just my mouth and my ears. That Indian hit me on the chin. Jammed my jaw back. Hurts under my ears."

Dan snickered. "You'll live. Build up that fire some. Bacon, skillet, coffee, and stuff are in the pack over yonder. I'm going to look around. Make yourself useful while I'm gone." He shrugged himself into his still damp sheepskin, picked up his rifle, and eased out to the mouth of the cave.

When he looked out, he was surprised to find that only about an inch of snow lay on the ground, and it was melting quickly. He was also a little shaken to see that it was almost full daylight. They had found the cave by last light. That meant that he had slept all night. He hadn't done that since he was a little boy. His mother wouldn't have liked that a bit. He had long ago formed the habit to be up and about, listening and looking, every two or three hours. He must have been at the end of his rope to lie flat through the whole night. He was lucky he didn't wake up to find his throat cut.

He stayed in the shadows at the mouth of the cave, sitting on his heels while he patiently looked at every inch of ground he could see. He started up close and moved his gaze back and forth, searching the terrain in strips, focusing farther away with each swing of his eyes. A soft Iroquois voice echoed in his mind: *Always look at the ground closest first —a close enemy is more dangerous than a far one.*

Only a few small trees grew in the narrow little valley to obstruct his view. Lush grass with speckles of fall flowers had absorbed and hidden the light layer of snow except for irregular patches clearly visible on the flat rocks. A stream, only a couple of feet wide and three or four inches deep, cut through the center of the valley, chuckling over five or six low waterfalls until it vanished at the lower end. Dan vaguely remembered coming here as a child. Only three or four acres, the valley was usually used only for an overnight camp since its graze was quickly exhausted by the horses. There was only one trail for men on horseback, which made the valley easy to defend but made escape equally difficult.

He flinched when a hand dropped on his shoulder. "Damn, kid, you got up on me, didn't you? You got a fine, light foot on you."

"Come eat, if you're ready."

Dan carefully moved away from the cave opening and walked back to the fire. He was surprised to find that the kid had found his sourdough and had made pan biscuits. Coffee was steaming beside the fire, and the skillet was full of crisp bacon. The kid had done pretty good considering there wasn't much to work with. Dan's tin plate lay on his folded blanket by the fire. "You eat already?"

"No, I figured I'd eat what you left."

Dan laughed. "Come on, you take half on this plate. I'll eat from the skillet. Don't ever eat after me, kid, 'cause I don't ever leave nothin'."

He was almost finished with his meal when the thought came to him. It hadn't been smart for him to snicker when the kid told about his jaw being sore. If he had been an Indian kid, that little fellow would be considered a full man, a warrior. He had been in a battle, and he had killed an enemy or, at least, wounded one. "Hell, that was a big Indian for a little twig like you. I saw that. He hit you a real lick, one good enough to drop a heavy man. How old are you, kid?"

"Eighteen."

Dan turned his head away and rubbed his hand across his face to conceal a grin. He figured that about fourteen, probably less, was more likely.

"How old are you?" asked the kid.

"I'm seventy-two," he responded with a straight face. "I don't hold with it, but if you're going to start a lying contest, I'll try to play. It's a dumb kid game though, and it might get to be a bad habit if you don't grow out of it."

The kid gave him a funny look. "You never told me your name."

"I'm loaded down with names. Daniel Webster Walker, Junior is my name on the white man's side of the street. Walking Hawk is my name when I'm on the Indian side."

"How do you do, Mr. Walker. My name is—"

"I already know your name."

"You do? How?"

" 'Cause I gave it to you. Fits you perfect in hard times, and that's the best test for a name."

"What name did you give me?"

"Your first name is Dumb. Your last name is Kid. Dumb Kid. It's got a fine ring to it, don't it?"

The kid didn't laugh, just hid behind a poker face. Maybe this little fellow needed more careful treatment. He had a good straight-at-you look. Dan was beginning to have a good feeling about him.

"Look, I was just fooling around. I didn't mean to make you mad. Everybody teases you when you're small. It's just in fun." Dan put his hand on the kid's shoulder and felt him draw away. Dan dropped his hand at once and turned to the cave mouth. "I better go take another look."

About fifteen minutes later, a hand touched his shoulder again. Dan looked back with a grin and accepted his steaming tin cup. "You would've got to me again, but I could smell the coffee. Little work and you would make a proper scout, kid, no foolin'." The grin on the little fellow's face made Dan feel good. Maybe he was over his touchy mood.

Dan settled his back against the rock wall. It was wonderful what food and a night's sleep could do for a man. He was sore and stiff, but he felt pretty good.

His eyes were still occupied with his patient vigil, but his voice was quietly friendly when he spoke. "Kid, this life goes by fast, and you don't want to wish any of it away or lie about how old you are. I remember when I was little like you. I couldn't wait to grow up. It'll happen before you know it. You're about at the time now when, all of a sudden, you're going to start growing about an inch a week. Next thing you know you'll be shaving regular, and your shoulders will be a yard wide. It comes on you quick."

"I can hardly wait," the kid said dryly.

"Well, it ain't all a bed of roses. You get that size and strength for a purpose. You need it to provide. That's what being a man is all about: providing. You'll have a big interest in girls all of a sudden; that's part of it, too. One of 'em ends up looking better than all the rest, and if you're lucky, you look better than all the other men to her. When that time comes, you got to look to your hole card. You need to have something to offer, or you make a hard life for your woman."

"You married, Dan?"

"Naw, not me. I don't have much of a good shot at it, kid. I got two problems. I'm half Indian. What we're going through right now tells you why a lot of folks don't smile at Indians. That fellow's blood on your shirt . . . friend of yours?"

"Yes, he was."

"Well, you see how it is. People find out I got that Indian blood, and first thing you know, somebody gets overheated. Then my second problem comes along. I get overheated too easy. It's a bad mix. I end up killing somebody and riding into the mountains."

"You don't look like an Indian. Your eyes are too light. Your hair is almost red. You're sure taller than any Indian I ever saw. How tall are you?"

"Oh, maybe three or four inches over six feet, I guess."

"I don't think I'd like to get that tall."

"Being tall helps sometimes, but sometimes it's a cross to bear. All the beds and blankets are too short. You always stick out somewhere. It's not so bad if you stay thin. If you get thick like me, if you get heavy, it's hard to find a horse that can carry you. It takes a lot of looking around to find a horse like Big Red." Dan paused and made a show of looking at the small form in front of him. "It's always light men, like you, they look for to ride in races and such."

"You don't look so heavy. What do you weigh?"

"No tellin'. Last time I got on a scale was a couple of years ago. Weighed 240. I guess it's still about the same. My britches still fit. What do you weigh, kid?"

"About half of what you do."

Dan was really enjoying this quiet talk. The kid had a good way of talking, like he'd had good schooling. This was a nice youngster, not dumb at all, probably just sick a lot. Dan remembered the small hands and feet he had massaged. Poor kid had better learn to use a gun; he'd never whip anybody. He'd probably never be up to a real day's work. "Like I said a while back, kid. You bide your time. You'll be up to 220 before you know it."

"I hope I never, ever, weigh that much," the kid said emphatically. Dan raised an eyebrow. "So hard to find a good horse, and all that," the kid added quickly.

"Well, I been thinkin'. We may have a tough ride out of here and maybe not. But if it gets rough, and you have bad luck, I ain't keen to put 'Dumb Kid' on a marker for you. It wouldn't be fit nor proper." Dan was feeling like a bully. The thought was troubling him that this poor little fellow must have taken terrible teasing all the time from bigger, stronger boys. "I think back on that cold ride, and you had a good chance to cry and whine, but there was no complainin'. Let's do the name-trade right." Dan came to his feet and stuck out his hand. "Howdy, partner, my name is Dan Walker, what's yours?"

"How do you do, Mr. Dan Walker. My name is Mistress Mary Alice Martin." The kid then sank into a graceful curtsy.

II

When Alice straightened from her curtsy, Dan realized that his hand was still extended. He no sooner dropped his when she extended hers, then when he reached for it, her hand dropped. This bit of comedy only made him feel more foolish.

"You a girl? No foolin'?" The words were out of him before he could stop them.

"No, Dan, not really. My parents just have an odd sense of humor about names for their children."

"Well, now, ain't that cute." Dan was feeling tricked and was getting madder by the minute. "Why didn't you say so before?"

"Dan, you don't go around saying, 'Howdy, I'm a man,' do you? Don't you just figure that people notice?"

"Yeah, that's so, but I ain't a skinny girl wearing pants, either."

"Thank you, Mr. Walker. Thank you very much."

"Aw, now, don't get sore, it probably ain't your fault you're sickly. Your folks must be hard up. It probably ain't their fault nor yours either. You don't look like you been eatin' good at all." Dan watched her face go rigid with anger and didn't see how this could come out any way but bad for him. "I can see me telling your daddy how much I enjoyed living with his daughter in a cave for a few days. He'll probably rush around to pour me a drink and get out his best cigars."

"That's precisely what he'll do. My father's a gentleman, and he treats other men as such until they prove otherwise." Her voice carried a sharp edge.

Dan's anger left him as quickly as it came. He found himself laughing in spite of himself. "You're really something, kid. Now you look and sound like a little princess out of a book. Or maybe a snooty rich girl right out of finishing school."

She gave a jerky, angry curtsy, quite unlike the graceful, polite gesture she had made earlier. "I regret that I am not the former, sir. But I am, indeed, the latter. My return home has been delayed by wild Indians and a sojourn in a cave with a half-breed."

Dan felt himself flinch and take an involuntary half step back. He forced himself to take a deep breath and hold a blank expression. It didn't work. She was watching too closely; he could feel her eyes on him. He had been caught too much by surprise. He instinctively tried to conceal the damage.

"Well, now, I figured to move around some today, ma'am. I'm a cautious man. I ain't one of those knights in shinin' armor. I don't think those boys would have done too good in this country; although, in their time, they probably did fine. Now then, I could use some help. While I'm out lookin' around, you could—"

"Dan, I'm sorry I called you a . . . a half-breed. I said that to hurt you, but when it did, it hurt me worse. Please, please let me take that back."

There was a long, terrible silence. He was shocked to see tears in her eyes. But there was no way he could help.

"No, ma'am. I can't do that. It wouldn't be right. You mustn't ever try to take back the truth."

There was another tense silence. Dan figured to walk away, but she caught him standing there looking her right in the eye. She started crying.

Dan figured himself to be an honest man, but this was something different. This was kid honesty. This poor little thing had been through a lot. He picked her up and walked back into the cave.

She stopped crying. It hadn't lasted long, thank heaven. He put her down, and she sat with her back to the rock wall, watching him. He went to his saddle and pulled his spare pistol. He sat down with his legs crossed and started cleaning his weapons. The silence stretched out, making him uncomfortable.

"The way this works, ma'am, is to have a good spare gun handy. That way you can clean one, and the other one's right at hand. It keeps a man from getting nervous and in a hurry when he's cleaning his tools."

"You get nervous if you don't have a gun ready to shoot, even for five minutes?"

He looked up with a grin. "Five minutes is a terrible long time, kid. You ever try to hold your breath for five minutes?"

"Dan?"

"Yeah?"

"I'm mortally tired of you calling me 'kid.' I really am."

Without answering, he came to his feet. He spun the newly oiled cylinder, flipped open the loading gate, and fed in cartridges, inspecting each one carefully. He settled the weapon delicately into its holster and drew. He knew that it was an almost invisible gesture to onlookers. The weapon came level, cocked, appearing in his hand like magic.

He stood rubbing and twisting his hands together for a moment. His movements copied those of a pianist he had once watched prepare to go on stage. He drew the weapon six or eight more times, twisting his body in different directions or spinning to aim behind him.

"What are you doing all that for?"

He knew his grin flashed brightly on his dark face. "Because being too slow would make me mortally tired, too, kid." He stood quietly, looking at her for a moment. "I'd rather not call you by any girl names on the trail. No tellin' what we might run into gettin' you home. You understand?"

She nodded. "I suppose so."

"Good. We've got to get moving tomorrow. I've got to get these horses out in the valley so they can graze. They haven't been fed for a day and a half. I've been giving them water from my canteens, and now that's gone. I'll have to watch them every minute. You got any folks?"

"Yes."

"Where might they be?"

"My dad owns the M Bar M."

He laughed shortly and shook his head. "Kid, you're always saying something ridiculous. Quit funnin'. If I'm to get you home, I got to know where to go."

"The M Bar M."

"Come on, kid, I've heard of that outfit. That's a big spread."

"That's correct."

"Yeah," he said doubtfully. "That's where you want to go then?"

"I was headed there before you took me for a pleasant ride through these here picturesque mountains." Her voice was abnormally low as she mocked his slow, serious manner of speech.

"I think I liked you better when you was a boy. You knew then not to talk smarty. I'd have kicked you so hard you'd have to unbutton your britches to see out."

She continued to mock his speech. "A proper gent don't talk nasty around a lady."

He stood there grinning for a moment. "You know how to use a rifle?"

"I bet I can shoot as good as you can, but maybe not as fast."

"Good. Your job is to take care of yourself while I'm gone and to watch me. If somebody takes a shot at me, try to make 'em nervous till I can get back here. First, I'm going down to that little stream to fill the canteens. After I get water back up here, I'm going to check all around before I let the horses out. Understand?"

"Yup," she said in that irritating imitation of his voice.

"Before I go, you want to clean that little toy gun you got hid under there?"

With a sheepish grin, she pulled a short gun from under her coat and sat down on his blanket. "Lend me your spare for a minute, will you?"

"What for?"

Her imitation of his voice came at him again. "The way this works, ma'am, is to have a spare gun handy. That way . . ." She stopped when he handed the spare gun to her.

He started to the cave opening, shaking his head. "I sure liked it better when you was a boy." He turned abruptly. "Were you foolin'? Are you really eighteen years old?"

She didn't look up from her work. "No, I was less than honest when I said that. I'm really twenty."

He snorted derisively. "Aw, are you really? You're full grown then? You ain't ever goin' to get bigger . . . nowhere?"

Her face was reddening, and her voice was stiff. "My legs are long enough to reach the ground, Mr. Walker. I'm almost five-and-a-half feet tall."

"It must be a burden to be mistaken for a thirteen- or fourteen-year-old boy all the time."

He could see a reluctant grin tug at the corners of her mouth. "That seldom happens, Mr. Walker. I imagine about as seldom as you being mistaken for a gentleman."

Their eyes held for a moment while she returned his smile. Dan said grudgingly, "Well, I reckon there's a female of some sort hidden in all that shapeless gear you're wearin'. You got the sharp tongue. I suppose half the young fellows in these parts have bled to death from it and left you a dried-up old spinster."

"My daddy has been sick a lot the last few years, Mr. Walker. Since I have no brothers, it fell to me to run the ranch. I guess my manner has been too businesslike and bossy for most men." Her voice had lost its bantering tone.

"It sure speaks poorly for the quality of the men around here, kid. It surely does," Dan commented softly before he moved away to take a look out the mouth of the cave.

Dan sat in the mouth of the cave and looked across the little valley, now lit by a brilliant moon. He loved this high country with its changing moods. The early winter storm that had savagely punished him yesterday had passed, leaving a clear, sunlit day with a wind from the south that had erased the snow. Even now, nearing midnight, he would have hardly missed the blanket around his shoulders with this balmy temperature. It felt more like late spring than fall.

The horses had grazed well on some of the prettiest pasture a man could want. It would be a good thing to move on at first light tomorrow. This good weather couldn't last. The meager traveling rations on his packhorse were going fast. Alice went at it in a dainty way, but she ate like a field hand. She was a wonder. Mighty easy to talk to and useful around the camp. He had been dead wrong about her. She was no tenderfoot.

She didn't put on airs like might be expected of a big rancher's daughter, either. Talking around the fire after eating tonight had been informative. Seemed her dad's health had been failing for some time. Alice had taken more and more responsibility for running the ranch. Two years ago, her parents had left to see some high-powered doctors, and she had gone to a fancy school. Her parents had been set on her getting as much education as a highfalutin city woman. Her father had been advised to live close to the attentions of his doctors, so he and her mother had not returned to the ranch.

After finishing school, Alice visited her folks for a while, but insisted on coming back to the ranch. There was some kind of trouble, and the spread was losing money. Ben Martin had borrowed a bunch of money to pay doctor bills. The bank insisted that a man named Alan Channing, a total stranger, be hired to manage the place since the Martins weren't there in person. Alice couldn't figure how a solid ranch operation could lose money with the cattle markets as good as they had been the last couple of years.

Alice Martin was no kid. After talking with her for three hours beside the fire that night, Dan figured she knew as much about ranching as anyone. He also figured that, if she found anything slack on the M Bar M, there would soon be hide and hair flying. It would be fun to watch. He had seen her knocked out by a big Indian, obliged to ride bareback in freezing weather till she fainted and fell in the snow, and then forced to live in a cave. She was the kind who just waded in and did what was necessary.

Dan figured that if the question came up, he would just tell folks that she had been civil to him up in this old cave. She didn't beat him up or hurt him in any way.

He was smiling when he drifted off to sleep.

Alice proved again that she was no tenderfoot when she helped him get ready the next morning. He noticed that she piled tinder close to the fire. She was leaving things ready for the next traveler who might seek the protection of the cave in bad weather. She was leaving things as neat as they had found them.

She started to protest when he lifted her into the saddle on Big Red. Shortening the stirrups, he said bluntly, "We may have to do some hard riding. Big Red can outrun any Indian pony in these mountains. I don't want you falling off, so maybe my saddle will help keep you up there. If things get tight, I don't want to have to fret about you." She put on an angry, straight mouth at his contempt of her riding skill.

He would have to ride bareback on the gray, but that didn't bother him. He had been riding a long time before he ever sat in a saddle. He was worried about his gear packed on that Indian pony. That pony wasn't a pack animal, and it would be hard to control if they got into a running fight. He tied the reins to Big Red's saddle and said, "If you have to run hard, kid, cut that hammerhead loose. There's a skinning knife on the saddle by your right leg."

They rode through a glorious, clear morning. Everything had a bright, sharply focused clarity that only seemed to exist in the clean air of the heights. Every breeze was loaded with the scent of pines and late flowers, accented by the early morning chill. It was biting cold in the shade but pleasantly warm in the sun. They had a brief climb out of the little valley and then were presented with a breathtaking view of reds, yellows, and shades of blue and gray in the ageless rocks of the sharp peaks around them. Dan could see for miles from the high trail.

Progress was painfully slow compared to the lung-bursting pace Dan had set for the run to the mountains. Several times Alice had to sit impatiently in the saddle for more than an hour at a time, waiting while he scouted the trail ahead.

Dan got his first look at the M Bar M in the late afternoon of the next day. Alice pointed out the main house first, the Martin residence. Then she identified the two barns, a bunkhouse, a residence for the foreman, and a cookshack with an extension on it for a dining room. The ranch looked prosperous and well tended even from a great distance.

They rode up to the M Bar M buildings just as the cook was whanging a triangle to call the hands to supper. Eight hands gathered to watch curiously as they rode up, and several of the men came forward to meet them when they recognized Alice. A broad-shouldered man with streaks of gray through his red hair helped her from the saddle and laughed when she hugged him.

"Alice, honey, are you all right? We been wild with worry. We found the wagons, and poor Jed and Charlie, but we been looking for you all this time. We followed a trail of two horses for a while, but it just petered out on the rocks. We were going out again in the morning."

"Red, this is Dan Walker. He fought off the Indians. We hid out in the mountains till we thought it would be safe to try to get home."

Red walked to Dan's horse and stuck out a gnarled hand. "Glad to meet you, Walker. I'm Red Cougan. Get down, man, get down. We got chuck ready." He turned to one of the hands and said, "Sam, go over to my house and tell Annie that Alice is home and to set another plate on the table."

A commanding voice cut through the clamor of welcome. "What the hell is all this?" A tense silence fell at once. A tall man, heavily muscled but running now to fat, swaggered from the front door of the Martin residence and stood arrogantly on the front porch. "What's going on here?"

"This here is Mr. Alan Channing, Miss Alice. Mr. Channing, this is Miss Mary Alice Martin." Dan caught a sense of anticipation, of relish, in Red's voice.

"Well, Miss Martin, I'm glad you've arrived. It's been almost impossible to get any work done around here with everyone wanting to chase around looking for you. Where have you been?" The man's tone was that of a person demanding an explanation.

"My escorts were killed by renegade Indians, Mr. Channing. I shall give more details later. Right now I would like to get something to eat, a chance to clean up, and a night's sleep in my own bed." Dan thought that her voice was cold enough to chill a meat house.

"Well, now, that might take some arranging, Miss Martin. Maybe you better plan to stay with Red and Annie in the foreman's house till we can discuss this. You see, I've taken the main house for my residence, and it might not appear seemly for you to move in." An expectant silence fell, and Dan saw the men looking away in all directions, some of them lifting calloused hands to hide grins.

He didn't have to wait long to see why.

"Mr. Channing, you must have misunderstood your instructions, sir." Alice's voice was loaded with venom, and her attitude was that of offended royalty. "You are employed to perform certain simple management tasks here in the absence of my family. You have no authority to move into my home, and the idea of your doing so is insufferable. For you to attempt to deny my entry is simply unbelievable."

There was no grinning among the men now. Alice's words were delivered with such cold anger that no one would find them amusing. Dan was afraid the woman was going to attack Channing; her body looked like she was going to leap at the man. He hoped she had forgotten the small gun she was carrying.

"Mr. Channing, it is my intention to dine this evening as the guest of Mr. and Mrs. Cougan. That may take as much as an hour. At the end of that time, I shall come home. When I enter my home, sir, neither you nor any evidence of you had better be in it. Should I find any sign of you, or that my family's property has been taken or abused, I shall take offense. Do I make myself clear, sir?"

The men were openly grinning now with snorts and guffaws breaking the silence following her speech. It was obvious that the crew had expected an explosion and were thoroughly enjoying it. Channing's face was crimson, his eyes wicked with fury. His voice was contemptuous when he said, "Now just a minute there, little Miss Queen of England. Just don't think you can walk in here and upset everything. You've got a lot to learn about business, so just get off your high horse."

Before Alice could reply, Dan asked, "Could I borrow a shovel?" The assembled crew shifted and turned to Dan, irritated to hear such an odd interruption in the middle of a tense situation. Surprise brought a complete silence.

"A shovel? Why?" Red asked.

"I might have some digging to do. I always like to bury the men I kill, unless I'm in a big hurry. I feel it's only proper."

"Who are you?" asked Channing. "I've never seen you around here."

"Not important. Anybody know what time it is?" Dan asked.

Red pulled out a watch and said, "It's five after six."

"You have till seven o'clock, Channing, unless you want to argue about it right now."

Channing's face showed both rage and caution. It was obvious that everyone present was against him, and he wanted no part of this oversized, ragged stranger who seemed to have come out of nowhere.

"Well, now, of course I wouldn't want to put Miss Martin to any inconvenience. No, sir, none at all. Where should I stay tonight, Miss Martin?"

"I would suggest that you stay in the bunkhouse, if the crew doesn't object, Mr. Channing. I would turn no one away at this hour. After breakfast in the morning, you may take your leave."

"Leave? Oh no you don't, missy." Channing's voice was smug. "I got to stay here if I'm going to manage this place, and your daddy signed a paper promising he would keep a manager appointed by the bank."

Alice's voice maintained a formal tone when she answered, "My father signed an agreement to keep a bank-appointed manager on salary as long as the Martin family was absent. A member of the Martin family has returned, sir. Your services are no longer required. You are dismissed." She turned and walked toward Red Cougan's house. On the way she hesitated and spoke to Red, who waved at Dan, flashed a big grin, and hollered, "Hey, Dan, come on and eat with us."

I I I

Dan was impressed by the spacious living room and the sense of comfort and warmth he felt when he walked inside the foreman's house. Annie Cougan was a smiling, plump woman with graying red hair that almost perfectly matched her husband's. She had tears in her eyes when she hugged Alice, saying, "It has been just terrible, honey. We couldn't imagine what had happened to you. We were worried sick."

Standing in this pleasant, clean room made Dan conscious of his filthy, ragged clothing and unshaven face. He stood awkwardly, shifting his shapeless hat around and around, much aware of the picture of clumsy discomfort he presented when Red introduced him.

With the direct manner of a woman who dealt with workingmen every day of her life, Annie shook Dan's hand and said, "You look like a mangy range bum, young man." She glanced at Red. "Take this raggedy thing around back and clean him up. Give him one of your shirts. Don't come back till I holler for you. Supper will be late tonight. I'm going to help Alice clean up and get her out of those awful rags. We'll look human for supper, gentlemen, is that clear?"

Red led Dan outside and said, "There's a pump over behind the bunkhouse. Towels and soap are always there. I'll get a shirt and bring it to you."

Dan nodded. "I got horses to see after, Red."

"Just get what you need off your saddle." Red raised his voice. "Joe! Joe, where are you?" An old man with a bad limp appeared out of the barn. "You eat yet?"

"Yeah. Cook fed me early."

"Good. Take Walker's horses and tend to 'em. Take his stuff over to the bunkhouse and dump it on a bunk."

Dan slipped his razor out of his pack and went looking for the water pump. He was almost finished shaving in the failing light when Red came around the corner with a shirt in his hands. "Here, this old shirt is way too big and long in the sleeves for me. It's about time I found somebody who could wear it. No need to shave in the dark. I'll light that lantern for you."

"Let it go. That light would hurt my eyes."

After a moment, Red replied, "Yeah, sure. I've known men to have that problem." He stood quietly while Dan finished shaving by feel. When Dan had tossed out the water and was donning his new shirt, Red said, "Never could shave worth a damn without a mirror, always messed up my sideburns and missed places."

Dan laughed. "Well, I don't have all that much of a beard. That makes it easier for me."

They walked to the house together. When they walked into the living room, Red pointed Dan toward a leather-covered chair. Before taking a seat himself, he walked casually around the room drawing the curtains across the windows. "Always like to make a cautious man feel at home."

Annie came bustling in. "My, my, look what a handsome man was hiding under that torn and dirty wrapper. You look much better, young fellow, much better, indeed." Looking pointedly at Dan's gun belt, she added, "There's a peg there by the door to hang your gear. You might as well be comfortable."

At Red's quiet, "Let be, Annie, let be," she glanced at her husband curiously, then turned a thoughtful look at Dan.

Alice spoke from the doorway. "Mr. Walker likes to keep his tools close to hand and in good working order, Annie."

Dan struggled to keep from expressing shock as he came to his feet. He expected her to look different. A change of clothes always altered a person, but he hadn't expected anything like this. He had grown accustomed to seeing her in crude clothing several sizes too large. It had given the impression that she was smaller than she really was, kind of shrunken.

He could tell that she was enjoying this. Her smile was pointed at him like a gun with a load of spite in it. Dan figured he had it coming. There certainly was nothing skinny about her. She wore a plain brown dress buttoned to the neck, but nobody could think her to be immature or boyish now. In fact, Dan found himself wondering if he had ever seen a prettier woman.

"Dust bother you when your eyes stick out like that, young man?"

Annie's laughing voice brought an unpleasant flush to Dan's face. He knew he was staring like a clod, and searched his mind for some comment to relieve the pressure of feeling so foolish. As always, it seemed to Dan, when he needed to say something quickly, he said something incredibly stupid. "Please don't tell nobody I thought you was a boy, ma'am. Please don't do that. A story like that could ruin a man."

Red and Annie both laughed, and Alice's smile warmed a little. The conversation at the table consisted mostly of Red and Annie dragging every detail they could from Alice about her adventure. It was a surprise to Dan how much she remembered—he had thought she'd been unconscious much of the time.

Dan felt that her description had far too many compliments directed at him. Twice he shook his head and tried to mumble a clarification, and both times when Alice challenged him to correct her, he didn't do too well.

After the meal, Red and Dan escorted Alice home, checked to be sure Channing had departed, and left her there. Before they parted, Red shook Dan's hand again and said, "We got a lot to thank you for, Dan. I'll be talking to you in the morning, but there's one thing that might not wait. Look out for Channing. He's vicious. He beat up one of our hired hands, almost killed the man. He fancies himself, and you called him down pretty rough in front of everybody."

The moment Dan appeared in the door of the bunkhouse, all conversation stopped. Four men at the table in the center of the room dropped their cards and came to their feet to greet him. Others rolled off bunks and crowded around Dan, introducing themselves and shaking hands. Dan noticed his gear on one of the bunks, walked over to it, and sat down. He heard another bunk creak and glanced over to see Channing rising to his feet.

Channing looked even bigger in the crowded bunkhouse. His eyes were glassy with hatred as he walked over and stood in front of Dan. "Seems you're a big hero, Walker. Everybody around here thinks you're quite a man."

Dan said nothing. He rolled back on his bunk and relaxed. Channing stood smirking. Dan figured that Red was correct. Channing's bad showing on the front porch had been working on him. Maybe he would be satisfied to blow off steam and forget it if Dan just ignored him.

"You act like you think you're red hot with a gun, Walker, talking big in front of the woman. You probably had things all your way out in the woods with her. Well, I don't think you amount to nothing without that gun."

It was plain now that the big man was determined to start trouble, had probably been thinking of nothing else. His remarks had crossed that invisible but still-essential line: They couldn't be ignored. Evidently he wasn't sure of himself with guns, but his great size indicated that he might be a very dangerous man in a no-holds-barred battle.

"Well?"

Dan didn't move, and Channing seemed confused about what to do next. "You got nothing to say?" He looked around, grinning at the other men, gaining confidence from Dan's lack of response. He was starting to enjoy himself. Dan just lay there watching. "Get up from there,"

Channing snarled, suddenly bending over the bunk and grabbing at Dan's shirt.

When Channing bent over him, Dan drove the edge of his fist straight up into Channing's exposed throat. Channing staggered back, making strained gagging motions, his eyes round with surprise and shock. He staggered against the table, spilling cards to the floor, and fell to his knees.

Both of Channing's hands were clawing at his throat, his eyes bulging, and his mouth wide open as he tried frantically to breathe. His face was turning a dark shade of blue. Struggling desperately he leaped to his feet and blindly dove headfirst into the wall. He fell to his knees again, curled in a ball, with his face on the floor. Dan still lay in his bunk, but every other man in the room was standing, horror written on every face.

One of the men, unconsciously holding a hand to his own throat, turned to Dan and asked in a voice that was almost a whisper, "Is he gonna choke to death?"

Every eye turned to Dan, who was lying relaxed, disinterested, on his bunk. Noises now came from Channing's quivering body like the whimpering, whining gasps of a strangling dog. Dan responded indifferently, "Likely. We'll know in another minute or two."

One of the men suddenly darted through the door. Retching noises from outside caused another man to bolt. Another said, "I'm gonna go get Red," and ran out the door. Channing, still on the floor, was up on his hands and knees. Each breath he tried to pull in made a thin, high-pitched whine. Every muscle in the man's body was jerking and trembling. A wet stain spread down his trousers.

Red charged into the bunkhouse. He looked down at Channing and then at the men standing around staring as if they were paralyzed. "What happened here?"

One of the men answered in a hushed voice, "This is awful, Red. Channing tried to start trouble with Walker. Walker done something to him, and Channing started choking. God, this is worse than watching a hanging."

Red dropped down beside Channing. "Can you talk?" Channing, his face now chalk-white, had toppled off his knees and lay curled against the wall. He shook his head feebly, making a whimpering noise with each breath.

Red turned and stood staring at Dan. Dan swung his feet off the bunk and stood. "Red, these men won't be able to sleep with that noise. I'll take him over to the barn."

An upraised hand stopped him. Red said, "I think you done enough for him tonight. I'll get a couple of others to do that." He selected two of the men, and they picked Channing up and started out with him. His legs dragged limply behind as the men went through the door with him. Red looked around and announced, "Gonna be a hard day tomorrow unless you men get some sleep."

The next morning at breakfast, Joe Ballas, the oldster with a limp, walked in grinning and said, "Red, you know I bunk over in the barn 'cause this bunch of crazies won't let a man sleep. Last night two of 'em brought a groaning wreck over there and left it layin' in the hay. Their idea of a joke on me, I guess. It kept me awake all night moaning. This morning I asked it if it wanted to eat breakfast. It just shook its head. I don't think it can talk. What you want me to do with it?" The talk around the table died out.

"Do you think he can ride, Joe?" Red asked.

Joe, grinning at Dan, said, "Maybe. Doubt it. He acts like he's afraid to move. Just creeps around real slow and hunched up. Want me to take him to town in the wagon?"

"Yeah, I guess so. Miss Martin wants him off the place."

"Well, I reckon he's ready to leave." Joe seemed to be the only one who thought his remark was funny.

A few minutes later when the men got up to leave, Red motioned to Dan to stay seated. He brought the coffeepot over and put it on the table. "You looking for a job, Dan?"

"Sure, but I'd be surprised if anybody's hiring at this time of year. What you got in mind?"

"Well, I lost a couple of the men I kept on permanent. I still got three or four temporary hands hanging around, but we don't need 'em. Seemed like Channing always wanted to hire too many men. But I can offer you a permanent job if you don't mind working a line camp this winter."

Dan considered the prospect of spending a lonely winter, likely snowed in, without enthusiasm. It would get him through the hard season, though, and the isolation would allow him to save his wages. He would have a nice stake in the spring. "I go alone or is it a two-man camp?"

"It's a two-man camp and it's well built. Our north range's been a big problem lately. We don't seem to be getting any increase up there the last couple of years. I can't understand it. That's always been the best pasture we have. I'm thinking somebody's taking our cattle, and the losses are hurting us real bad. The camp is new; this is the first time I've kept men up there."

"Sounds like you got trouble."

"Might be. Joe Ballas will be with you."

"The old man?"

"Listen, Dan, make no mistake! That's a hard old man. He's the best shot with both rifle and handgun on the place. He can track like an Indian. I'll bet he would have tracked you and Miss Martin down if it hadn't snowed. He said then that whoever had Miss Alice was trailwise and smart. He says that he learns a lot about any man he trails. Only thing was, he was dead wrong about you."

"About me?"

"Yeah, he told us you were big but old, like him. You surprised him. He said that he never figured a young man to know all the tricks you used. It seemed to tickle him. Another thing, Dan, I asked him to go to that camp before. He said no, unless he went alone. I couldn't send a man up there by himself, expecting trouble and all. He said if he had to wet nurse one of our cowhands it would just get him killed."

"What changed his mind?"

Red leaned forward. "He came to me before breakfast this morning and said that he'd go if I hired you to go with him. Dan, that old man is a loner, won't even sleep in the bunkhouse with the others. He don't associate with nobody, even eats alone, but I think he's taken a liking to you."

Dan was curious. "Why'd you hire a strange old man like that, Red?"

"I didn't. I came here before Miss Alice was born, but he's been here even longer. He and Ben, Alice's daddy, have known each other forever. Joe comes and goes as he pleases. Sometimes he's gone for months. One time he was gone two or three years, nobody knows where. He's also close with the Martins, so you be careful not to say anything about 'em, careless-like. I warn everybody I hire about that. That old man is dangerous. He might kill you." Red smiled. "Dan, I nearly fell over when he walked in with that big grin on his face this morning. That ain't like him. He ain't got no sense of humor at all."

"When do we go?"

"The sooner the better. Might's well go on as soon as Joe gets back

from taking Channing to town. Let's see, it'll take him a day to get there
and a day to get back. With the day he spends there to buy stuff, you
want to figure it will be three or four days at least."

"It seems early in the season to put men in a winter camp."

Red shook his head. "Naw, you need to get up there in time to cut
more wood before the snows come. We cut some hay for the horses
when we built the cabin, but you might want to cut some more. You
need to hunt some fresh meat, or you can slaughter one or two head if
you have to do it. Get to know the country. If you was to get lost up
there in bad weather, you might be in serious trouble."

"If we find somebody fooling with the stock, how do you want it
handled?"

Red looked startled. "Whatever works, just so they don't do it no
more." There was a brief silence. Then he added, "Don't bring 'em
down here. I never held with women watching hangings."

Dan was looking forward to a cold, lonely winter. He had ridden
beside Joe Ballas since early morning. Dan quit trying to talk to the man
after getting no responses to a couple of comments. Joe just looked away
and acted like he hadn't heard a thing. They rode ahead of the heavily
loaded wagon driven by Sam Dalton, one of the permanent M Bar M
crew. Dan's gray packhorse and a spare mount for Joe came along behind
the wagon.

When they pulled up in front of the shack, Dan liked what he saw.
The building was made of logs, backed against a mountain in such a
manner that it would be difficult to approach from behind. In fact, to do
so would require some careful climbing on foot. There were two rooms,
one for the men and one in which to stable the horses.

He had offered to help with making up the list of things needed. Joe
had told him flatly that he would see to it. When Dan came around to
help load the wagon, it had already been done. Thus, Dan was surprised
at the amount of provisions they had to unload, especially when he lifted
off three cases of ammunition. He made no comment until after Sam
left the next morning to return to the ranch.

"You ever talk, Joe, or do I send smoke signals?"

To Dan's surprise, Joe turned with a friendly grin and said, "Sure,
Dan, we can talk now. I don't like to talk in front of any of those half-
baked cowhands. It's a waste of time and effort. Most of the time they

don't listen, but when they do pay attention they don't understand nothing. I noticed you looking at our grub. Look like we got enough?"

"Yeah, for four or five men, maybe more, and enough ammunition to start a war."

Nodding, Joe said, "that's about the size of it. I been telling Red for two years that we been gettin' robbed blind up here. We're going to fight rustlers, Walker. Any man who will steal cattle is likely to be a man who would bushwhack, too, so we start acting like we're at war right now. The simplest way to rustle cattle is to kill the men guarding them."

He paused to light his pipe before continuing. "I figure to find a couple of places to stash grub and ammunition. If somebody gets hurt, he might get to a stash easier than he could get back here. I brought enough to hide away to keep us going if somebody burns this here shack." Grinning, he added, "Look what happens when you invite an old magpie to talk."

"Red don't listen to you?"

"He surely does, but Red's had an awful time holding things together this last two years since that feller Channing came. He's had to work around Channing on mighty near everything that needs doing. At times it looked like Channing was trying to run the ranch into the ground. Red would have quit about the second day after that fool arrived if he and Ben Martin weren't close friends. With Ben being sick and all, Red's just hung on and swallowed his pride, trying to do things right. I bet this ranch ain't made ten dollars profit in the last two years. If Red hadn't been here, the Martins would have lost their shirts by now."

"Well, Miss Alice Martin seems to have solved that little problem with Channing quick enough."

"That's another thing I better let you know about. Some jaspers figure they can't work for a woman. They figure a woman don't know enough about things, I suppose. Well, let me tell you something: Ben's health started slipping a long time ago. Lots of times, when she was just a little bitty girl, she would bring her daddy's orders out to Red. Now old Red got used to her saying, 'Daddy says to do this, and Daddy says to do that.' But Red ain't stupid, no sir. About the time Miss Alice was about fifteen years old it dawned on him that Daddy wasn't saying much of anything. Hell, Walker, that girl has kept the books on this ranch since she was twelve. She did it better than Ben could even when he felt good."

Dan could hardly picture the situation Joe described. A ranch the size of the M Bar M was a complicated business, requiring experienced planning and sound business judgment. "Must have been a big load for a little girl, and a lonely job at that. Doesn't sound like she had a chance to have any fun at all."

Joe snapped his fingers. "That reminds me. There's going to be a dance in town in a couple of weeks. Won't be no more social stuff after that till the winter's over. Miss Alice told me to send you down for the dance."

Dan laughed. "Dancing ain't my strong suit, Joe. Besides, it looks like we got all we can handle without running off to fool around at some fiddling contest. Now that I'm up here, I figure to stay till the job's done . . ." Dan drew back at the change in Joe's expression.

Joe's face had gone rigid, his eyes fixed on Dan's with an expression of cold anger. "I'm disappointed with you, Walker," he said harshly. "I stood here talking till my throat is sore explaining things to you. I thought you was listening, but maybe your head is as empty as them others. I feel mighty let down."

"What's got into you, Joe? How did I let you down?"

Joe looked exasperated. "After all this talk, you don't understand yet? Well, I'll lay it out so a blind and deaf man can understand it. Miss Alice said for you to go to the dance. When Miss Alice tells a man on M Bar M property to dance, he starts to jig. She's the boss, hardcase, and don't ever forget it. So rest your mind on it, you're going to a dance."

IV

Joe Ballas was an irritating, clever, domineering old man. When Dan suggested that they cut more wood while the weather was still pleasant, Joe agreed that it was a fine idea. Dan took down the ax from the wall, sharpened it, and started work. After an hour of steady chopping, he sat down on the woodpile, mopping his face, and said, "Want to take a crack at it, Joe?"

Joe glanced at Dan from where he was seated beside the door of the cabin. His eyes had been endlessly surveying the surrounding land. "No, I'll just keep watch. I do that better."

The next day, cutting hay, Dan leaned on the scythe, mopping sweat again, and asked, "I don't suppose you'd be interested in swinging this thing while I rest a minute or two?" Joe looked amused. "Go ahead and rest," he responded from his seat in the shade, but he made no move to touch the scythe.

That night Joe showed Dan some work he had done on the cabin. He mentioned that he had waited until after the rest of the crew had returned to the ranch. "Those fellers would tell everybody in the country if they knew." Five of the logs in the back wall of the cabin had been cut and so cleverly rigged for removal that, unless shown, Dan would never have noticed them. "Nice to have a back door if there's a fire," Joe said with a grin. "Now look here, youngster, at how I stacked your wood."

Dan could see how the stacked wood along the edge of the cliff behind the cabin would provide cover to anyone leaving the cabin by the hidden back exit. The stacked wood provided cover almost as far as a low patch of rocks at the base of the cliff.

"The way I figure it, we won't have no trouble until bad weather sets in good. Then, I figure they'll try to catch us in this here cabin unawares, burn it with us in it, or shoot us when we try to get out. That way they can make it look like we was careless and burned the cabin down on ourselves. I think they'll try it at night. They know I'm a tracker. They might think I'll be hard to bushwhack outside the cabin."

Dan nodded, saying nothing.

"You're part Injun, ain't you?"

Dan nodded again.

Packing tobacco into his pipe, Joe had a satisfied look on his face. "Thought so. Makes sense. You been well schooled by somebody. You know how to make good jerky?"

Dan nodded again.

Joe's eyes had an amused twinkle. "Grindin' on you, ain't I?"

Dan nodded again.

"Ordinary case, you'd whup my ass and be boss up here. Grinds you that I'm old and got a limp and bossin' you around. Don't seem fair, right?"

Dan nodded again.

Joe actually laughed out loud. "Well, you're tough enough to whup me, but you don't feel it'd be a fair fight, me being old and half-crippled. It's a good thing you feel that way. I don't need you, son, not at all. If you was to lay a hand on me, I'd have to kill you. It would be sad, too. Miss Alice is some taken with you. That would bother me."

"Yeah, Miss Alice is some taken with me. Everybody noticed that. I was hanging around the ranch waiting for you for three days. She never came out of the house, not one time. She got enough of me when we were together. She probably nearly fired Red when he hired me, if she even noticed."

"You go up to the house? You go up to say howdy and pass the time?" Joe's voice held amusement.

"A man with any sense at all stays away from the owner's pretty daughter unless he's packed and ready to ride."

"Think she's pretty, eh? Way I heard it, you was mighty slow to notice."

"Who's been talking to you? What do you know about it?" Dan had been hoping that this kind of talk wouldn't get started. Everyone would have a laugh on him till some joker carried it too far. Then there would be trouble.

"Oh, I hear things. Don't much go on that I don't know about. It's an advantage I get from listening instead of talking all the time."

"Well, tomorrow it's time for me to ride. I got to see what's up here, where the cattle are and all," Dan said. "I'm tired of this cabin, tired of cutting wood and hay, and I'm getting tired of you, old man."

"We'll both ride tomorrow. I drew up a map, spent some time on it. Let me show you the lay of the land on the map. Then tomorrow you follow me around. Stay a hundred or maybe two hundred yards behind me. No reason for us to make it easy for somebody to get at both of us at once. Another thing, I got places picked for us to cache food and ammunition. Every time we leave here, we carry supplies along to our hideouts. When we hide stuff away, fill the empty packs with sticks. If somebody is watching, they won't know where we unloaded anything."

Dan was gaining confidence that he knew his way around the enormous north pasture. He had also gained great respect for Joe Ballas as a cook. The old man was full of surprises. He went off by himself one day and returned with four hens tied to his saddle. In response to Dan's questions, he just said, "Need eggs now and again."

Dan was about to climb into the saddle one morning when Joe walked out of the cabin. "Where you headed?" Joe asked.

"Planned to go along the rim. Lots of cattle up there. Figured to drift 'em down some. If the weather should come on us quick, some of 'em might get caught up there and we'll lose 'em."

"Never mind that. Them cows got sense enough to take care of themselves. They got by without us up here just fine before somebody started running off with 'em." Joe dug a roll of bills out of his pocket and extended them to Dan. "Advance on your wages. Picked it up before we come up here. You head for town. There's enough money here for a new hat, new boots, and one of them black suits they got in the store. Told Jesse to hold a big 'un for you. Can't have no M Bar M hand going to a dance looking like a scarecrow."

Dan had forgotten about the dance. He was not happy with the idea of leaving Joe alone up here. He wasn't interested in going to the dance either, but a look at Joe's face told him that there was no use trying to dodge the trip. "Where's this dance to be?"

"Big barn at the Stenholm spread. It's only about four miles from town. The dance is tomorrow night. If your suit needs sizing, there are town women Jesse gets to do that stuff."

It was an easy ride for Dan. He had a good idea from Joe's map and directions where the town was located. His first view of Buckhorn was from a mile away, and he was surprised. It looked like a good-sized town.

He took a good look as he rode along the dirt main street. There was a livery stable, a saloon, a bank, a general store, a blacksmith's, even a hotel. Several small houses were scattered around. Dan grinned and muttered to himself, "Not exactly New Orleans, but it's an honest-to-goodness town."

He swung out of the saddle in front of the general store. When he walked in, a small man with a huge waxed mustache came to greet him. He stuck out his hand and said, "Howdy, I'm Jesse Robers. What can I do for you?"

Dan took the hand and answered, "Dan Walker. I need to get some clothes to wear to a dance I gotta go to."

Robers grinned. "Sounds like you ain't that sold on it. I been expecting you, Walker. Heard you was full-sized. That's just fine. I got some nice stuff that will fit you."

"You been expecting me?"

"Yeah, some of M Bar M is already in town. Miss Alice was by here this morning. Said you was big as a house. She was worried we might have to trim down one of our tents to fit you." Robers was businesslike as he plucked a measuring tape out of his pocket. "Let's see if this is going to be as easy as I think."

Evidently it was. Robers brought a coat and Dan shrugged into it. It needed to be tucked in a little at the waist. Robers was going to pin it for altering when Dan stopped him. He liked the looseness of the coat around the gun at his middle. There was a little more difficulty with the trousers, which were much too large for Dan around the waist. However, Robers said, with his mouth full of pins, that he could get them cut down in a couple of hours. "You'll be a real dude at the dance, Walker. Nothing to worry about. I'll have this stuff cut and sewed to your size and ready for you before noon tomorrow."

Dan selected a new pair of boots, a new hat, and three new shirts. He asked, "You know the right size shirt for Red Cougan?"

"Sure. I got the size for everybody at M Bar M."

"What color does Cougan like?"

"Red, like that shirt you're wearing. That looks just like one of his shirts."

"It is. I owe him one. I'll take another one just like this."

Dan told Robers that he would come by to pick up his new clothing the next morning except for the boots, hat, a pair of pants, and a shirt. He carried those items with him across the street to the hotel. The clerk, as soon as he heard Dan's name, handed him a key. Dan looked puzzled, and the clerk said with a grin, "You're new. M Bar M always takes a bunch of rooms for the dance. Miss Alice said you were coming."

"Where can a man get a bath and haircut in this town?"

"Bathhouse is behind the hotel. I keep the fire going all the time for people coming in for the dance. Towels are up in the rooms. Just go any time you like as long as it's still daylight. I ain't heating water in the nighttime."

"Haircut?"

"Tom Tolar, over to the blacksmith shop. He does good work, both blacksmithing and barbering, if you don't mind him being a damn squaw man."

Dan turned and started up the stairs without answering. He found his room and took a quick look around to find his towel before he headed for the bathhouse, carrying his new boots and work clothes. He was relieved to find the bathhouse empty. He disliked the attention some men paid to the fact that he went to great pains to keep his guns handy, even when bathing. He poured clean hot water into his boots, took a quick bath, and jerked on the new pair of pants and shirt. He did a fast job of washing his dirty clothes in the same water he had used for his bath. He poured out the water from his boots and pulled them on.

Dan hated the stiffness of new boots. He made a practice of filling new boots with water, letting them sit for a while, then walking them dry. He figured that saved him getting blisters by stretching the leather quickly to fit his feet. He was going to have to wear them to the dance, since the old ones were almost worn to shreds.

He walked across the street and into the blacksmith shop. The fire in the forge was banked, only a few coals showing among the ashes. "Anybody home?" Dan called in a loud voice.

The back door banged inward and a tall, squarely built man with a full beard came ducking through. "Didn't hear you, friend. Not much doing today, so I was sitting on the bench in the sun out back. What can I do for you?"

"Fellow over at the hotel said that a man could get a haircut over here."

"Sure, come on out back. The light's better outside, and I just hang one mirror on the wall and another on the fence. It works real good."

Dan followed the man out the door. He sat on a high wooden box while Tolar hung up two large mirrors. Tolar laid out his clippers, scissors, razor, and shaving mug on a packing crate. He unfolded a sheet and pinned it around Dan. "You must be the new hand at M Bar M, I reckon?" Dan waited to nod till he was sure the clippers wouldn't remove a hunk of hair.

Dan could see Tolar's grin in the mirror when he said, "We been a little bit curious to meet you, Walker. Most of us have known Miss Alice and her folks a long time. We heard you came along just in time to do her a good turn. Everybody is mighty curious about you. We don't see many strangers come through these parts."

"You been having Indian trouble? Nobody at the ranch seemed to worry about it once Miss Alice got home."

"Didn't nobody tell you? Old Joe Ballas took a good look at them Indians you shot. They ain't from around here." Dan stiffened in surprise. He wasn't fond of big talkers, but it was absurd that Ballas hadn't mentioned this to him. "We ain't had trouble with Indians for years. Get along fine." Tolar's voice hardened. "Fact is, my wife is an Iroquois."

"So was my mother," Dan said quietly.

"Is that a fact? Well, ain't that a rare thing now. Lots of folks don't even know there's Iroquois in this part of the country. The fur companies hired a bunch of 'em to come here and teach the mountain Indians how to do things right. The Iroquois are different, what with bein' Christians and educated and all. I know plenty of people who don't know the difference; they just think an Indian is an Indian. My wife and I run into . . . uh . . . hard times now and again. Some folks take a dim view when a man marries an Indian. I suppose your daddy runs into it, so you know what I'm talking about."

"I run into difficulty sometimes, but my dad doesn't have any problem. My mother died a few years ago. Dad's married to a white woman now."

There was a long silence while Tolar did his work. Then he asked, "Why don't you take a look in the mirror? You got nice thick hair. I didn't take off much. Man with thick hair can look bushy real easy if it's cut too short to lay down nice."

Dan nodded his approval.

"How about a shave? I'll throw in the shave free."

"In that case, sure. You giving free shaves with haircuts?"

"Not normally, Walker. Fact is, I kinda owe you. I'm the tallest man in these parts. Sooner or later most of these local boys want to see if they can tear down my meat house. It's mighty tiresome sometimes. That Channing fellow had been talking pretty smart to me before, but he ain't talking smart to nobody since you came. In fact, he almost can't talk at all, just a kind of funny whisper."

"Channing still around? I figured that he might have drifted on, since Miss Alice ran him off the M Bar M."

Tolar laughed like a man who enjoyed doing it. "Way I heard it was that Miss Alice politely invited him to leave. You was the one what run him off. Heard you nearly killed him without even getting up from your bunk. You just laid there yawning while he crawled all over the floor choking near to death."

"Stories always get bigger with each telling," Dan said dryly.

"Well, I ain't seen Channing around town for days now. Maybe he lit out. Everybody has to make a living, and nobody was giving him the time of day. I got no idea where he come from in the first place."

Tolar was finished. He whipped off the sheet and shook it. Dan paid him and was about to leave when the big man said quietly, "One other thing, Walker." Dan turned to face him again, gaining a clearer idea of the man's imposing size when standing face to face with him, at close quarters, for the first time. Dan was surprised that he had to look up to meet Tolar's hard eyes. The man was a giant.

"I been sort of known around here as the best man at hand-to-hand fighting. Just old country knuckle and skull fights at the dances, you know. Well, I got a couple of kids now, and I figure it ain't fittin'. I figure to settle down some. Anyhow, that fellow Channing, he came over and bought me a drink at the saloon last week. Said he'd give me twenty bucks if I busted you up good at the dance tomorrow night. I told him I'd think it over."

The big man was shifting uncomfortably from one foot to the other. Dan kept his voice friendly. "Don't sound like much of a prizefight, just twenty dollars."

"Well, you being almost as big as me, them boys wouldn't like nothing better than to see us tangle. They'd think it'd be a good show. Guess it would, too." Dan could see that the man was trying to say something that was hard for him. He stood patiently, waiting for the big fellow to work it out.

"Uh, you see, my wife will be there. She's been working real hard to learn white man's dances. She's all excited about it. I never took her to no dance before." He cleared his throat awkwardly, spat to the side, and stood rubbing his face while he watched for Dan's reaction.

Dan nodded approvingly. "That's nice. She'll have a good time. She'll be nervous and excited, everything being new to her. You'll want to stick close to make sure everything goes nice for her."

Tolar's face brightened. "Yeah, you got the drift. I don't want to get into no fight this time. Them boys are going to try to get us to have a go at each other, though. I thought, if it's agreeable to you, we could make a big show of being friends, like we knew each other a long time. If you're taken with the idea you'd like to try me on, I'd consider it a favor if you'd put it off till after the dance. Sort of postpone it, if it ain't inconvenient or nothin' for you."

Dan laughed and put a hand on Tolar's massive shoulder. "How about us putting that off forever? Is that long enough?"

Tolar's big smile showed his relief. "Shake on that, Walker. That's a load off my mind. That's mighty fine."

The two men shook hands, grinning at each other.

"What about the twenty dollars Channing offered you to bust me up?"

Tolar shook his head and his grin got even wider. "I sure hate to give it up. Twenty dollars is a bunch of money, but he didn't give me none of it yet, and I didn't agree to nothing, so I ain't obliged. I'd rather my wife have a good time than to have that money. Besides, I ain't seen him for a while, like I told you, and he might've skipped town. Say, Dan, I just thought of something. Why don't you drop by and have supper with me and the wife this evening?"

Dan noticed the shift from "Walker" to "Dan" in Tolar's last comment. He figured that he had passed some unknown test and was getting a chance to make a real friend of this big man. There was something about Tolar that appealed to him. Maybe Tolar felt the same way. Some men just seemed to get along well together.

Tolar pointed to a cabin set back in a little clump of trees. "Just come on by a little bit before dark. We'll be watching for you."

"That's real nice of you, Tom. After living with Joe Ballas for a couple of weeks, it's going to be a pleasure to be around someone who'll say a few words once in a while."

Tom Tolar laughed. "Yeah, I know. Old Joe is a real easy talker, ain't he?"

Dan walked to the hotel and laid out his rolled-up ball of wet clothing to dry in his room. Then he went downstairs and rode Big Red to the stable. He walked the short distance back to the hotel. The first thing he did when he was inside his room again was to remove his boots. They were almost dry. He sat on the bed and took a heavy curved needle from his bedroll. He took a wicked, narrow eight-inch throwing knife from his old pair of boots. He used the knife to cut a piece of leather from one of his old boots, which he sewed into the new one. The knife vanished into its new home in his right boot.

Working swiftly, he laid his spare pistol on the bed while he cleaned and oiled the weapon from his holster. As soon as he finished and reloaded the first weapon, he cleaned the spare. He removed the lid from a small round tin of grease, dipped the tips of his fingers into it, and carefully rubbed it around the inside of his holster. He tested the interior of the holster with careful fingers before replacing the pistol. He lifted the weapon from the holster and dropped it back several times before he was satisfied.

He stepped out into the hall. As soon as he saw that he was not observed, he slipped a short piece of black thread around the latch and under a splinter in the door facing. He would be able to feel for that thread in the dark. It would tell him if anyone had been in his room while he was absent.

When Dan came in sight of the well-built cabin that Tolar had pointed out to him, he stood for a moment admiring the carefully fitted log walls. If Tolar had built this house himself, he had a rare talent with an ax. Neat beds of fall flowers still in bloom and a porch swing gently swaying in the breeze gave the place a comfortable, homelike appearance. A horse standing at the hitching rail in front caused Dan to wonder if there was another visitor. When he stepped up on the front porch, the door opened before he could knock. Tolar stood there with a grin of welcome and said, "Come on in, Dan, come on in. Thought you was never going to get here."

Dan stepped inside, and the first thing he saw was Alice Martin, sitting in a big leather chair and looking at him with a wide-eyed, startled expression. Tolar was obviously delighted when Dan stiffened in surprise. "I think you two met once before. Leastwise, that's what I heard."

Alice gave Tolar a smiling glance and returned her gaze to Dan. She said, "I suppose you're as surprised as I am, Dan. Tom didn't tell me you were coming. I'm glad to see you."

"Same for me, Alice. Once we got to the M Bar M, seemed like you kind of vanished. I think this is the first time I've seen you since we came down from the mountains."

"I've had lots of work to do. It took me several days to get our books figured out. There are still several gaps where I can't imagine what that man Channing was doing. For a manager hired by Ira Rice to represent the bank, he kept terrible records. I don't understand it. Everything seems to be costing more than I remember, and we've had to hire more men than before. I wasn't hiding. I was working."

"Alice usually stays here with us when she comes to town, which ain't often enough," Tolar said. "The hotel sometimes gets a little loud when the boys have been doing some drinking." Dan saw Tolar's eyes shift to the side, and he turned in time to see a tall Indian woman come into the room. "This is Katherine, Dan, my wife." Tolar snapped his fingers and corrected himself. "I meant to say, 'Mrs. Tolar, may I present Mr. Walker. Mr. Walker, this is Mrs. Tolar.' Was that the right way, Katherine?"

Dan knew that his eyes had registered shock, and he fought to control his expression. This was the most beautiful Indian woman he had ever seen. Her movements as she advanced to greet him were smooth and graceful, her expression calm and confident. She was dressed in ordinary white woman's clothing, but her dark coloring and high cheekbones clearly indicated her heritage. She flashed him a smile and said, "How do you do, Mr. Walker," in a low voice.

"How do you do, Mrs. Tolar. I gather from Tom's remark that you're having some trouble teaching him civilized manners."

Her smile widened as she said, "And Tom tells me that you are part Indian, Mr. Walker."

"Yes, ma'am."

Tolar put his arm around her and announced proudly, "She can read and do sums and all kind of clever things, Dan. She's been showing me, and I think I'm about to get the hang of it. She's a good teacher, got lots of patience."

"I can cook, too, Mr. Walker. Dinner is served."

They seated themselves around a large table, and Dan asked, "Where are the children? Didn't you tell me you had a couple of youngsters at home, Tom?"

Katherine answered, "They're too small to sit at the table when company comes. I fed them and put them to bed earlier in the evening. Tell me, do you dance, Mr. Walker?"

Somewhat taken aback, Dan said, "Yes, ma'am, I do. My daddy saw to that. He insisted that I take dancing lessons when I was a little boy. Most humiliating thing I ever went through. Not to be immodest, ma'am. It ain't one of my proudest achievements, but I know most of the steps well enough to keep out of people's way."

Katherine said in a flat, matter-of-fact tone, "I don't think I need tell you of the social problem that stems from being Indian. Tom has been reluctant to take me to dances. I never learned to dance in mission school. That's one thing they never taught us. He's decided to take me tomorrow night, and we could use your help. Tom has attended many . dances, but I gather that he seldom goes near the music. It seems that he engages in other vigorous exercise." She gave Tolar an amused look, and he grinned back at her. "Would you be willing to help us, both of you, to learn to dance . . . this evening after dinner?"

Dan laughed with such pleasure that he saw Alice look at him with surprise. He loved to dance, and teaching this graceful woman would be an easy task. The whole idea of having to come to the big dance was beginning to sound better if he could look forward to having some friends among all these strangers. Besides, his concern about Joe Ballas was probably silly, like worrying about a mountain lion. "Ma'am, that would be an honor and a pleasure. I'll be glad to dance with you until that grinning man-mountain over there runs me off." He turned to Alice. "How about you, kid? You think you can train that big bear to dance?"

Alice gave him a furious look and asked, "What name did you call me, sir?"

A sudden silence fell with all movement at the table suspended. Dan, having felt relaxed and expansive, straightened in his chair, suddenly brought up short. He didn't know what had happened. "Name? Name?" His mind was blank.

"I thought I asked you not to call me 'kid' anymore. I thought I made it clear that I didn't like it."

Dan carefully placed his fork on his plate. "I beg your pardon, Miss Martin. It was an unguarded moment. I forgot . . . that is . . . it was an accident. Honest, kid, I wasn't thinking. Oh, I did it again."

His face nearly went into his plate from the force of the slam on the back he received from Tom Tolar. "Haw, haw! She sounds just like Katherine! Haw, haw! Just like Katherine when she gets on my poor back. Ain't nothing to do but duck, Dan, duck!"

Alice was doubled over laughing. Dan knew he shouldn't have been surprised, but he was. First he had thought she was a no-account, soft, tenderfoot boy. Then he figured she was a skinny, underfed daughter of a down-and-out family. Then she turned out to be the beautiful, well-schooled daughter of a big rancher. He was just getting her placed in that role, but now she was showing the same teasing, rough brand of humor found in a bunkhouse full of hired hands. The woman simply didn't seem to fit into a mold; every time he thought he had her figured out, she changed into something different.

V

Daniel Webster Walker, Sr., leaned back in his great chair and smoothed his graying beard reflectively. He was seated behind a broad desk of polished, gleaming mahogany. The large room was richly furnished, more like a tasteful study in a wealthy man's home than an office.

Walker considered himself to be in the prime of life. At fifty-five, his weight was the same 250 pounds it had been when he was twenty-five, and he still wore clothing of the same size. "Big Dan" was accustomed to towering over everyone with his six-foot four-inch frame. His booming laugh and genial expression concealed his true nature from all except a few close business associates. Most people regarded him as an oversized, good-natured, untutored man of below average intelligence who had been lucky enough to become modestly wealthy. They thought it mildly odd that Big Dan had courted and won the hand of the Widow Whitson.

Margaret Whitson, a tall, graceful, patrician woman was thought to be fabulously wealthy. Her husband, lost at sea several years ago, had been an astute businessman with all the advantages of inherited money. However, her wealth and beauty did not compensate for her arrogant manner and acid tongue. Her brutally honest conversation and no-nonsense attitude caused many of the ladies of high social standing to flinch when her name appeared on a guest list. Furthermore, many of the social set regarded Mrs. Whitson as past her prime at fifty, with two grown sons, although all admitted that she looked much younger than her years.

It pleased the giant Walker to recall the first conversation between him and Margaret. They had been introduced and paired off for dinner at the home of mutual acquaintances. She had taken his arm as they walked through a garden of roses, looked directly at him, and asked, "Is it true, Mr. Walker, that men of large size tend to be dull-witted?"

With the big grin that was his trademark, he responded, "Yes, madame, I regret it, but it must be true." He watched the mixture of contempt and disappointment appear in her eyes before he added, "That must be the reason I have looked forward to meeting you so much, madame. I have heard that your conversation is honest and straightforward. We, the dull-witted, like that. We know where we stand."

He had walked several steps to let that sink in properly before he continued. "Besides, a man of my obvious wealth and beauty is constantly being molested and disturbed by nubile maidens. I have been looking forward to a peaceful evening with a harmless old woman."

She had inhaled sharply in surprise. "You are insulting, sir! You are no gentleman."

Maintaining a quiet, friendly tone of voice, he responded, "No, madame. As you were implying, I am merely simple. We dull-witted men always pay our debts. If someone says something nice to us we return the compliment. If someone says something mean, we keep our powder dry." He could see a beginning of a smile in her eyes.

"Perhaps we could be friends, Mr. Walker."

"No, madame, not perhaps. It's our destiny. I would like to call on you, Mrs. Whitson. I find you attractive."

Her expression had turned speculative and her voice uncertain when she replied slowly, "You presume much on short acquaintance. You sound like a fortune hunter, sir. I believe you to be of modest means, while my relative wealth is well known."

"Ah, yes. You surprise me, madame. I was warned of your candor, but you still astonish me with your honesty. I suggest that we start our friendship with a mutually profitable business transaction. I would like to call on you tomorrow afternoon. We can begin to arrange at that time for me to purchase all of your assets. You can easily divide the money between your sons. Then your tiny fortune can be dismissed as a barrier to our open friendship."

"Tiny fortune! Why you . . . !" Suddenly, she burst into delighted laughter and stepped close to him. "If you are bluffing, Mr. Walker, you have fallen into a terrible trap. I accept your offer. If you have insufficient funds, I shall see that the news of your bluff is all over town by nightfall tomorrow. You will be a laughingstock."

"I have noticed that many men laugh at me, Mrs. Whitson, until they come to try to borrow money."

Big Dan laughed out loud in the empty office. Margaret Whitson, whom he had long called "Grit" in private, had become more than a friend. She had filled the aching gap in his life since the death of Gray Bird, Little Dan's mother. She had laughed with genuine good humor after their marriage when he told her of the group of detectives and informants he kept on retainer. Their sole purpose was to inform him of the composition and extent of things like the Widow Whitson's "tiny" fortune and other matters of business interest to him.

The two Dans, father and son, had discussed the Whitson properties, how they would integrate with enormous advantage into the Walker holdings. They had agreed that Margaret's two sons were magnificent young men with strong characters and excellent educations. If Big Dan could attract their interest, their youthful energy, talent, and experience gained from managing their mother's properties made them exciting prospects. Their services would increase tremendously the potential profits of the combined assets of the two families. The two Dans hoped that the Whitson sons would use the money from the sale of their mother's properties to increase the holdings of the combined families in the many Walker enterprises.

Big Dan figured that things had been going too well to last. A cold-blooded plan for a marriage of financial convenience had turned into a true love match before it could be consummated. Astounded, but enormously pleased, he had watched the growth of a powerful sense of brotherhood between Matthew and Mark Whitson and the distant, uncommunicative young Dan. Margaret's affection for young Dan completed the circle of an intense family bond without blood kinship.

For four years, business had been good, profits had rolled in, his holdings had been freed from all debt, the family had grown closer together, and everything had gone well. Then tragedy struck with shattering speed and violence. Two hot-blooded brothers of a young woman Mark had been seeing became enraged at some imagined slight. Mark and the young woman had a spat, the two brothers attacked Mark with pistols, and young Dan killed them both. The entire incident had taken only minutes.

Young Dan had disappeared without knowing that he had a chance to be cleared of legal fault. He had taken action to defend his unarmed stepbrother from a mortal threat. The courts had called his actions justifiable homicide and had cleared him, but it had taken six months, with the final decision coming this very day.

Big Dan had figured that his son would communicate with him somehow, but he had heard nothing. Dan figured he knew his son. The boy did things thoroughly. Once he decided to run, he wouldn't do it halfway. He would run long, not short; he would travel far. He would be far enough away that news of his being cleared would almost surely fail to reach him. Big Dan shifted his weight in his chair. "He's twenty-four years old now, if he still lives," he mused aloud.

The door opened and Margaret stepped into the room. Big Dan knew it would be his wife before he turned his head toward the door. No other person would dare enter his office without knocking, nor would anyone else have been allowed past his clerical staff to take such liberty. She gave an amused look at his relaxed form and said, "Sorry if I woke you."

Big Dan came to his feet and bent to her kiss. "Old men like me take to sitting and dreaming, Grit. I was just sitting here feeling sorry for myself about Little Dan. I guess something happened to him. Surely we would have heard from him by now if he . . ."

"Was still alive?" she finished for him. "Is that what you wanted to say?"

"I think maybe I brought this on myself, Grit. I never gave that boy an inch all his life. Gray Bird and I were determined that our only boy would be all things to all men. We taught him to be self-sufficient in every kind of situation. He probably thinks he'd be a failure if he got in touch with me now. He knows I'd try to help him, and he fears that I'd get hurt by being involved. He sees himself as a big embarrassment and threat to the whole family, a fugitive killer."

With a glance at the closed door, she pushed him gently into his chair and perched on his knee. "You see him as a product of unusual training, a man who has been trained from the time he was a baby to be both a successful Indian warrior and an educated, efficient white businessman. I see him quite differently."

"Yeah, I know," he responded with the voice of a man who knows he's going to hear something he has heard before.

"Now, really, Dan. You listen to me. That is a very sensitive boy. You and Gray Bird assured that he was taught all those things about business, mathematics, dancing, weapons, hunting, tracking, and so on. I suppose he's a very dangerous man if pushed. It only took him a few seconds to kill those two poor misguided men when they tried to hurt Mark."

She shifted from her perch on his knee, curling gracefully into a kittenish ball in his lap. It was a smooth, trusting, intensely feminine movement. He found such openly loving gestures from this wife of his, this woman with such a fierce, arrogant reputation, to be irresistibly appealing. A brilliant woman, sharply impatient with the superficial silliness of so many of her gender, she could teach them all when it came to womanly tenderness, passion, and loyalty. Big Dan knew a trace of a hard smile came to his lips with the thought that he and his wife fooled most of the world. He was thought to be a genial bumbler and was growing richer by the hour. She was thought to be a shrew and was an incomparably generous, thoughtful partner.

She softly combed his beard with subtly perfumed fingers. Big Dan found no contradiction between the loving caresses and the matter-of-fact voice when she continued to speak. Grit was not a woman for baby talk. "I had the opportunity to know the real Dan, the one behind the false front. I found out that he's very sensitive and reserved. He's a special kind of man; he'd rather die than embarrass someone he thinks trusts him. You kept him so busy learning a hundred skills that he never had time to have friends like a normal boy. I think that's why his feeling for Matt and Mark is so strong. He has so few friends that he puts so much feeling, such great importance, on the few he has."

"You're winding up like a clock. You've been thinking about this a long time. I can feel it like a train coming down a track right at me. You're about to issue orders."

"Don't interrupt. You just sit there and listen. I want you to spend big chunks of your cash. If anyone can afford to spend some money, it's you. You also have political influence, which will help. I want you to institute a search all over the country. If you find him and tell him all's well, he'll come home in a minute. Until then he's going to stay away for fear of causing you trouble."

"Impossible, Grit. This is a big country. He's surely using a different name, maybe several different names."

She turned and straightened until her nose was almost against his and looked into his eyes. "For a man who reads people's minds in business negotiations, you have a peculiar blind spot, big man. That boy loves you beyond most men's understanding. He'd be fed to lions like an ancient Christian before he'd deny being a Walker." With their noses almost touching, she sat looking into his eyes as silence fell.

Finally, her voice harshly challenging, she said, "Name the biggest bet you can think of, Big Dan. I'll bet that you can find him by searching for a man named Walker. Name your bet." She drew away, rose to her feet, and stood looking down at him. "Or, if he's with the Indians, you'll find him by asking for Walking Hawk. You can bet on that, too."

Big Dan could feel the heavy tension building in the air that evening. He looked around the table at the faces that had come to mean so much to him. Margaret's was composed, but her fingers were nervously busy spinning the wine glass in front of her. Mark Whitson, the younger of her sons at twenty-two, had retreated behind his card-playing mask. Matthew, the elder at twenty-five, was wearing a similar expression, unwittingly emphasizing the remarkable physical resemblance shared by the two brothers. Dan couldn't help grinning at the two of them.

"Gentlemen, the house rule not to discuss business during a meal has been scrupulously observed. I thank you for that courtesy. Now, let's have it. I can't take the suspense any longer. Whatever it is, we'll work together to repair the damage or whatever is necessary."

"You haven't told him anything, Mother?" Matt's voice was tense.

"I do not believe it appropriate for a lady to meddle in men's affairs," she responded loftily. When all three of the men burst into laughter, Margaret's expression began to soften, her eyes sending a smile to each of them in turn.

"Well, let's have it. What's going on?" Dan asked.

Matthew and Mark eyed each other briefly before Matt turned to Dan. "Two items of business, Dan. First, my brother and I have decided to take legal action to change our names. We've chosen to take the name Whitson-Walker. However, we felt that we should ask your approval in case you might object."

"Object!" the word exploded out of him. "Why, that's the finest compliment I've ever had in my life. I presume you've discussed this with your mother and obtained her approval?"

"Yes, sir, we have. You know it's been ten years since our father was lost at sea. We both remember him with great affection, but we think . . ." Matt stopped and cleared his throat. "We think this would indicate the state of feelings under this roof. We feel that you're a true father to us, and we would like to have the honor of bearing your name."

Dan knew that his face was growing flushed, and he could feel tears in his eyes. As he made a casual show of mopping his face with his handkerchief, the thought came to him that these two strapping young blond, blue-eyed men looked much more like his natural sons than did his own.

They came to their feet when he did. They both had a tense look, as if wondering what he was going to do. "I can't just sit here. I think I must be about to burst with pride. Seems to me it's time for some huggin'," Dan said hoarsely as he reached for Matt. Mark came around the table quickly to join in the embrace, arriving at the same time as Margaret. They all stood wordlessly together in each other's arms for a moment before returning to their seats.

"There's another thing, Dan," Matt said when he had returned his own handkerchief to his pocket.

"You boys are knocking me over tonight. I was all braced for something terrible. What's next?"

"Well, it's about money, Dan." Mark had now assumed the role of spokesman. "Matt and I would like to sell you some of our assets that we received from Mother. That is to say, we want to sell you some of the assets we bought with the money she gave us. We're going to need quite a lot of money, we think, in the near future. We want to keep these properties in the family if we can. Also, we want to do some traveling, so we figured we'd better warn you and help you pick some people to do our work for a while."

Dan was stunned and his voice clearly showed his shock. "Sell out? Leave? Where will you go? You don't need to do this to take a vacation, even a long one. Is something wrong?"

"We want to go look for our brother," Mark said simply.

Dan turned to Margaret, but a tiny shake of her head and a twitch of a shrug disclaimed any prior knowledge on her part. He sat very still while the silence in the room continued. Slowly, Dan lowered his head and rubbed his forehead in thought. No one moved. Finally, Dan raised his eyes, again directing a questioning look at Margaret. This time she smiled, as if reading his mind, and nodded. Matt and Mark sat quietly while their mother and Dan sat looking at each other.

"Gentlemen, there need be no talk of you sacrificing your inheritance. I think you have too modest a perception of how wealthy a poor Scot with a smart little Indian wife can get. Trading furs and saving and digging a little gold and shrewd investing and modest living and good luck and time can do wonders. I think we will have sufficient funds to do a thorough job. Our problem is going to be planning and proper organization. It seems to me that a search can be done in a businesslike manner just like any other enterprise, and a good time to start seems to be right now. Shall we begin?"

Margaret rose from her seat and started to the door. Her husband and her two sons came to their feet and exchanged surprised glances. "Grit? Aren't you going to help?"

She turned back to them as she opened the door. Lamplight caught the shine of tears on her cheeks. "Oh yes. I'll be back in just a few minutes. I wouldn't miss this conference for anything."

Dan was puzzled. "Where are you going then? Are you all right?"

"I'm fine, thank you. I'm just going upstairs to our bedroom for a moment. I have an urge right this minute to say thanks for the men in my life." She stepped out and closed the door quietly.

The three men stood looking at each other in an embarrassed silence for a moment before Dan said, "Gentlemen, your mother is a good woman and a smart one. I hope you both can find someone like her. But that kind of woman can sure put a load on a man to be better than he knows how to be."

VI

Dan rode till he was in sight of the Stenholm ranch buildings. He was sure that this was the correct place. There were wagons parked all around the main buildings, and there was already a crowd watching the cooks at work around a smoking fire trench.

He changed direction to ride into a clump of trees. He put on his new clothes, careful not to drag the legs of his clean suit trousers on the ground when he got into them. Jesse Robers had laid out a fancy white shirt with a frilled front for him to see when he went to pick up his new suit. "You better buy that," Robers had commented flatly. "I don't have much call for nice stuff in a big size like you wear. You ain't going to find a perfect fit like that every day."

Dan had looked up from the price tag with a grimace and Robers had added defensively, "You ain't going to get the owner's wife to wash and iron a fancy thing like that every time you buy one, either." Dan's glance moved to the quiet little woman smiling at him from where she was folding and stacking dry goods onto a shelf. Sweeping off his new hat, Dan had bowed and said, "Mrs. Robers, I'm deeply obliged. A clean and properly ironed shirt can make a shabby-looking man into a well-dressed gentleman. I am in your debt."

He looked back to find Robers looking amused. "My, my, smooth manners and fancy talk from a gun-totin' bunkhouse brawler." Dan had cursed inwardly. He should have been up in the hills with Joe Ballas, not down here attracting attention and causing curious talk. That had been a serious mistake. He must be careful what came out of his mouth if he wanted to fade into the background.

Dan felt at cross-purposes about coming to the dance anyway. He loved to dance, had received many compliments in happier times on his ability. It always seemed to surprise people for some strange reason when a big man moved around gracefully. Why should that be considered unusual? He liked to be around people having a good time, too, but there was a smoldering resentment in him. Much as he might enjoy it, he hated being ordered to come. It reminded him of his rage at being ordered to dancing lessons when he was an awkward boy, and close contact with girls had made him hot and uncomfortable.

He rode slowly toward the crowd, looking for M Bar M people. He had seen them leave town long before he saddled Big Red. When he drew closer, he finally saw some of the familiar hands around the fire trench helping turn two halves of beef. Red Cougan came walking out of the barn when Dan stepped out of the saddle and called, "Hey, Walker, take your horse over there to the M Bar M wagon and put him on our picket string." Dan nodded and climbed back into the saddle for the short ride to the wagon indicated by Red's extended arm. He stripped the saddle off Big Red, dropped it with the others on the ground by the wagon, and walked toward the group around the cooking fire.

Men came forward to introduce themselves and shake hands. There were several remarks that it was lucky for everyone that he came by at the right time to help Alice Martin. Dan quickly came to realize that the M Bar M was the largest ranch in this part of the country, and the Martins were highly respected and admired by their neighbors. Several men offered Dan a secret pull at bottles hidden in their coats. He always declined with thanks, saying that he had already had too much and didn't want to fall down in his new clothes until after the dance.

Dan realized that he had, out of habit, dressed too well. Most of the men were wearing normal range attire, just their newest and cleanest. Red walked by and said innocently, "Mr. Walker here is spending his vacation at the M Bar M. He's actually a big banker from back East. He's thinking about buying two or three towns to play with." The group standing around laughed, and Dan laughed with them.

"Yeah, that's right, but I was looking for something with a railroad through it and a couple of gold mines real close." The laughter broke off when a buckboard came into sight.

Someone in the group said, "Here comes that damn squaw man." Another voice said, "Aw, let him alone. Tolar's a good man, and his wife is a nice woman." Dan could feel the tension around him as the men shifted uneasily. It was obvious that opinions were divided in the community about Tom and Katherine.

When she and Tom pulled up in front of the ranch house, Dan saw that Katherine was wearing a dust coat long enough to reach her ankles. Tom dismounted and helped her down. Conversation had all but stopped while the men stood watching. Alice Martin appeared on the front porch and walked to meet Katherine. Tom scanned the groups of men standing around and started toward Dan as soon as he spied him. "You wanta take off those prissy clothes before I whup you, Walker?"

"Don't come around me, Tolar. I just had a bath," Dan snarled. Tom straightened from his menacing, glowering approach and stuck out his hand, grinning.

Dan could hear the change in the breathing of the men around him. All of them had backed away during Tom's approach. They were caught by surprise when the two men stood shaking hands and grinning at each other rather than coming to blows. Tom looked enviously at Dan's fancy shirt and said, "Ain't that a pretty thing. Can I touch it?"

There was a scattering of snickers when Dan said, "Keep your dirty hands off my new shirt. That's for the ladies to admire, not no grubby blacksmith."

"You and Dan know each other already, Tom?" asked Red Cougan.

"Yeah, me and Dan got into a fight one time," Tom said with a straight face.

"Who won?" The question came from somewhere in the group.

"We did. Started out with eight dumb cowpunchers crowding us up in a little saloon and making too much noise. When me and Dan finished, it was real quiet, and we was all alone, 'cept for the bartender. Me and

Dan like things to be quiet so we can think when we're drinkin', don't we, Dan?"

Dan nodded solemnly. "Actually, we like it quiet so I can think and Tom can drink, to tell the truth. We got confused one time about that. I did some drinkin' while Tom tried to do some thinkin'. We both got an awful headache."

The men were still laughing when there was a call for help to set up tables. The women were ready to bring food from the house, and it was time to take the beef off the fire and start cutting it into portions.

Since each group of guests had brought its own tables, dishes, and eating utensils, the crowd broke into family and ranch groups for the meal. Favorite foods had also been brought along, but the dishes were divided and passed around so all could have a taste of favored recipes from other homes. Dan heard conversation indicating that some of the guests had ridden a hundred miles to get to the Stenholm dance.

The Cougans sat at a table a few feet away from a longer one for the crew. When Dan approached with his plate loaded with beef, Red waved him to a seat across from him. Mrs. Cougan was already seated. Dan looked at the remaining empty chair and asked, "Will Miss Martin be eating with us?" When Red nodded, Dan came to his feet. "I'll serve a plate for her."

Mrs. Cougan smiled at Dan. "That sounds nice. Any of the other men around here would have said, 'I'll git her some grub,' but you don't need to do anything. Here she comes with a loaded plate."

After the meal, everyone picked up his own plate and filed past tubs of water that had been placed to heat over the cooking trenches. What would have been a big cleanup job for the women was finished in minutes with everyone washing his own. The women went back to the house to change into their party dresses for the dance, and the men began lighting lanterns. It was still early in the evening, but the lanterns were already needed in the dark interior of the huge barn. Dan watched while the short, fat Stenholm, obviously enjoying his role as host, walked around sprinkling water to settle the sawdust that had been spread on the hard-packed earth floor.

Red Cougan walked up to Dan and spoke casually. "Watch the front porch. When the women start coming out and standing around on the porch, look for Miss Alice. You escort her from the house to the barn." Dan gave him a questioning look and pointed at himself, wordlessly asking if Cougan really meant the comment for him. Cougan nodded and said, "Yeah, you, Walker."

Dan was beginning to feel that this was going too far. He didn't care for people who were always looking for a chance to feel insulted, but he was mad enough to saddle Big Red and ride out right now.

He didn't feel like a stranger to Alice. Their ride into the mountains and back had been an unpleasant introduction, but their evening of dinner and dancing with the Tolars had been relaxed and informal. The conversation at the table with the Cougans today had been nothing but casual small talk. There had been ample opportunity. Why hadn't she simply asked him to escort her from the house to the barn? But no, she didn't do that. Instead, she sent the foreman with another order. One minute she seemed friendly enough, the next minute he was being indirectly ordered around like a gigolo.

He wondered. She said that she had been to school. Surely she had been taught something about social graces. Was he supposed to be so honored and so ignorant that he didn't detect the insult? First, he was ordered to the dance. Now, he was ordered to escort her from here to yonder at the dance, without ever a simple request or invitation from her. Always, it was orders through someone else. Were these the actions of an unbearably arrogant, spoiled woman? Dan's head jerked when a new thought struck him. Why was he so angry? Why did he give a damn?

Dan was tempted to make her wait when Alice stepped out on the porch, but he was embarrassed to think how small and mean that would have been. He went at once to the steps, extended his hand, and asked, "Miss Martin, may I walk you to the dance?"

It seemed to Dan that she looked surprised and a little flustered as if she were very pleased and flattered. "How considerate of you, Mr. Walker." She put one hand in his while she lifted her long skirt a little with the other as she came down the steps. Then she put her hand lightly on his arm for the short walk to the barn. Her light blue gown enhanced the color of her eyes. The dress was also a perfect shade to complement her blond hair. Dan found himself feeling proud to walk beside her. She was easily the best-looking woman on the place. They had taught her how to walk, at least, in that school she attended.

"You are lovely this evening, Miss Martin. Your dress is perfect for you. It does wonderful things for your eyes." Dan slipped into the conversational pattern in which he had been trained before thinking about it. He felt her turn. Her expression was openly curious when he looked down.

"Dan, you don't sound like the same man all the time. Every once in a while you say something like that, and then act like you're going to bite your tongue."

"If they play a waltz tonight, I'd like a dance, if your dances aren't all promised." Dan figured that he needed to get her thinking about something else.

She laughed and said, "We don't have dance cards out here in the country, Dan. I'll wait for you when they play a waltz. Don't forget and leave me standing there."

It was a square dance, and it was fun for Dan. They only played two waltzes. During the first one he found Alice to be a graceful, delightful partner. By the end of that waltz, many of the dancers had stopped to watch them, and there was a spatter of applause when the music stopped. Dan was halfway through the second waltz when he realized that nobody else was dancing. Everyone stood around the walls of the barn and watched. When the music stopped that time, everyone applauded, and Dan found himself bowing while Alice curtsied to the onlookers.

"I'm determined to stop being surprised by the things you do, Dan," Alice commented while they walked toward Red and Annie. "I should have been prepared when you said your father made you learn to dance, but I wasn't ready for this. Are you casually good at everything you decide to do?"

A flicker of surprise showed through her amused expression when he responded, "Yes, but no man can dance well without a good partner. Thank you for the pleasure." She flashed him a delighted smile and seemed to be searching for a retort when he bowed, spoke to the Cougans, and walked away.

Dan went to say hello to Tom and Katherine Tolar. She was wearing a striking dress of a deep wine hue with a white shawl and sash. The dress provided a superb accent to her dark, glowing beauty. When she saw him coming, she extended both her hands in a charming, openly happy greeting. He took and held her hands and stood admiring her for a moment. "Tom, it's a good thing your wife is a real beauty. Otherwise, the prettiest dress at the dance would be wasted."

Tom laughed while Katherine blushed furiously, obviously flattered to the point of discomfort. "That's what I been telling her, Dan, but I can't say it neat like you do. She don't pay no attention to what I say anyhow."

"How are you doing with dancing the paleface way, Katherine? Are you finding it easier with music like we told you it would be?"

"Oh yes, Dan. We've been having a wonderful time. Thank you so very much for helping us, but it was worth coming just to see you and Alice dance together."

A pinch-faced young woman standing nearby said in a brittle voice, "Maybe we should get some drums so the squaw could do some dances she knows better."

Tom's face hardened and a stricken look crossed Katherine's as Dan turned quickly to the speaker. "What a wonderful idea. I've spent a lot of time with the Indians, and it's a wonder how graceful some of their dancers are. Why I've seen some little children in those villages dance so well I bet people would pay money to see it."

A cowhand standing beside pinch-face asked, "You spent a lot of time with Indians, Walker?"

Dan laughed, "Yeah, my mama and daddy treated me like I was half Indian." Several people joined in the ripple of chuckles that went through the listeners. They all froze into shocked silence when Dan added, "Maybe it was because my mother was Iroquois."

Pinch-face looked sour and said, "You ain't no half-breed. You don't look Indian at all. You're just saying that to shine up to that squaw."

"Ma'am, my daddy taught me to be respectful to a lady whenever I run into one. He cautioned me to be special careful to do that when she had a husband or a brother as big as a grizzly bear. If you watch me close when I'm around Mrs. Tolar, you'll see how well I remember what my daddy told me."

"Well," she sniffed, "seems to me you ought to tell decent people you're a half-breed, so there won't be no mistakes."

"I just did, ma'am. I wouldn't want you to make any more mistakes."

She turned to the cowhand and said, "George, are you going to let him talk to me like that?"

George, glancing from Dan to Tom, looked like a man tied to a railroad track watching a train coming. He probably weighed about 150 pounds with his boots full of water. Tom Tolar's talents were well known, and the story of Channing's fate in the M Bar M bunkhouse at Dan Walker's hands had run through the neighborhood like a prairie fire. His voice was strained when he said, "Walker, maybe you oughta apologize."

Instantly, Dan said, "Miss, I apologize if I have said anything to make you mad."

Without another word, she turned and stalked away. The puncher stepped forward and stuck out his hand, saying, "I'm George O'Connor, from the Circle J. Thanks for getting me off the hook, Walker. I been seeing Cindy for a while, but I didn't know she had such a mean streak. A woman with a mouth like that can get a man killed. I hope you ain't mad at me either, Mrs. Tolar. I'm real sorry about this."

Katherine gave the red-faced O'Connor a warm smile and said, "I remember you, George. You're Bill O'Connor's youngest son, aren't you?" When he nodded, she added, "Don't let a little thing like this ruin your dance, George. You just forget this and have yourself a good time."

"Thanks, Mrs. Tolar. I'm mighty relieved I didn't have to take these two men outside and give 'em a lickin'. It might have taken me a long time to get it done. The dance might've been over before I could get back."

Tom clapped young O'Connor on the shoulder and said, "George, I ain't seen your dad or your brothers yet. Are they here?"

"Yeah, Tom, they're around someplace."

"Well, if I don't see 'em, say hello to 'em for me, will you?"

"Sure, Tom. Well, I'll be moving on. See you later." He moved away with obvious relief.

Tom said, "Thanks, Dan. You're as quick with your mouth as a snake. I never can think of things to say in time. Women kill me. Can't just bust 'em one like you can a man. I ain't had no real trouble learnin' to dance the way you teach it. Suppose you could teach fast talkin' too?"

Dan, in a perfect imitation of broken English, responded, "Injun teach white brother. White brother carry tomahawk. Man talk bad, hit man on head, take scalp. Woman talk bad, no hit head, no hit elbow, no hit knee. Woman need head, elbow, knee to carry wood, do work. Hit woman in mouth. Woman no need mouth for work."

Katherine was looking away with her lips in a tight line to keep from laughing when Tom asked sincerely, "Where can a man find a good tomahawk?"

"I go. I find for white brother." Dan walked to where the Cougans were seated with Alice on bales of hay. "It's getting late for me. If you'll be all right with Red and Annie, Miss Alice, I'd like to start for town."

She came to her feet and curtsied. "I'm staying the night here, Dan, so I'll be fine. It's very flattering to have you concerned about me. Thank you."

Surprised and pleased, Dan couldn't remember his parting comments to Red and Annie. Alice's candor had him off balance again, made him feel small for thinking harsh thoughts about her earlier. Again his training took over and he bade them good night. Then he shook hands with Stenholm and thanked him for hosting such a pleasant social gathering.

It didn't occur to him until he was riding back to town that an ordinary cowpuncher would probably have simply walked out of the barn, straddled his horse, and departed. Well, to hell with it. You could never tell about cowhands anyway. Some were educated, cultured men. Maybe rendering a few simple courtesies wouldn't draw any particular attention to him.

The night was as black as a pit; clouds had gathered to block the light from the stars. Fortunately, Stenholm had worn a twin path from his ranch to town with his wagons, so there was no trouble finding the way. The sight of the livery stable was a cheerful one with a lantern glowing in front like a beacon. Suddenly, Dan felt as if a cold hand touched him. He didn't remember the lantern burning there last night. Was this a special gesture from the owner, a convenience for those staying in town after the dance, or was it something else?

Dan turned Big Red into a small grove of trees and thought it over. He was tired from a long day, but he had a bad feeling about that light. If an unsuspecting man rode up to the stable, he would be blinded and present an easy target for someone hidden inside. Dan debated with himself for five minutes before he decided that the risk wasn't worth taking.

He slid from the saddle and took off his coat and shirt. He took his moccasins and leather leggings from his saddlebags and carefully folded the white shirt back into the bag. He shrugged back into the coat. His black suit was fine for this type of stalking, but that white shirt was as bad as carrying a candle. He sat down in the grass, removed his boots, and laced on the moccasins and leggings tightly. He pulled a short cord of rawhide from his saddlebag, tied his boots together, and hung them across the saddle. He dropped his hat on the pommel. He took the knife from his boot and slipped it into a sheath in his right legging.

He had about two hundred yards to go. If someone was lying in ambush inside that stable, they would probably be watching the area lighted by the lantern. Unless there was more than one in there and they were extremely good at this kind of work, there would be no lookout at the rear of the building watching the dark side. Dan smiled grimly to himself. He was probably going to a lot of trouble for nothing, but a man only dies once, and he wants to put it off as long as he can. The only other light in town was in the hotel. Dan looked between the buildings as he moved behind them on the opposite side of the street. He could see through the open hotel door that the clerk was dozing at the desk.

Dan was able to keep other buildings between him and the stable for all but the last thirty yards. Even then, he had partial concealment from the corral fence as he moved toward the building. He was thankful for the unusually black night, but the reflected light from the lantern took away some of that advantage as he drew closer. Dan moved very slowly; he wanted to be able to breathe gently, especially after he got into the building. He could see now that the back door leading to the corral was open.

He reached the back wall without difficulty. As he slid along the wall, he could see nothing. As he felt his way, the gentle Indian voice whispered in his mind, "Your name brings you great honor, my son. The elders picked that name for you because you can move without noise. They say you walk as quietly as a hawk flies. It is a name all warriors will respect. The spirits have told the medicine men that is the reason your father's name among the white men is Walker. The son is like the father."

He paused at the back door to listen. He heard horses stamping, moving, chewing, breathing. Five minutes passed, then ten. Then a clear whisper, "I gotta have a cigarette. I got to move around some, too. Hell, this is dumb. When that damn Walker rides up, he ain't gonna be able to see or hear nothin' in this here building until it's too late anyhow."

"Shut up. Keep still."

"Damned if I will. He may be hours away havin' fun while we sit here like stumps. I got to pee."

Dan heard scuffling of steps in the loft and splashing of liquid. He stepped through the door and froze against the back wall.

"Jesus, that's better. I was about to bust."

"If you don't get quiet, I'm going to bust you for good. A hundred dollars apiece for one night's work is good money. Channing ain't generous. He'd of killed this hombre himself if he thought it would be easy. You keep ready to shoot and then hit the saddle fast. After it's done, we gotta git outta here before the whole town comes down on us. Now git still."

Dan had them located. The restless one was in the loft. The other was in the first stall from the front door on the left side of the building. There was more light coming in the front door from the lantern than he liked. He dropped to a crouch and slid the knife from his legging, keeping it behind his leg until he could cover it with his coat. The soft Indian voice reminded, *The light of one star shining on the blade of a knife can cost a careless warrior his life.*

A long, lingering, drawn-out fart echoed through the building followed by muffled snickering. The man right in front of Dan on the ground floor said in a disgusted whisper from his seat on a bale of hay, "Gawd's sake! You're worse'n a damn hog." Dan covered the man's nose and mouth with his left hand, pulling the seated man over backward against him. With the same movement, he drove the knife into the man's throat and dropped his weight on the sprawled man to prevent any movement. The only sound was the tiny noise of ripping cloth as Dan drove the knife in again, lower, into the heart. Dan held the man in an iron grip with all his weight on him until all twitching ceased. He removed the knife and carefully wiped it clean on the body.

The gasping, suppressed giggling in the loft continued. The whisper came again. "Wasn't me. Must've been one of them damn horses."

Dan could see the ladder leading to the loft clearly. His heart sank. He had to hope that the man in the loft was looking out into the lighted area around the lantern. If he was doing that, his eyes would be useless if he looked behind him toward the dark area where the ladder entered the loft. Slowly, Dan started up, placing his feet as near the edge of each rung of the ladder as he could. He tested each rung, applying his weight slowly. He wanted no squeak of loose nails.

Dan raised his head above the level of the loft floor, prepared to leave the ladder and drop if necessary to avoid a shot. The second man was seated beside the loft door. He had propped the door open about a foot. His eyes were fixed on the opening, his face clearly illuminated by the light from the lantern.

The fellow seemed to feel Dan's presence at the last moment and turned to look over his shoulder. Dan drove six inches of steel into the man's right eye. Again, Dan dropped his weight on his man, smothered the convulsive twitching until the body was completely still, and wiped his knife on the body. Dan ran his hands over the man, found a money belt around his waist, and emptied it. As he put the money into his coat pocket, the voice in his mind said quietly, *Anything on the body of a warrior you kill belongs to you.*

Quickly, Dan covered the body with hay and slipped down the ladder. He searched the second body and made the same exchange of money from a belt to his own pockets. He dragged the body into an empty stall, rolled it against the wall, and covered it thoroughly with hay. He crept out of the building, paused to wash his hands and his knife in the watering trough, and faded into the shadows on the way back to Big Red.

Twenty minutes later, Dan rode down the main street, spotless in his unwrinkled new clothes. He dismounted in front of the hotel and walked inside to find the clerk still dozing at the desk. "Hey, what're you doing still up?" he asked, pretending to be surprised.

The clerk's head popped up from the desk, and he replied grumpily, "Boss makes me stay here on busy nights. Says somebody has to be here to keep drunks from shooting the place up or burning it down."

Dan slumped against the desk. "I'm beat down, just plain wore out. Tell you what, if you'll unsaddle my horse and bring my old saddle up to my room and take my horse over to the stable, I'll give you a dollar. Would you do that for a tired man?"

The clerk jumped to his feet. "Sure, that ain't no trouble at all. I need to move around some anyway or I'll turn into a statue behind that damn desk."

Dan moved one plodding step at a time up the stairs, pretending to be so tired that each step looked like the last he would have the strength to make. By the time he reached the top of the stairs, the clerk came up with Dan's saddle over his shoulder. Dan pretended to fumble with the door latch while his fingers slid over the black thread. It was in place. Dan threw open the door and motioned the clerk ahead. As soon as he dropped the saddle into a corner, Dan gave the fellow a dollar, propped the chair against the closed door, folded his new clothes carefully, and went to bed.

VII

Dan awakened in his usual cautious manner, scanning the room and listening before he moved. The window was a square of soft light in the dark room. His inner clock had awakened him just prior to sunup. He came to his feet, splashed water on his face from the bowl on a small table by the wall, and surveyed the street through the window. No one was moving around. Dan stood thoughtfully, rubbing his wet jaw for a moment. He stepped across the room, found his razor, and flipped it open to test the edge on his thumb. He jerked the belt from his pants. With the buckle in his left hand, he pinned the other end of his belt to the floor with his foot while he stropped the razor on the leather.

He moved the small table with its bowl of water closer to the window and stood watching the street while he shaved without lathering his face. The door of the stable swung open and a cowpuncher from M Bar M walked out, leading four horses. Dan's body stiffened. Big Red was one of the horses following the man out of the stable. The puncher walked to the front of the hotel and tied the animals to the hitch rail. He vanished inside.

Dan packed his gear and was about to open the door when he heard footsteps coming down the hall. There was a knock on his door.

"Walker?"

"Yeah."

"I got that big red horse of yours out front. Everybody is gonna be eatin' breakfast downstairs in just a minute. Come on down."

"Right." Dan opened the door and stepped out, carrying his saddle. "I was just coming down. Thanks for bringing Big Red over for me."

"Think nothin' of it. No need for all of us to walk all the way down there."

"Yeah, but I owe for feed."

"Naw. M Bar M pays for us when we come to one of these wingdings.

It's a bonus we get for workin' for good folks." The puncher grinned. "We gotta buy our own whiskey, though."

Dan finished his breakfast and was walking toward the door of the hotel dining room when Red Cougan waved him over. "Headin' back to the north pasture?"

"Where else?"

Cougan grinned. "Need anything?"

"Can't think of anything."

Cougan nodded and turned back to his food without further comment, so Dan walked out of the hotel, saddled Big Red, and headed out of town. He wondered how and when the two men in the stable would be noticed under the hay. He had not heard any comment about a lawman, nor had he seen any sign of one. It seemed like almost everyone in this part of the country had been at the dance, but Dan had seen no sign of a star on anyone's shirt.

Dan was eager to get back to Joe Ballas, but there was no sense in wearing Big Red out on uphill trails just to make a few minutes difference. Relaxing in the saddle, Dan wondered if it wouldn't be better for him to keep riding right on out of this country.

He had been roped into saving Alice. Hell, anybody would have done that. Dumb kid or woman, it made no difference. Some things a man just had to do. When he rode into the M Bar M with her, and that fellow Channing talked so smart, he should have kept his mouth shut. Big Mouth Walker had to show off. No, that wasn't it. Dan knew he had no need to show off in front of these people. What would be the point of that? The idea was absurd.

He had just become accustomed to looking after Alice during that ride, and he hadn't quite shaken loose from it when Channing challenged her. If that incident had happened ten minutes later, he would have watched with detached interest and minded his own business. But maybe he wouldn't have, either. She had seemed so small and tired, and Channing had acted like such a damn horse's ass.

The thought came to Dan that Channing must be insane. He had no idea what a ranch manager's wages might be, but paying two outlaws a hundred dollars each to kill a man was crazy. Channing seemed to have left the country, but his hate must have been clear out of control to send men back to kill somebody over a bunkhouse fight. Two hundred dollars! It would take a top hand a long time to save that kind of money. Since his first try failed, would Channing try again? Where was he now?

Would he have enough money to send others to try again, would he decide to try it himself, or would he come to his senses and forget the whole thing?

Remembering the heavy money belts, Dan fumbled in his coat pocket and drew out a wad of crumpled bills. Idly he smoothed the money and counted it. Rolling it tightly, he slipped it down into the buckskin rifle scabbard, tamping the bills down with the muzzle of the weapon. Those two outlaws had not been down-and-out range bums, not carrying over six hundred dollars cash in money belts. Being an outlaw must pay good around here. How? Where would they get that kind of money?

Dan thought grimly how little six hundred dollars would have counted with him at one time. He reminded himself not to think about the past. He had to figure something out for a future. There was nothing for him here. The stay up at the north pasture with Joe Ballas might keep him out of sight for a while. The more time that passed the better. Maybe his trail was growing cold by now anyway.

Dan almost reined Big Red to a halt. Why not ride on? Why hang around here waiting for a crazy man to try to kill him again? He could ride a long time on that money in his gun boot. Dan smiled grimly at the thought that Channing had unwittingly provided him traveling money.

Joe Ballas needed Dan Walker like he needed a boil on his butt. That old man had once gone four days without saying a single word. Big Red was more company. At least Big Red would whinny hello in the mornings. Still, he was only one old man, and there was no telling what he was up against. It wouldn't be right to ride off when the old man was counting on him, even though the contemptuous old bastard had made it plain that he didn't count on Dan for much. On the other hand, Dan had caught Joe several times watching him and nodding to himself as if in satisfaction or approval.

The picture of Alice, looking up at him as he walked her to the dance, came to him. By damn, she was a pretty woman, but pretty women were everywhere you looked, everywhere you went. Still, he felt a tension, a special lift, every time he thought about her. Smart woman, Joe said, running the biggest ranch in this area when still a young girl. Dan had no interest in helpless women. Gray Bird had been a big influence in his life, and she hadn't been a stand-around, do-for-me person. Margaret was the same way, tough and smart, although she wasn't as gentle about it as Gray Bird had been. Margaret could take off hide with her tongue.

There was no sign that Alice needed or wanted his help, and that was probably why he found her so interesting. She was attracted to him. Once a man grew out of callow youth, he learned to read the signs. Best to stay clear of her; Dan knew himself well enough to know that he was getting too interested. Hired hands just shot themselves in the foot by getting interested in the women in owners' families.

Dan felt a pang of regret. He enjoyed the company of women, but seldom felt anything special for any particular one. In another time and in some other place, Alice might have turned into something special.

Rustlers, of course! M Bar M was losing money, and Joe was sure cattle were being stolen from the ranch. That would explain the money on the bodies of those bushwhackers in the stable. But how could a ranch manager hired by the bank have any connection to rustlers? It didn't make sense. If a prosperous ranch failed under his management, Channing would suffer loss of reputation, would be held responsible. How would such a man have any contact with rustlers except over gunsights or under hanging trees? But how could a ranch manager know how and who to hire to do murder? Just knowing where to look for hired killers was an unusual thing among honest men.

Dan wondered if those men in the stable were locals. There was no way he could find out while isolated in the mountains with Joe Ballas. The talk about them would probably have died down by the time he spoke to anyone again. He couldn't ask, would have to wait until someone volunteered news of the discovery of the bodies and whether or not they were identified.

If rustlers were hitting the north pasture, where would they live? There had to be some kind of hideout. This country was sparsely settled. As far as Dan knew, the nearest town was several days' ride away. There would be no place to market large numbers of cattle, so a large herd would attract a lot of attention. They must be driving them off in small numbers. Where could they be sold in the middle of the winter?

The answer was that it didn't make any difference if he and Joe kept their eyes open. Cattle couldn't be sold until they were stolen from the ranch. The mere presence of riders might stop the problem. Plenty of men would consider stealing if they were hard up enough, but most men wouldn't want to go through a shootout for a few head of cattle. Nobody had said anything at the dance about rustling. The subject would surely have come up if the problem was widespread. Neighbors would be quick to warn each other about that kind of problem.

Dan found himself wondering why he was spending his time worrying about problems other than his own. In the space of a few months, he had lost his own home, his family, and his position as the only natural son of a very wealthy man. The two men who had tried to kill Mark had died in seconds and he had run, almost like a reflex action. Dan knew that his father would not allow his son to go to jail. He simply wouldn't let it happen. No telling what he might have done. Likely everything the old man had worked for all his life would be lost. The only rational solution was to leave, to prevent his own misfortune from destroying everything.

Then, almost without thinking, he had killed three of the four Indians attacking Alice and her escorts. Maybe he had killed all four. There was no way for him to know whether Alice had killed the one she had wounded or whether his own shots had finished him. With his background and blood, Dan knew that killing Indians should not be any easier than killing whites. White men thought of Indians as "them." In a sense, with his Indian blood, Dan was one of "them," too. Still, those killings didn't bother him much. What else could he have done? Just like stepping in to save Mark, there was no choice, no chance to find another way.

The killing of those two outlaws last night had been completely different. He could have avoided them, maybe. Also, there had been no crisis, no hurry. He had calmly stalked them, learned their intentions, and then deliberately killed them. The whole incident was different. There is nothing distant or hurried about killing with a knife, no standing back, no chance for indifference. It is an intimate act to knife a man and hold him in your arms while he dies.

How could a cultured, educated, decent man feel nothing but satisfaction? By all rights, Dan thought that he should feel sick and depressed, horrified and shaken. He didn't, and it concerned him. For a certainty, he had killed at least seven, maybe eight, men in a few short months. His only feeling was that he had either not had a choice or had done the right thing. He felt nothing else. Yet, it seemed he should feel bad about it. Was he different from other men? Was something wrong with him? Even soldiers, he had read, felt remorse and sadness for those they were obliged to kill. Even soldiers had nightmares and felt guilt and pain in the quiet of the night.

Dan remembered his mother's quiet voice as she read the Bible aloud in the evenings. "A soft answer turneth away wrath," she had read, turning to Dan with her voice filled with wonder. "There is powerful wisdom, great medicine in this magic book."

But then, on another occasion, a visitor said, "Love thine enemies." Gray Bird had nodded in agreement and said, "Of course, all great warriors love their enemies. What would a warrior have to do without enemies? Look at their faces when they tell of great battles. Few speak of women with such a light of love behind their eyes."

His father had roared with laughter and said, "Your mother is gentle as a lamb, son, but she lives in a savage world just like the rest of us."

A savage world. Yes, maybe that was to be his world now that he was on the run. Maybe his parents had known somehow and wanted him to have a chance. Why else had he been taught to use all kinds of weapons and been obliged to practice almost every day? What else could be the meaning of the endless hours of practice with a pistol? A pistol has no meaning except for the killing of men; nobody hunts with a pistol. Was there something about him that his mother and father saw and feared would doom him to be a grim fugitive?

Dan wished he could talk to his mother. The thought brought a sad smile to his lips. The vicious, uncaring killer wants to cry to his mama and have her tell him that everything will be all right. He wished he could have had time to say goodbye to Big Dan. There might have been time, but he had been afraid to face his father. Big Dan would have tried to help and would have been pulled into the trouble.

The picture of Mark came to his mind, too proud to run, standing there facing two men determined to kill him over some trifling slight. Dan wondered if his own back would be so proudly straight if he ever had to look certain death in the eye. Right now it might not be too difficult. If a man already feels he has lost it all, he can face all kinds of things. Maybe that was the answer. Perhaps killing came easy to him because he didn't give a damn anymore. Dying could come easy for the same reason. Maybe that's what it means to be a savage, to be so down and without hope that nothing really matters.

Again the sad smile played across Dan's lips. It was going to be a great winter. He and Joe Ballas were perfect for each other. Joe was an old man so mean he wouldn't have anything to do with ordinary people, while Dan was a heartless killer so mean he couldn't be tolerated by decent people. They were two of a kind, like matched bookends.

Dan came in sight of the cabin in mid-afternoon. He stopped Big Red in a grove of trees and took a slow look around the place. Joe must be outside somewhere; there was no smoke coming out of the chimney. The weather was already cold enough up here to make a fire comfortable even at midday. Joe's horse was gone. He started to ride on in when something stopped him. Something wasn't right. Dan sat back in the saddle and took another look. He ran his gaze across the small corral, the cliff behind the house, the trees nearby. Then his attention focused on the cabin. The door wasn't completely shut. At this range, Dan couldn't tell for sure, but the door looked to be slightly ajar.

Dan sucked in a quick, deep breath. Joe had never said a word about it, but Dan had watched him carefully shut that door every time they left the cabin. He always stretched a hair or a piece of thread or did some small thing somewhere on the door to indicate to them whether or not it had been opened in their absence. Wordlessly, the old man always glanced at Dan to see if he had observed. He expected to be understood without speech. Joe Ballas would never leave that door partly open. It would either be all the way open or all the way shut if he were the last man to touch it.

Dan slid from the saddle to the ground, moving slowly, by inches. Well hidden in the brush, he quickly pulled off his boots and donned his moccasins and leggings. He put his hat on the pommel and drew the rifle from its boot. Dan didn't tie Big Red, just dropped the reins to the ground. The big horse was trained to stay "ground-hitched" until Dan came for him or whistled to call him. Dan slipped through the woods until he reached a better vantage point. Now there was no doubt. The door was open two or three inches.

Dan scanned the surroundings patiently. An hour passed, then another. Dan switched his position four or five times, moving a little closer to the cabin each time, taking advantage of each move to see things from a slightly different angle. The afternoon was passing; the sun was dropping fast. Dan's grim grin came back. It was easy for the damned to be patient. He felt no hurry, no excitement, but he did feel very much alive and alert. He figured he was getting accustomed to hunting people who dared to hunt him.

A small movement caught his eye. He found Joe, crouched behind some rocks, looking right at him. The old man had spotted him and had moved deliberately to catch his attention. Relief flooded through Dan. It was good to know that the old man wasn't lying dead in the cabin while somebody waited to get Dan next. He saw Joe's sign language signal to stay where he was. He settled in for a long wait, wondering what Joe was planning.

Dan stayed put until dusk was fading into darkness. Joe had vanished, but Dan had seen him working his way toward him. Finally, in the last of the light, he saw him again, only twenty yards away this time. As soon as Joe saw his gesture of recognition, he moved easily and quickly to Dan's side in the concealing brush.

Grinning like a happy child, Joe gripped Dan's hand and asked, "How was the dance?"

"I had to fight off a hundred pantin', grabbin' women. What's going on up here?"

"I been having a hell of a good time. It was a strain on my character, but I held off to share the fun with you. Thought you'd never get back. There's two of 'em. They're both in the cabin waitin' for me to open that door so they can blast me to kingdom come. I got their horses they had hid away in some brush down yonder. I found a better place to hide 'em. Damn nice stock, too. We can find use for 'em."

Dan made a show of shaking his head and twisting a finger in his ear as if it bothered him.

"What's wrong with your ear?" Joe asked.

"Nothing. I just forgot how much you talked all the time. Just getting my ears loosened up for it again."

"Hell, boy, we didn't have nothing to talk about before. This here is different. This here is fun."

VIII

Joe's face was that of a man twenty years younger. The painful limp and slow movement that had been so obvious before had not been evident at all when he moved up to Dan in the gathering darkness. Dan thought of his father's old hunting dogs, stiff-legged and half-blind, leaping and jumping around like happy busy-tailed puppies at the sight of a man carrying a rifle or shotgun. Hunting is born and bred into some creatures.

"What do you think we ought to do, Joe?"

Joe answered without hesitation. "Take one or both of 'em alive if we can. Get 'em to talk. That'll be easy. Then kill 'em both."

"Take them prisoner and then kill them?"

"Hell, yes!" He started speaking as if he were counting off the points he was making on his fingers. "We got to find out where they come from, how many we're up against, who's running this here rustling. Then we got to kill 'em or they'll come at us again. We got to read the book over 'em, boy. They come here to kill us. We can't let that get to be the fashion."

"How do you want to go about it?"

"I figure they been in our cabin since about noon. They think I'm late now, and they're expectin' me any minute. After it gets dark real good, they'll figure I decided to camp out somewhere. I expect 'em to relax a bit—one or both of 'em might even go to sleep. If we work it just right, maybe we can get in our back door without no noise and grab 'em before they catch on."

"There's going to be a moon tonight," Dan replied. "Soon as you move one or two of those logs, the moon will shine in that cabin like lantern light. Unless they sleep like dead men, they'll hear those logs move and blow your head off with good shooting light."

"Yeah, but I got those logs smooth as glass so I can move 'em quiet." Joe's voice was showing some doubt. "I was plannin' to wait till moonset anyhow."

"How about trying some kind of trick?"

"Like what?"

"How about you bringing their horses up close and turning them loose? A horse will come on up to the cabin. You know how horses like company. In the moonlight, those two will recognize their own horses wandering around, and they might come out to get 'em and check around. They don't have a good ambush with their horses standing around the cabin anyhow. Maybe we could get the drop on 'em."

"What if they don't fall for it?"

"If it don't work, we don't get our heads blown off, either."

Joe snickered quietly through his nose. "I'll go along with it. Where you gonna be when I bring the horses up?"

"When you're facing the door of the cabin, I'll be to the left, just around the corner. If only one comes out, you get him and I'll go for the one still in the cabin. If both come out together, you take the one on the right and I'll take the one on the left. If one hangs back, I'll take the one behind and you take the one in front."

In the gathering darkness Dan could barely see Joe's nod of agreement. "Walker, be ready to move when I say, 'Put 'em up.' I reckon you'll be closer'n me to 'em. Likely I'll have to shoot mine if they put up a fight. You're gonna have the best chance to grab one from behind to do the talkin' later. That's good with your size. We'll soon find out if you can handle another man as easy as you handled that Channing feller. Watch out for yourself." He started to move away.

Dan grabbed a handful of shirt to stop him. "Wait, Joe. We got to plan what to do if they don't fall for it."

"If they don't, you stay where you are till I come up to the cabin to join you. We'll try my back door." He slipped away and was swallowed by the dark.

Dan had no trouble in the early night darkness before moonrise. In an hour he was safely crouched beside the left wall of the cabin with a nicely balanced stick of firewood he had picked up on the way. The only way he could be seen from inside the cabin now would be for one of the occupants to lean out the window on this side. He was only in his position for a short time when he heard whispers, but he couldn't hear the words.

Another hour passed. The moon rose, bright and full. Suddenly the sound of walking horses was plain in the stillness. There was no sound inside the cabin. First one, then two horses came into sight, ambling along, stopping, shifting direction now and then, but working their way toward the cabin. There was no sign of Joe, and the horses showed no indication of being herded. He must have brought them up until they could see the cabin and turned them loose, hoping they would react as planned.

This time Dan clearly heard an explosive whisper. "Damn! Them's our horses. They must've broke loose." Although Dan had not heard anything, they must have swung the door all the way open. The speaker had to be standing right in the door for Dan to hear him so clearly.

There was a mumble from inside and then the clear response, "I'm goin' out there to hide them horses again. Git out here and cover me. I ain't likin' this none." The speaker stepped into plain sight, a rifle at his hip. Dan could almost have reached out and snapped his suspenders.

The man looked over his shoulder, but Dan was invisible, crouched in the shadow of the cabin. The man wasn't looking Dan's direction anyway; he was looking back to see if his partner was covering him.

The second man stepped out and moved to a position right in front of Dan. He stood there so close that Dan was afraid his presence would be felt if not heard. Joe's voice rang out, "Put 'em up!" The blasting of shots drowned out the dull thud of Dan's firewood club smashing into his man's skull. The man fell face down and lay without a quiver. Dan dropped the club and drew. The other man was down and still.

"Are you all right, Joe?"

"Why, hell yes! You tend to yours, and I'll take care of mine. You get your man alive?"

"Yeah, if his head isn't bashed in."

"That's good." The body in the moonlight jerked as two more shots smashed into it. Joe appeared magically, as if he grew out of the ground. "I hate to walk up on a man who looks dead in the dark unless I can make sure. It's creepy how some of 'em come back to life and try to put lead into a trustin' man." He walked to the dead man and kicked him over onto his back. After taking a good look at him, he walked to the unconscious one and also jerked him onto his back. "Never seen either one of 'em before. Strangers." He walked back to the dead man and searched the body. When he came back he was carrying the dead man's guns.

"Drag sorehead there inside while I light a lantern," Joe said, stepping through the door. When Dan pulled the unconscious man inside, Joe continued, "I got some rope over in the corner. Search him real careful and tie him to that center post. Throw all you find on him here on the table with this stuff." He threw the contents of the dead man's pockets on the table.

The unconscious man was so completely limp that Dan had some trouble holding him in a sitting position to tie his hands behind the post. He pulled the man's boots off before tying his feet. Watching, Joe said, "Somebody taught you a thing or two along the way. I like a partner who does good work. Only thing is, if it had been me, I'd of hog-tied him and then tied him to the post. If we don't make it easy to take him outside once in a while, this cabin is gonna smell like an outhouse. We might have to teach him for a while before he learns to sing."

Dan untied the man's hands and retied him as Joe had suggested. "I got a horse I'm fond of out there in the dark. I'm going after him."

"No, you ain't," Joe replied. "I got one out there too, but I know where mine and yours both is. I'll go get them horses. You build a fire and keep an eye on sorehead there till I get back."

Dan had the fire going under the pot of beans and was slicing venison to put in the skillet when he heard Joe's bobwhite whistle at the door. He went to the rope strung on the wall several feet from the door. The rope was tied to the bar on the door, allowing the bar to be lifted while he was standing well off to the side. Joe came in grinning from ear to ear. "Aw, it's so wonderful to come home to a warm fire and a lovin' wife cookin' somethin' good on the stove."

"Those two helped themselves to your beans while they were sitting around all day. They must like cold beans."

"Anybody as clumsy and dumb as them two should have a good meal for coming up against me and you, Walker. They was condemned men as soon as they took the job. When I seen you coming today, I was afraid I was gonna have to fire a shot to warn you off, but you caught on quick. What tipped you?"

"The door wasn't shut all the way."

"Well, I didn't see that myself at first. I circled around, found tracks, and trailed 'em to where they hid their horses. There wasn't no reason to hide their horses unless they was up to mischief." His voice was hard as he continued, "I think somebody who knows me has been talking to 'em. Ordinary thing would be for two men to just ride in on an old man, act friendly, get the drop on him, and shoot him. Somebody told these two that wouldn't work with me or they'd have tried it. That would be a lot easier and quicker than all this clever stuff."

"There were two men laying for me in the stable in town after the dance."

"What happened?"

"They weren't up to the work any better than these two. When I left town nobody had found them yet. I covered them with hay when I finished with them."

"You must've shot 'em awful quiet." The old man's eyes were eager with interest.

"Didn't shoot them, Joe."

"You carry a firewood stick home with you from the dance?"

"No, but I didn't want to make a fuss. It seemed better to keep things quiet."

"Used that skinny little knife, by Gawd! Indians and mountain men always like things quiet. Haw! That'll give some bastard something to think about! Somebody sent two for you and two for me, and we got all four of 'em. Haw!" The old man did a remarkably vigorous, leaping dance. "We got somebody on the run, Walker. We're a fire under somebody's butt, and he's gettin' desperate as hell. Ain't no damn gang nowhere can lose four men without it hurtin' 'em bad. Haw!"

"Seems to me our luck is stretching thin. We don't even know who is after us or why."

Joe quit his wild dance, dropped back onto the wooden box chair across the table from Dan, and spoke around a spoonful of beans. "Sure we do. We know the why part. Somebody is taking thousands of dollars worth of M Bar M cattle, and we're in the way. We'll find out who is doin' it and how as soon as sorehead over there wakes up."

Dan got up and went to the unconscious man. Blood had dried in his hair and in a couple of streaks down his neck. Dried blood had also left a track down from one ear. He was breathing. Dan went back to the table. "Just thought I'd take a look. He's been out quite a while now."

"Gettin' hit with a twenty-pound stick by a bull like you would give most fellers cause to pause," Joe said with a wicked grin. "You git sincere when you hit folks. I admire sincerity in a man."

Joe grabbed the plates and scrubbed them vigorously in a pan of soapy water, rinsed them in hot water from the kettle over the fire, and set them upside down on the table to air dry. "It's a shame sorehead slept through supper, but he probably already ate anyhow. Let's see what these boys had in their pockets." He whistled in surprise when he felt the weight of the two money belts and dumped wads of bills out on the table. "Looky here! Hey, Walker, looky here."

"Yeah, the two who were waiting for me in the stable were loaded, too. Carried the same kind of belts. Prosperous men." While Joe laboriously counted the piles of money, Dan looked at the rest of the items on the table. They were unremarkable, simply the usual pocketknives, tobacco pouches, and cigarette papers to be found in the pockets of men anywhere. Neither of these men carried letters or anything else that would identify them.

"Them Indians you killed, Walker, had over two hundred dollars each on 'em. Fancy that. Most Indians don't have no want nor need for cash money. Ain't that a curious thing? I kept that money for you. Figured you left in too big a hurry, trying to get Miss Alice to a safe place, to pick it up. That amounts to almost nine hundred dollars. Funny how that slipped my mind till just this minute." He looked at Dan with an evil grin as he divided the money on the table into two equal stacks. "Your half here is a little over four hundred more." He pulled a tight but bulky roll of bills from under his shirt and put it beside one of the stacks while he picked up the other. "You're on your way to becoming a rich little feller."

"Joe, do you suppose those Indians who killed two M Bar M hands and almost got Alice are part of the same gang that tried to get us? Seems like all these bushwhackers are flush with money."

There was a long silence while Joe stood frozen, his hard eyes on Dan. "You figure all of this dirty work has been hired, from start to finish? Maybe so, Walker, maybe so. It would be hard to hire a white man to kill a white woman around these parts. An Indian might be more practical. A killin' is a killin', and that's the practical fact of it." He stood staring off into space for a long time. Then he turned to Dan with a sour smile. "If you have it figured right, then whoever's behind this trouble has lost eight men, not four. He probably figures you're plumb bad luck for him, Walker. Losing eight men in a month is enough to make a man stop and think, ain't it?"

A strangling gasp of pain turned them both toward their prisoner. The man was struggling, half-conscious, against the ropes. He kept trying to straighten his legs, which was choking him. When Dan hog-tied him, he passed a rope around his ankles that ended up around his neck. The rope was short enough so that it would only allow the prisoner to breathe if his knees were kept bent.

Joe went to the bucket of soapy dishwater and picked up the dishrag. He came to the prisoner and said gently, "Quit kickin' now, sonny. You're all tied up." He scrubbed the man's face roughly.

"Ow! My eyes!" The tied man was throwing his head weakly back and forth. "My eyes are hurtin' terrible. Got somethin' in my eyes!"

Dan brought a tin cup of clean water, shouldered Joe aside, and bathed the man's eyes. Joe, without hesitation, walked over to a couple of branding irons hanging on the wall. "Might as well get the tools warmed up and ready." He shoved the irons into the fireplace.

The prisoner looked up at Dan with bleary eyes and said, "Thanks. Felt just like I had lye soap in my eyes there for a minute."

Dan pulled a box closer and sat down. "You did, my friend. That mean old man washed your face with a soapy dishrag. You see what he's doing now?" The man twisted around awkwardly to see Joe working the

irons in the glowing coals in the fireplace. A muscle quivered in his face
when he turned his head back to Dan.

"Da da da da dum, te dum, te dum," Joe hummed to himself as he
waltzed around the small room, holding an imaginary partner in his
arms.

"That crazy old man is almost out of his mind with joy at the prospect
of working on you as long as it takes. He hopes it'll take several days.
He's hoping you're tough as hell. He's hoping you won't talk till the very
last minute."

It took him two tries before he could get it out. "Last minute?"

"Yeah, the last minute before you die."

"Wh-what you want me to talk about?"

"Who hired you to come up here?"

"Feller named Dutch MacRae. Don't let that crazy old bastard at
me."

"What's this fellow MacRae look like?"

"He's the boss, but he don't stay with us or go with us when we work.
He just comes and gives us orders and brings the bills of sale and takes
his cut. He's a big, tall man. Dark hair and eyes, getting fat around the
middle, has a face that stays red lookin' all the time. Always dresses in
real fine clothes."

"He brings bills of sale to you?"

"Yeah, they're already signed by somebody named Channing. We
gather up the number of M Bar M cattle on a bill of sale and drive 'em
off a hundred miles or so and sell 'em. Ain't never no big bunch, but it's
safe, 'cause we got a proper bill of sale. We give half the money to Dutch
and split the rest."

"How many men in your bunch?"

"There was ten, but four was Indians, and they rode off one day and
never came back. There's six left now, I think, but some ride out and
some ride in. It ain't a steady bunch. We usually work in pairs, so
sometimes we're taking cattle every which way, all at the same time."

"You only take M Bar M stock?"

"Right."

Joe's cheerful voice came from beside the fireplace. "Just about ready,
yes, sir, any minute now."

"Look, I'm doin' all I can. I'm answering all your questions. Make him
quit that. That old man is crazy. He don't sound like he's right in the
head."

"You're right. He's a little off, but he won't bother you if I tell him not to."

"Man, that's good. He scares the hell out of me. Why do you let him stay around? I'd be afraid to go to sleep with him dancing around like that. Does he think he's dancing with somebody?"

"No, he's just excited right now. He didn't think you were going to be helpful. He likes to change people's minds."

"I'm doin' the best I can. You can see that, can't you?"

"Sure. How many cows do you take each time and where do you take them?"

"We take them to the mining camps and different small towns around. Hardly ever take more'n twenty or thirty head at a time, but we keep at it regular during the winter. We got us a little camp about ten miles from here; it's at the old Slanthole silver mine."

"What did you get paid for this job?"

"A hundred bucks. I didn't want to get in on no killin', but my partner said we would do it, and I was so damn scared of him I was afraid not to go along with it."

"Do you know where MacRae lives?"

"Naw, but it can't be far away."

"Why not?"

"Hell, the last time I saw him, he was in bad shape. He was real sick, and I don't think he would try to ride far considerin' the shape he was in. Hell, he could hardly talk. Kept holding his throat and talking in a kind of whisper, acted like it hurt him to say every word. He told us not to try to fool that old man, said he was liable to shoot on sight."

"All ready," sang Joe Ballas. He came waltzing across the cabin with a white-hot branding iron.

A wordless little cry came from the helpless man, and his eyes flicked from Joe's spinning figure to Dan's face. His eyes were white with terror. "Ask me something more," he pleaded. "I'll tell you anything, but don't let him at me."

Dan came to his feet. "We won't need that this time, Joe."

"Aw! You said I could. You promised." Joe's face crumpled like a child about to burst into tears while the glowing iron waved back and forth only fractions of an inch from the face of the cowering prisoner.

"Joe, put the iron back in the fireplace and come back over here." Joe trudged back to the fireplace, shoulders drooping in frustration, and threw the iron down on the hearth. He came back reluctantly, his face a malignant mask. "Joe, look at this man real good." Joe leaned forward and peered fixedly into the cringing man's face as Dan said, "The next time you see this man, kill him. Kill him."

Joe stood there staring, then started dry washing his hands and smiling. He said in a pleased voice, "Now that sounds like fun. That'll be nice."

Dan untied the trembling man, picked up the lantern, and helped him to his feet. He practically had to carry the man outside. The poor devil didn't have the strength to get into the saddle unassisted. As soon as he was in the saddle, he leaned toward the opposite side, and Dan thought he was going to fall to the ground, but then he heard the racking sound of retching. Dan stuffed a hundred dollars in the man's shirt pocket and said, "Head south, it's warm." He heard the word "south" being numbly repeated over and over and the chattering of teeth as the horse walked slowly away.

When Dan went back in the cabin, Joe was striking a tragic pose by the fireplace. "I'm a wasted man, son. I was born for the stage. The flower of my art is lost in these here deserted wastelands far from the bright lights and my adorin' public."

IX

"I think you might be right after watching that act. To tell the truth, you were making me jumpy, too, Joe. I got to where I was afraid to turn my back on you. I knew you were a mean old codger, but that was quite a show."

"Mean? Me? I just wanted to kill that poor, broke-down little coward bushwhacker. I ain't the one what sent him out into a freezin' night, soakin' wet with cold sweat and with pee-pee drippin' down his britches leg. I didn't run him off with no coat, no boots, no gun, no hat, an' no money. You done that, not me."

"I put a hundred dollars in his pocket. He's got ridin' money."

"I reckon your idea to let him go may be a good one. I'd have killed him my own self, but I don't think that one will come back at us. He just lost all the sand in his craw. Maybe he'll be a good, fast messenger. Maybe folks will hear from him about how much fun it is to mess around with M Bar M."

"I don't think he'll be talking about what happened here. I think that was a quiet man who just rode out."

"I'll tell you what I think. You need to ride down to the ranch tomorrow. Miss Alice and Red need to know what's been goin' on around here."

"Yeah, they need to know about this. That's true. You've been here a long time, though. Seems like you'd be the one to ride down there."

Joe shook his head. "I'm a contented old man, sittin' up here feedin' the birds and pettin' the rabbits. I ain't the one doin' a calf-eye at the boss."

"Look, Joe, I need this job for the winter. After that, I'll probably be riding on. There's no chance for a rich woman like Alice to be interested in a drifting, penniless saddle bum. You start talking like that, and I'll get fired and have to go riding off into cold weather."

"*Pen*-ni-less, is it? That's a nice, fancy word. Most saddle bums would say they was busted or broke. It sounds like an advantage when a man is *pen*-ni-less, plumb high-tone. It's also mighty refreshing to an old man like me to hear somebody say how poor he is when he's got almost two thousand dollars in his poke. It's right modest."

"I have a bad feeling about that money, Joe. The way we got it figured, that's money from stolen M Bar M stock. Seems to me that money should go back to the ranch. I plan to give my part of it to Red."

"Do tell." Joe's hard eyes were fixed on Dan with a glitter of amusement. "I suppose you think I ought to give my cut to the ranch, too?" His voice was heavily sarcastic.

"Seems to me that's for you to decide."

"My, my, ain't that nice. You gonna leave that up to me, are you? I ain't never spent the winter with no choirboy before. Maybe I'll be spoutin' the gospel by spring." He threw a wad of bills on the table in front of Dan. "You take that money down tomorrow." He stood staring at Dan for a moment. "I'm beginnin' to take a fancy to you, son. That makes me skittish. I been through a lot of disappointments in my time." He climbed into his bunk and stared at the roof. "One more thing."

"What?"

"You might like to take a little ride with me when you git back from the ranch. I'll be ridin' over to the old Slanthole mine."

"Yeah?"

"If there's anybody there, I figure to give 'em a choice. They can ride on or they can die. Makes me no difference either way. Then, I'm gonna burn the whole place down. Since you're gettin' to be a regular partner, I don't want to hog all the fun if you want to come along. Seems to me that's for you to decide," he finished in a prissy, mocking voice.

The next morning, the two men walked down the slope from the cabin and found a pleasant spot where the soil appeared to be deep. Dan wasn't surprised to find himself stuck with the job of digging the grave. When the hole was deep enough, Joe threw a rope around the stiff, cold body of the outlaw, mounted his skittish horse, and dragged the corpse callously over the rough ground to the gravesite. Joe dismounted, pulled his rope loose and kicked the body into the grave. Dan flinched when the dull thud echoed from the bottom.

Joe removed his hat, drew a small Bible from the inside pocket of his coat, and read in a clear, steady voice. He slapped the book shut and nodded to Dan. "You can cover that thing up now. That's the end of it." He mounted his horse and rode the short distance to the cabin. Dan filled the grave while the old man sat in a chair tipped back against the front wall, smoking and watching.

Dan saddled Big Red, mounted, and sat looking down at Joe. Neither said a word. Dan wheeled away and rode down the slope. He figured that Joe was more like a snake than an old hunting dog. He just lay around hardly moving till something caught his interest. Then, bursting with energy, he struck with blinding speed and accuracy.

He was obviously back in his bored mood this morning, virtually motionless and wordless, and he was limping around as if he were almost a helpless cripple. Dan shook his head as he remembered how that old man had seemed to float over rough ground in the dark and how he had danced around the cabin. He must spend 99 percent of his time faking. Dan wondered how many men had been dropped into holes after misjudging Joe Ballas.

Dan was in no hurry, and he figured that he had plenty of reason to exercise caution. It was dusk before he rode up to the ranch. He went to Red's house and tapped on the front door. He could hear Red's chair scrape in the dining room as he got up to walk to the door. When the door opened, Dan said, "Sorry, Red, I didn't mean to interrupt your supper."

"Come on in, Dan. What are you doing here?"

Dan removed his hat and walked into the house. Red indicated a chair with a flip of a hand. Dan said, "Look, I'll go over to the bunkhouse and say hello to the boys. When you finish your meal, just holler and I'll come back."

"Have you eaten yet, Dan?"

"No, I'll just pick up something from the cookhouse."

"Set another plate, woman," Red yelled. Dan heard another chair move and Annie Cougan walked into the room. "Why, Dan, how nice to see you. Come in and eat with us. We've got plenty of everything, and you're mighty welcome."

"Thanks, Annie, but I don't want to intrude. I need to talk to Red about some things that have been happening. I got a bunch of money I need to get rid of too, frankly."

Red chortled, "You come to the right place for dropping off money, Dan. I can always find a use for it. Come on, tell us your story over supper." He shoved Dan toward the dining room. Dan walked into the room and looked right into the eyes of Alice Martin. Red laughed and said, "Don't look so surprised, Dan. Alice eats with us all the time since her folks ain't here. I don't believe you've met our banker. This here is Ira Rice. Ira, this is Dan Walker."

Dan shook hands with the small, narrow-faced, nattily dressed man who seemed to rise to his feet reluctantly. Dan smiled at the memory of one of his father's favorite comments. "Watch out for horses and men that have their eyes too close together." When they were all seated with food in front of them, Red asked, "What's the news you rode all day to bring down from the mountains?"

Dan was caught. He didn't want to discuss this kind of news in front of a stranger. He also didn't like Rice. To others, that might seem unfair, but Dan had compared notes with his father too many times to ignore his instincts. He had been trained to form an instant impression of people and to proceed very cautiously if that impression was a bad one. Dan had been sitting quietly beside his father in important business conferences while other boys his age had been playing games.

"Red, I hope this won't make you mad at me, but my daddy taught me not to discuss business when food was being served. He was real stern about it. Dad said it insulted the cook," Dan said, smiling.

Annie applauded and crowed, "See, Red, see there, it's rude to mess up a nice meal talking business. I always told you it was."

Red gave Annie a tired look but turned a grin toward Dan and said, "No hurry. We got all evening to talk. Ira will be spending the night. He rode all the way from town on business, and it's too far to ride both ways in one day."

After the meal, they all walked into the living room and Red asked, "Now, what's this all about, Dan?"

Dan took Red by the elbow in an iron grip and moved him toward the door. "I don't want to bore Miss Martin's guest with ranch business, Red. Why don't we excuse ourselves for a few minutes? Glad to have met you, Mr. Rice. Will you ladies excuse us please?" Alice was already seated and looked as if she were going to protest. Her expression was one of controlled anger.

Out on the front porch, Dan said in a low voice, "Let's take a walk, Red." The foreman's expression was mystified, but he went along with it. Dan walked him over to the empty cookshed, and they lit a lantern and sat at the long table. Dan said, "I think when I spill all this, you'll see why I didn't want to talk in front of any strangers, Red." Dan started with the business in the stable after the dance and related the events that followed, along with his and Joe's interpretation of all that had happened.

He was reaching into his coat for the imposing roll of bills to hand them to Red when the door slammed open and Alice stormed into the room. Her eyes were cold with anger as she spoke to Dan. "I have seen some poor manners in my life, but this takes the prize. You come walking in uninvited, eat, and then physically drag Red away from his guests for half an hour. I wouldn't blame Mr. Rice if he was to be very much insulted by all this, and this is not a good time to have him upset with us. I'm sure there can't be anything so important and private to justify acting this way. Just who do you think you are?"

Her eyes popped wide with surprise when Red said flatly, "Don't say nothin' more till you know more, Alice. Don't say another word. You owe this man more than you know. Set down there and listen."

Her face was stiff with anger, but her expression showed how reluctant she was to contradict her foreman. She sat down and said harshly, "Let's hear it."

Dan was calm and relaxed. He had faced anger from much more imposing people than this young woman. He went through the story again from start to finish. At the end, he dug out the huge roll of bills and put it on the table in front of her.

The silence made the pings of the cooling cookstove seem loud in the long, narrow dining room. Alice touched the slowly unrolling mound of money with a tentative finger. "How much is here, Dan?"

"Just over twenty-four hundred dollars."

Red gave a gusty sigh and dropped his elbows on the table. "Well, I'll be damned. I'll just be damned." His voice was almost a whisper.

Alice turned eyes as round as those of a wondering child to Dan and said, "I think I owe it to you to tell you what has been happening. Mr. Rice rode all the way out here to tell me that he must have a two thousand dollar payment within ten days or he is going to cancel a loan to the ranch. The ranch is collateral for that loan. He's ready to foreclose, in other words. If I paid him that much money from our account at the bank, it wouldn't leave enough money to meet the payroll till our roundup."

Dan gave her a cool smile. These paltry sums of money didn't impress him, but he knew very well how small sums can greatly influence large fortunes at critical times. "Seems as if your immediate problem is solved. You must be saying the right prayers."

"Why are you giving us all this, Dan? There isn't any proof this is M Bar M money. You and Joe have just made a series of guesses. Why don't you just ride away? You could buy a good business with this much money. You could start a nice ranch of your own."

Dan looked directly into her eyes. "I have become romantically inclined toward a person here in this area and am reluctant to just ride away." His voice was very low to match the formality of his speech. He leaned toward her earnestly. She straightened and a curtain seemed to drop over her eyes, as if she were drawing back. Both she and Red were rigid and still in the tense pause that followed. Red had a pained look on his face; he looked like he wanted desperately to be somewhere else. Dan continued, "I hope to be able to announce my engagement in the spring."

The pinging of the stove again seemed loud in the silence of the room. Alice finally asked, "To whom?"

"To Joe Ballas."

All three of them sat for a frozen second, then Red slapped the table with the flat of his hand and yelled. He jumped up and fell against the wall, then staggered across the narrow room to the other wall, convulsed with mirth. He wobbled over and pointed at Alice and groaned breathlessly, "He gotcha, Alice. He got you and me both. That was the most beautiful sucker punch I've seen in a coon's age. Aw, that was neat."

Alice sprang to her feet, her eyes looking like they were about to shoot sparks, her face flaming. Red, still chuckling, said, "Aw, come on, Alice. This ain't no time to play offended lady. Forget bein' a lady for a minute and be a range boss and a good sport. Come on, now."

A smile started and she covered her face with both hands. "Oh Dan!" Her voice was strangled. "That was mean. That was just awful!"

"But funny," prompted Red.

"Oh, it was not. It was awful," she said, laughing behind her hands.

Red flopped back into his chair and gave Dan a speculative look. "Alice, you was about to get into a sticky, gooey thank-you act, and Dan shot you right out of the saddle. That was neat. Wait'll I tell Annie."

Alice sat down and said, "A thank you is hardly enough, it seems to me. What do you say to a man who brings in a fortune, throws it on the table in front of you, and says, 'Here, take this. Your troubles are over'?"

Dan sat looking directly at Alice when he said, "I've been doing some more thinking while I rode down here today. Maybe your troubles aren't about to be over. Not yet. How come your banker hired a man like Channing? Where did he come from? If we have this figured out right, Channing is leading a gang of rustlers and trying to hire killers to get you, Joe, and me. I can see why they want Joe and me out of the way. We're out there guarding cattle they want to rustle, but why you, Alice? Another thing, that bushwhacker who was so eager to talk to us said that they only took M Bar M cattle. What's the sense of that? A thief would usually take whatever was available, it seems to me."

"No, didn't you say that they felt safe since they had bills of sale signed by Channing?" Alice asked.

"Maybe that's enough reason. Maybe that's all there is to it. But it seems to me that you better be very careful, Alice. You may be in grave danger. Channing has dropped out of sight, but he's still sending men here to try to kill people. I don't understand it. He had a good thing here for a while. Now that's all changed, but why is he trying to have you killed? He tried to get you killed before you ran him off, or could even get back to your ranch."

"Maybe he tried that because he was afraid I would fire him as soon as I got home."

"I might have to take blame for that," Red said. "I did some talking to him about what a sharp manager you are." Red shook his head, and gave Alice an apologetic look. "I might have set you up without knowin' it."

"I'll bet Annie and Ira Rice are wondering what happened to us," Alice commented. "What will Rice think when I hand him this huge pile of cash all of a sudden after acting sad and broke for two or three hours?"

Red came to his feet. "Just get a good receipt with me and Annie to witness it." He turned to Dan. "Soon as Rice heads for town tomorrow, come up to the house. You, me, and Alice need to talk some more."

Dan nodded. "I got a suggestion. Alice, you might cut off any questions from Rice by using the same snooty voice you used on Channing. You're mighty convincing on a high horse. Just tell him how much you appreciate his interest, but you are sure that some details of M Bar M business would bore him."

"Snooty voice? Convincing on a high horse? I need to think a minute before I decide if I like that," Alice responded while Red stood behind her trying to rub a grin off his face.

Dan started for the door. Alice's voice stopped him. "Dan?"

"Yeah?" He looked back at her.

"Thanks."

"Sure." He winked and walked out.

Dan took a quick step aside as soon as he was through the door, standing in the shadows to let his eyes adjust to the dark. He couldn't help hearing Red's voice. "Alice, honey, do you notice the difference in Dan's way of talkin'?"

"Yes, I do. When he forgets himself, he sounds like a very highly educated man. He does a lot of polite things. When I told him who I was up in that cave, I gave him a curtsy, and without even thinking, he bowed. He didn't bend over, like most cowhands would. He bowed; there's a difference. I don't think he even realized he did it. It's enough to make me wonder if he's even pretending when he says he's half Indian. Did you see how indifferent he was to all that money, like it was small change? Strange, don't you think?"

"Alice, I believe that part about him being half Indian. That's the only thing he's told us about himself. I don't think he's a liar. I don't know any white men who would go into a dark stable and use a knife against two armed men tryin' to kill him. The thought of that gives me the shakes. Did you notice how he told that story? 'I heard enough to know they'd been hired to kill me, so I killed 'em.' He told that like I would say, 'My hands was dirty, so I washed 'em.' Didn't seem like nothin' to him, nothin' at all. Man kills easy like that, seems like he'd make me nervous bein' around him. But he don't."

"Well, he sure makes me nervous."

"You? Why should he upset you? You been saying he's a perfect gentleman all this time."

"Oh Red, I like him, and I want him to like me. But I think he's just riding through, running from something, and I don't want to make a fool of myself."

"Aw, Alice, don't you worry about that. You got too much sense to do that. Besides, we ain't mentioned the most important thing about him that should make us feel good."

"What?"

"Honey, Joe Ballas likes him. I've knowed Joe for twenty years, since before you was born, and I ain't never seen him make a mistake about a man. Joe's mighty careful, and that's a fact."

Dan picked his way to the bunkhouse, silent as a big shadow. His instinct had told him that Alice was interested. To hear her say so made him feel good, though. Mighty good. Dan found himself wondering if maybe he had already run far enough. He didn't know much about the so-called long arm of the law, but he hoped he was out of reach here.

Yawning, he slipped into a bunk and lay there staring at the ceiling. Thinking about the fact that he might have to ride away from here bothered him. He narrowed that down in his mind to one simple fact. He didn't want to leave Alice behind, for her to become just another memory. His breathing seemed tight when he thought about her. Seemed like he ought to be able to pick out the reasons why. Maybe it was because she was pretty, had a lot of spunk and was a good dancer. He yawned again. There were lots of women around like that. Suddenly his eyes popped wide open. He sat up on the bunk.

It was ridiculous to be thinking like this. What was he doing? He wasn't safe anywhere. Suppose he settled here and started a family. It would destroy him to go to jail, or worse, and leave a family behind. He tried to picture Alice as his widow with a couple of his children, and the thought was horrible. He could almost hear her saying, "Your daddy was a wonderful man till they hanged him for two murders." He felt closed in, as if the bunkhouse was a cell. He needed some air. In seconds, Dan was walking to the corral.

Big Red trotted over to the gate as soon as he caught Dan's scent. Dan hadn't had to throw a rope at that big horse since he was a colt. In five minutes, Big Red was headed for the north pasture as if he had read Dan's mind. Dan would stay there till this trouble was cleared up if he could, but he had to stay away from Alice. She was too decent to be pulled into his kind of trouble. As soon as Dan could be sure the threat to Alice was over, he would ride on to Canada.

Dan vowed he would not see or speak to Alice again. He was so filled with rage that he hunched over in the saddle and his whole body shook like a man trying to lift a weight too heavy for him. The changes in his life were really beginning to fall on him like a crushing weight. His family was lost to him forever. Now, for the first time in his life, he found a woman interesting enough to daydream about, and he didn't dare risk trying to win her. There seemed to be no escape from a hostile fate. It was then Dan decided that Channing and all who worked with him were dead men. His thinking was bitterly clear. "What the hell, after the first murder, what difference can a few more make? I'll clean this up fast and get out of here. And if one of them gets me, that's a damn small loss to anybody."

X

Dan rode into sight of the cabin just after first morning light. He had made much better time coming back than on the trip down. Dan was sure that no ambush threat existed at night, so he had not lost time taking the extensive precautions that had slowed him the previous day. Riding up to the cabin at night had not appealed to him, not when it contained a cautious, quick-shooting man like Ballas, so he had stopped and slept about three hours beside the trail. He stopped Big Red and hailed the cabin from a distance of a couple of hundred yards. Joe stepped out and waved him on in.

He whistled the gray horse to him and spread a dry blanket across his back. Then he transferred his saddle directly from the tired red horse to the gray. He roped Joe's horse and saddled him, too. Joe walked out of the cabin, blinked at the already saddled mounts, and said, "Come on in. I got breakfast cooked."

Dan walked in, sat down, wolfed down eggs, bacon, biscuits, and two cups of coffee without a word. While Joe washed up, he cleaned his weapons. As he slipped the last round back into his pistol, he asked, "Ready?"

Joe nodded, picked up a can full of coal oil, walked out, and swung into the saddle. Dan mounted the gray and followed. Joe knew where the Slanthole was; there was no need for conversation. Although the distance to be covered was only about ten miles, Joe's caution and the broken terrain slowed them. When they came into sight of the old abandoned mine it was already late afternoon.

The Slanthole looked like an old deserted Buckhorn, a collection of dilapidated buildings on a valley floor with a string of smaller shelters around it and extending up the side of the mountain. The route Joe selected brought them to a point of rocks overlooking the whole area of the old mine. He dismounted, moved cautiously to a good viewing site, and sat scanning every building. Dan did the same. After fifteen minutes, Joe asked, "See any sign of rustlers?"

"No. No horses, no smoke, nothing." Dan continued his scan of the broken porches, cracked and missing windows, doorless entrances, and other signs of disrepair and decay in the little ghost town.

"Let's do what we come to do. Watch yourself. Cover my back while I work."

Dan didn't bother to answer. He let Joe get about fifty yards ahead, then followed him. In less than two hours, they were sitting on the rock overlook watching again. Joe had sparingly splashed a little coal oil on a wall of each building, lighted it, and moved on to the next. Now they sat and watched fire consume what had once been a small mining town.

Sparks and smoke spiraled skyward as the dry old buildings burned with a frightening, fierce, almost explosive flame. Columns of darting, glowing sparks and firebrands spun and danced in the air when roofs collapsed. Some of the falling roofs seemed to draw the walls inward with the force of their fall. When other roofs caved in, the walls blew outward like the blossoming of brilliant, flashing, flaring flowers.

Joe said softly, "Shame, ain't it? That was a good overnight stop for a wanderin' man. Place to sleep dry and stay warm. When it becomes a meetin' place and hideout for rustlers, though, it can't be allowed to stand. I know a good place tc camp. Let's get to it while we still got good light. We'll rest the horses and head back to the cabin in the morning."

Dan stopped on the way and built a small fire. Joe cooked them a sparse meal. Then they rode another two miles before they stopped and unrolled their bedrolls. Neither of them was the type to risk sleeping where the smell of a fire might reveal their location during the night. Dan took the first watch.

His anger at fate had carried him through his night ride, but watching the fire had taken something out of him. His own fury seemed to burn out along with the old mine buildings. Without the anger, he simply felt empty and tired. Joe looked at him with a quizzical expression several times and acted as if he were about to speak, but he never did. Dan thought, I never before fully appreciated a man who keeps his mouth shut.

Ira Rice allowed himself a grimace of distaste when he heard the light tapping at the door of the bank. He opened the slot in the heavy door to be sure it was Channing and that he was alone before unlocking and opening it. Channing slid through the door quickly and Rice closed and relocked it at once. The big man looked around the dimly lit bank foyer with its heavily draped windows before flashing a hard grin at the banker. He walked without a word through the small foyer and into the cubbyhole Rice called his office. He walked straight to the only comfortable chair in the room, the one behind Rice's desk, and sat down.

Rice remained standing. He didn't expect this conversation to last long anyway. "Channing, the things I hear lately indicate that you aren't going to be able to keep your end of our bargain." The insolent smile on the big man's face started fading as Rice had anticipated it would. He continued, "I've been hearing some things that sound like you've overstepped yourself, got slapped down and run off. Sounds to me like you're out in the cold." Rice pointed to a narrow little straight chair. "Get out of my chair, sit hcre, and I'll hear what you have to say."

Channing rolled to his feet, the grin now a forced grimace, and walked from behind Rice's desk. He spun the straight chair around and sat down with his arms crossed across its back. It was exactly what Rice had expected. The man was clever enough, but there was something weak in him. Rice, outweighed by at least fifty pounds, shorter by at least six inches, and unarmed, still had confidence he could control the larger man.

Rice settled himself comfortably and started the conversation along lines planned to keep the big man on the defensive. "Did you hire those renegade Indians to attack Alice Martin?"

The cocky grin now forgotten, Channing looked more like he had bitten into something sour. "Seemed like I had to do somethin'," he muttered in a hoarse, strained voice. He had picked up a habit of holding his hand to his throat when he spoke. "Cougan can't read or write, but he's a damn sharp foreman. All he could talk about was how that woman was so good at the books and knew every little thing about the ranch. I couldn't get the job done with somebody like her hanging over my shoulder. Besides, I figured that if she was out of it, her parents might cave in and sell out real easy."

"When I offered you this opportunity, I set certain rules to be followed. There were to be no big drives of cattle to attract attention, no killing, no trashy range riders in the town of Buckhorn spending money like fools. The idea was to bleed that ranch down so we could take it over quietly for the cost of a few small loans. You could make a small fortune selling cattle you didn't own, and I could get a choice ranch for a fraction of its value. Those rules seem simple enough to understand. You have broken them, and by doing so, you have ruined two years of patient work."

The big man was shifting uneasily, making the small uncomfortable chair creak plainly in the silence. He glared at Rice and looked like he was about to make a denial, but his gaze slipped off to the side. "Would've been over by now 'cept for that damn Walker. He killed four of my men when he stepped in and saved that Martin woman, and now four more've vanished. Then somebody burned down my meetin' place at the Slanthole. There ain't a board left standin' out there."

Rice sat back, trying to conceal the shock of what he had heard. This thing was completely out of control, much worse than he had believed. "Four men killed! Four men missing! An abandoned cluster of mine buildings as big as this town burned to the ground! This is insane. It sounds like a wartime damage report. What have you been doing?"

Channing's face was red and sweaty, but his mouth was set in a grim line. Rice thought the big man looked like an overgrown, petulant child. Perhaps he had made a serious mistake with Channing. The man had seemed perfect for the job, but now he looked completely different. From a reasonably intelligent, well-dressed man willing to shortcut the law for a safe profit, he had changed into a wild, erratic, murderous fool.

"At first, I thought that damn Walker would ride on through after saving the Martin woman by shootin' my men and then hittin' me with a sneak punch. But Cougan hired him for some reason. That surprised me. Cougan don't have nothin' good to say about the driftin' gunslingers that come through once in a while, and he was always gripin' about me hiring too many men." He paused to rub his throat, and Rice waited, leaning forward like a stern schoolmaster hearing a story from a misbehaving student.

"I ain't a gunfighter, and this Walker is full of dirty tricks. I tried to get Tolar, the blacksmith, to mess him up, thinking that would run him off. Tolar wouldn't do it. I was pretty mad, so I paid two men to kill Walker after the dance. Hell, while I was at it I went ahead and sent two more men to kill that old man up at the north pasture, that Joe Ballas. I figured with Walker and Ballas out of it, I could sweep that pasture clean and be done with it before anybody knew what was happening."

"You blundering fool." Rice's voice was almost a whisper in the small room, but he spoke with such venom that Channing drew back. "You sent men to kill Walker. That must be the two men they found in the stable. Two men were stabbed to death and hidden under the hay in the stable right here in Buckhorn. You sent your hired killers into this town, into Buckhorn?"

Channing was now sweating heavily and unable to meet Rice's angry eyes. "I didn't care where they did it," he mumbled looking at the floor. "Maybe I forgot to tell 'em to stay away from Buckhorn."

"Idiot! I suppose the other two missing men are the ones you sent to get that man Ballas?"

"Yeah. They might've taken what I paid 'em and just rode off. One of 'em wasn't eager to do it, but the other one was a good, tough man. I don't know what happened."

Rice sat back and took a couple of deep breaths. His mind was spinning. He needed time to sort this mess into some kind of order. His original plan to take cold-blooded advantage of Ben Martin's illness and take over the most prosperous ranch in the area was turning into a farce.

Murder and violence was not the way to do business. Sharp business practice, taking advantage of others' misfortunes, was the road to wealth and power. It was even permissible to make use of crooks like Channing if proper distance could be maintained.

"How many M Bar M cattle have you sold since Walker came?"

"None. How can I do that? Our game was to sell 'em straight and safe with a proper bill of sale. I can't sign 'em anymore. Hell, it would be like signing a confession to rustlin' now. The trick was to make the people buying them think that they were dealing with temporary drovers from the ranch. Hell, I got no more men. I even lost the place where I been meetin' with 'em. You're the one insists that they never come to Buckhorn. I didn't run no prison camp out there at the Slanthole. Soon's them boys would get some money, they'd want to ride to a town to have some fun. Now I got a problem. Proper men for this kind of work have to be picked careful. Some of these riders will pull a gun on you if you ask 'em to do a little rustlin'. I'm goin' to have to ride all over the country to find some more men I can trust to keep their mouths shut."

"You tried to get Alice Martin killed and lost four men. You tried to get Ballas and Walker killed and lost four *more*. I'm not impressed with the men you pick. On the other hand, this man Walker is into everything. I went out to put pressure on Alice Martin. That's a very cool young woman, but I thought I might be able to put her under such financial strain that she might listen to an offer for the ranch."

Hope on his face and obviously eager to talk about something else, Channing leaned forward and asked, "You think we got 'em broke enough to take over right now?"

"I thought we were close. I swear that Martin girl was being evasive when I demanded payment of the interest plus some of the principal on the loan. They certainly don't have enough in this bank to pay and keep afloat till roundup. Then she and Walker had a long talk somewhere outside the house, and suddenly she came up with two thousand dollars in cash. I think Walker gave it to her. Could they have sold some cattle or something? Where else would a drifting gunslinger come up with that kind of money, and why would he give it to her?"

"He sure looked ragged when he brought her back to the ranch. He didn't look like a man with that kind of money, although he was ridin' one of the finest horses I ever saw. Did you say my men in the stable had been stabbed?"

"That's what I heard."

Channing seemed to shrink. "What kind of a man is this Walker? I figured him to be a broke, down-and-out gunslinger. Has anybody heard of him before? Where'd he come from? Everything was goin' good before he came into it."

Rice was sitting back in his chair now, relaxed. "It doesn't matter. The important thing, though, is that you've made such a mess of everything that our original plan may be ruined. The whole area is buzzing with talk. Everybody is nervous. You need to get back out of town while I try to figure out if there is a new way to do this. I'll get in touch with you if I can think of something. Otherwise, our association is ended."

Channing seemed stunned. "You mean you're quittin'? Givin' up when we're so close?"

Rice said coldly, "I planned to take over a ranch. You were supposed to run a ranch into the ground with extra expenses and stolen stock. You ended up planning a series of murders instead. If word got out that you were involved in trying to kill a woman, you wouldn't be safe within a thousand miles of here. You made good money from stealing cattle. Let it go at that, unless I can think of something. In the meantime, I think you had better look for other work. This is getting too dangerous."

Channing lost the embarrassed schoolboy expression, and a look of harsh anger settled on his glistening red face. "Maybe so. Maybe your part of the plan is busted, but there's still lots of cattle up there to be taken if a man knows how. It'll take me some time to find the right men, but I ain't through with it. I ain't givin' up, not till I get even with Walker for that sneak punch he pulled on me. I ain't sure if I'll ever talk right again; I might always sound like a sick frog. Maybe seeing him down and dead is what I need to feel right again."

Rice said nothing at first, just sat meeting Channing's furious glare. After a brief silence, he said firmly, "I am a businessman. Vengeance and personal feelings of that sort are not businesslike. What you do is your own affair. Do not involve me. However, I wish you luck." He stood up and offered his hand. When Channing took it, he continued, "You are, I think, making a mistake. I hate to see that. Take my advice. Ride away from here with your pockets full of money and look for a new game."

Channing grinned and said, "You're a bloodless little bastard, but I like you. You brought me in on this deal, and I made a bunch of money. You always been straight with me, and that's a good thing. You don't think I'm very smart, but that's fine with me. I been puttin' money in my pocket all along, but you don't have nothin' but the regular interest on a loan. I got the best of the deal."

After they shook hands, Rice dimmed the lantern, peeked carefully out the curtains of the bank foyer, and let Channing slip out into the deserted street. After closing and locking the door behind him, Rice walked back into his little office. Sitting in his comfortable chair, he reached into a drawer of his desk, pulled out a bottle and a sparkling clean glass, and poured himself a drink.

He started to raise the glass to his lips, stopped, went to the lantern and adjusted the wick so that the room was again brightly lighted. Then he raised the glass between him and the light and watched the warm color of fine bourbon move before his eye.

He lifted the glass a bit higher and said aloud, "Here's to you, idiot, simpleton, fool. Go get your cattle. Go try to kill dangerous men. Get your barbaric revenge and savor it. I wish you well. If you succeed, I'll be the owner of the largest piece of choice property in this part of the country. My best wishes." The bourbon, smooth though it was, bit his throat and he coughed. Hell, he might as well have another.

Sitting with the glass close under his nose to enjoy the fragrance of the good whiskey, Rice studied the circle of light thrown by the lantern on the ceiling. Channing had been correct about the change in luck that had suddenly upset their plans. It all coincided with the arrival of the mysterious Walker. The man was clever. At the dinner table, he had avoided talking while Rice was present by merely insisting on good manners. He was a man of contrasts, pretending to be an ordinary rider but wearing a gun in an indefinably more dangerous way than other men.

Walker was there to frustrate Channing's vicious plan to have Alice Martin killed. Perhaps it was only a coincidence, but Walker appeared again just in time to provide Alice Martin money when she needed it, money from nowhere. There was no way it could have come from the bank without Rice knowing about it.

A chilling thought came to him. Could Walker be some kind of range detective secretly hired by Ben Martin to look after his ranch and his daughter? The man's table manners had been worth watching. He ate with an unconscious grace and politeness. He also failed to show the awkwardness and nervousness that a common hired hand would have displayed with his foreman and a female owner. He had more of an air of being in command than of being a hired man. There also appeared to be an aura of tension between him and the Martin woman. Rice took a tiny sip of his whiskey. Maybe there was more to this that a cautious man should know.

He had attributed that little feeling of tension to male-female attraction . . . but it could be something much more dangerous. It might be a shared secret about who Walker really was. It was odd. When Alice Martin had returned with Cougan she was obviously excited, showing the high color and bright eyes that could signal romantic stimulation. Smiling cynically, Rice reflected that it could also signal the delivery of badly needed funds. It might even signal being relieved of responsibility in a difficult situation by being told exactly how to handle it. Alice Martin and her foreman had both come back to the house suddenly full of confidence and with the attitude of having some shared secret.

Success in business required taking risks, but Rice decided that he would watch from the sidelines from now on. There was no proof that he had been involved in anything illegal or unethical. Channing was the only one who could implicate him. The best thing that could happen would be for Channing to steal enough cattle for the original plan to work and drop a prosperous ranch into Rice's hands.

Mentally picturing Channing against Walker made Rice shake his head with pity for Channing. The only way this could go bad now was for Channing to be captured and to talk—but if Walker caught Channing stealing M Bar M cattle, there would be little chance for talking.

Rice felt a fine sense of satisfaction as he turned out the lantern and quietly left his small bank building. He felt safe, but also in a position to profit if events favored him. Now he had only to watch and wait.

XI

Big Dan looked at his son's likeness on a wanted poster. In large print across the top he read, NEEDED: DAN WALKER, ALIAS WALKING HAWK and across the bottom, $2,500 REWARD TO THE MAN WHO TELLS DAN WALKER TO COME HOME, ALL PROBLEMS ARE SOLVED.

"That has to be the most unusual wanted poster I ever saw, and it still worries me. It looks like a reward poster to bring a fugitive to the law, and some man who can't read might try to do just that. We run the risk of someone getting hurt trying to capture Dan. I sure wouldn't want to try. Would you, Mark?"

Mark Whitson-Walker shook his head with a frown and said, "It might not be a good idea. Maybe the poster should only have printing on it. Then only men who can read will be able to make sense of it, and the risk of misunderstanding would be reduced. I had one made up that way for you to look at." He dropped the other poster on Big Dan's desk. "This one has no picture and the same words as the first one, but a physical description has been added. Dan's tall enough to stand out in a crowd. That might help somebody to notice him."

Matthew Whitson-Walker grinned and said, "The Pinkerton Agency said that they would help with the distribution of the posters, but it's going to cost a fortune. They say they can hire riders to deliver the posters to the Indians on reservations, hire people who know how to get them inserted in selected newspapers, and they even think they can talk the railroads into putting them up in their depots. Dan, the Pinkerton men I have talked with think that many of the newspapers will pick this up as a feature story: 'Fugitive Scion of Wealthy Family Cleared of Charges,' or some headline like that."

Big Dan's first remark was directed to Mark. "Use the poster without the likeness. The other one looks too much like a wanted poster." Then he turned to Matt and asked, "What kind of expenses are the Pinkertons estimating?"

Matt handed him a voucher with a Pinkerton letterhead. "This will cover the first month. They will have two dozen agents on it full time, and the whole agency will accept it in addition to the other things they are working on now. In other words, all their agents and informants will be alerted."

"What do they have to report as of now from their attempts to trace him?"

"They think he headed west and north. As you know, Big Red is missing, and that tall gray horse is also gone. That's almost all we know so far. They have found nothing, and that makes them think he's avoiding trains and other public modes of travel. They think he headed west because the law out there isn't too eager to pick up men wanted in other jurisdictions. It makes sense to me, Dan. He might head for the more sparsely settled areas. Many outlaws do that successfully. The Pinkertons think that he might go to the areas where he traveled with Gray Bird when he was living with the Indians."

Big Dan leaned forward intensely. "He might go to Gray Bird's people. They thought a lot of him, so he knows they'll hide him. His breaking the white man's law will mean nothing to them. I can't predict him, though. He might be afraid of causing them trouble and stay away from them, too."

Mark added, "Another thing that makes me think the Pinkertons have made a good guess about his direction of travel, Dan, are the things Matt and I found missing. His favorite guns are gone, and they aren't city guns. His little hideout guns for use in the city were left behind."

"That's one thing that has made our search difficult from the start, Dan," said Matt. "He's equipped by training to hide in either city or country. For all we know he could have left these clues to confuse the law. He could be sitting in some office somewhere, pretending to be a clerk until the furor dies down. All we can find missing, though, are the kind of clothes he would use if he rode for the mountains, rode into Gray Bird's type of wild country."

"His accounts weren't touched, so he left with very little money. That indicates to me that he planned to live off the country. If he planned to hide in a city, I think he would have tried to get his hands on some of his money," Big Dan said. "Matt, tell the Pinkertons to proceed. Tell them to conduct a general search, but they are to concentrate the most effort in the Northwest. He might be heading for Canada or already be there by now. We'll do it this way for a couple of months. If we don't find him by doing this, then we'll figure out something more to do."

Mark stepped closer to the big mahogany desk. "I'm going to head in that direction. Travel in that part of the country would be more pleasant if it weren't winter, but that's my hard luck."

Dan looked amused. "There doesn't seem to be much for you to do up there at this stage of the search."

"It would give me a better feeling that I'm really doing something. What's that old saying, 'If you want something done right, do it yourself'? Matt will still be here ready for frontline duty if anything interesting comes up, and you'll be our reserve."

"Reserve? Him? I don't think your father fits that role well at all," Margaret laughed. "I will handle the reserve job, thank you. Your father and I can freely substitute for each other when it comes to running our business interests. The three of you can go wherever you please; the real business head of this family will take care of the expenses." Margaret's voice was now matter-of-fact. "I'm the only one in this family who hates to travel, so I'll stay home in comfort and count our money while you men dash around the country."

"Done! The Walkers and Whitsons start their march to the battlefield," Big Dan agreed while Mark and Matt nodded.

"How about your companions?" Margaret directed the question to Mark.

"I have selected three," he responded. "All are sober men, proficient with weapons, and two of them know something about the Northwest. We'll be leaving tomorrow by train. I may pick up local men in the area after I get there."

Margaret turned her eyes to Matt in silent question. He shrugged. "I also have three men. We are ready to go to the scene of any hot clue that comes up."

Big Dan said solemnly, "If I end up doing any traveling, it will be alone. I work better that way, unless I find me another woman along the trail."

While both her sons ducked to hide grins, Margaret responded acidly, "There's no fool like an old fool."

Snag Mathis had hidden his horse and pack mule in a dense clump of woods a hundred yards away. He worked his way carefully to the fork in the road where he was to meet his man. The meeting was to be thirty minutes after full dark tonight, so Snag had slipped into the area in the early morning darkness. He picked a spot carefully from which he could see all approaches. That done, he methodically scouted through the surrounding ground to ensure that there was no hidden observer. When he returned to his selected spot, he was positive that he was alone. He settled down, alert as an animal, to await the man's arrival. He opened a heavy leather carrying case, removed a large, powerful telescope, and began a patient surveillance of his surroundings.

Snag carried no watch. He found the ticking too noisy for his line of work. Other didn't seem to notice the racket, but watches boomed as loud as drums to his sensitive ears. His was an unusual profession. In fact, he knew of no other man who made his living in exactly the way he did.

Snag Mathis was an ambush killer who had several significant qualifications for his line of work. Two important ones were a complete lack of conscience and a truly superb ability to hit targets from very long ranges. His heavy Sharps .50 caliber rifle was equipped with the best telescopic sight money could buy. Another significant advantage Snag brought to his work was a bottomless well of patience. He loved his work; the only time he became impatient was when he wasn't working.

An old wound had changed Snag from a handsome young man into a scarred, bitter beast. A bullet from a drunken, carousing drover had struck him, an innocent bystander, in the mouth. The bullet had ripped through his teeth and torn his right cheek wide open. One tooth remained in the upper front of his mouth, thus his nickname "Snag." The muscles in his cheek were torn away, leaving a sunken mass of scar tissue from mouth to ear. The jawbone had been shattered and had healed improperly, leaving his face misshapen and his speech an awkward mumble. On the rare occasions Snag went to town, he held a bandana around his lower face to hide his scars. He never allowed anyone to see him go through the messy torture of eating.

A few carefully selected men, mostly bartenders, knew about him and sent customers to Snag. Every prospective customer paid a hundred dollars to the contact man for an appointment. The bartender kept the hundred whether or not Snag took the assignment. Snag would kill anyone—men, women, children, or whole families. His price was six hundred dollars per death. One hundred dollars of this fee went back to the bartender as a bonus when the job was finished.

His only requirement was that the victim must not be in a town; he worked only in the countryside. He was the most efficient solver of the homesteader problem available, and several otherwise respectable ranchers had employed him. Like the customer he was preparing to meet today, they had hired a shadow, since he never allowed them to see him other than as a shape in the darkness, and he never spoke to them.

The inability to find honest work because of his disfigurement, the awkwardness of eating and speaking, and the horror and contempt in all human eyes that looked at him had combined to turn an ordinary young man into a vessel brimming with hatred. Snag Mathis hated all human beings; he had killed for enjoyment before he discovered that it could be enormously profitable. Years of living alone like a solitary animal had taken a fearful toll. Mathis had no idea that he was insane; he wouldn't have minded had the thought come to him.

He traveled through the country like a ghost. Few ever saw him, but stories were told about him around firesides. Most who heard the stories figured that they were just tall tales. As the years passed and his hair turned a dirty gray, the good side of his face became permanently fixed in an evil grimace as ugly as the wounded side.

Mathis went through elaborate preparations for each meeting with a new customer. This was, in his opinion, the most dangerous part of each job. He never knew when a bartender might betray him for some unknown reason or some trick might be involved. His customers were instructed to bring the money for the job in cash, the whole amount to be paid in advance, no bargaining. They were to bring a description, a picture if possible, of the intended victim along with a sketch map showing the victim's location. They were to recite all they knew about the victim's habits, lay the money, map, and pictures down when Mathis pointed out a spot on the ground. Then they were to ride away. They were instructed not to ask him any questions; he would not speak.

The sun made its way across the sky while Mathis continued his ceaseless vigil. The wind from the north had the frigid cutting edge of winter now, although the ground was still free of snow and ice. Motionless, Snag was prepared. He was always prepared. Seated on a folded blanket and wearing a dull brown sheepskin coat with the wool turned out, he was as comfortable as if seated inside a snug cabin beside a warm fire. Unaware of him, squirrels and deer fed nearby. He watched with grim amusement when a fox caught a young rabbit and dragged its body triumphantly out of sight.

As the last light of day was fading he saw a lone horseman coming slowly along the road. He was a big man, heavy in the saddle, with his collar turned up and his hat pulled down against the wind. Snag watched the rider with contempt. The man rode with his eyes fixed on the road in front of his horse. Hell, the man might as well be asleep in the saddle. Snag figured that he could kill him with a smooth stone from a creek bed, just walk up and knock him off his horse. The temptation was strong, but this was a customer. After a last scan of the surroundings to ensure that no other person was approaching, Snag crept from his vantage point to a spot close to the fork in the road.

When the man reined his horse to a stop at the fork, Snag cocked both hammers of his shotgun, his favorite weapon for close work. The man recognized the signal to start talking and did so in a shaky rush, speaking in a hoarse, odd voice. "I want you to kill two men. One old one with a limp and one young one who is big and tall. The tall one rides the prettiest red horse you ever saw. They live in a cabin on the north pasture of the M Bar M ranch. They're both tough and ready for trouble. I think they've killed four of my men. I got a map in this bag along with twelve hundred dollars. The map shows where the cabin is located."

Snag held the shotgun well out in front of him to be sure the man saw it when he stepped into view in the weak starlight. He held the weapon with his right hand and swept his left in a sweeping, obvious gesture in the poor light. He pointed to the ground beside the man's horse. The horse was getting jittery and prancing around. The man asked, "You'll take the job?" Snag repeated the pointing gesture, then raised the shotgun. The bag dropped to the ground. Snag lowered the shotgun and waved the man on down the road. The fool hesitated just long enough to see the shotgun rise again before he put spurs to the horse and galloped on down the road.

Snag waited until the man was out of sight before he darted across the narrow road, snatched up the canvas bag, and faded into the blackness of the trees. Slipping the bag into a large pocket inside his sheepskin coat, he approached his horse and mule with infinite caution. If someone had managed to approach, they might try to ambush him here. Snag knew that most men tended to relax a little when they came back to their horses. He had lain in ambush for a couple of alert, careful men once, waiting for them to return to their horses. They had relaxed at that critical moment and paid with their lives. Finally, he was satisfied that there was no trap. He mounted and rode very quietly into the night.

Snag had ridden about four miles before he reached into the recesses of his coat and brought out a handful of fire-dried venison cut into tiny cubes about the size of raisins. He stuffed them into his mouth, leaving his hand across the lower part of his face to hold his torn lips together on the right side. Snag was eating the only way he knew how to do so without saliva drooling down his chin. The small cubes of meat soaked in his mouth and released a flavor he liked, and he could swallow them without going through the painful effort to chew.

He rode for about ten miles, stopped at midnight, and slept till dawn hidden in a thicket. He rose almost the instant he awoke and focused his telescope on his back trail for fifteen minutes of intense observation. Then he made a small fire no larger than his spread hand to heat a tin cup of water for tea. He drank with his head tilted sharply to the left, so the liquid would not run out the ruined right side of his mouth.

He put the cup back in the pack, roped it to the mule, saddled his horse, and rode about two miles across rocky ground. He dismounted in another cluster of fir trees and reached into his coat for the canvas bag. He counted the money carefully, folded it as tightly as he could, and packed it into one of four money belts around his waist. He glanced at the crude map briefly before tearing it into tiny pieces and releasing them into the icy wind. He had ridden the north pasture of the M Bar M, but it had been several years ago. No matter—he never forgot country once he had explored it.

The big stupid customer said that these two men had killed four of his own men. Snag wished that speech weren't so hard for him. He would like to know how those killings had been accomplished. Maybe these two were gunslingers. If that was the case, he was not concerned. The fast draw was no help out here; that fancy work was nice in saloons, but it was useless in the wide open spaces.

On the other hand, if these men were riflemen, bushwackers who had taken out four men from a safe distance, then they might be competent woodsmen. That would make the job more difficult. A man who ambushes moves with care and stays alert to avoid having the tables turned on him. The man said that his targets were ready for trouble. Snag felt a mild sense of discomfort. He hated to take risks. He liked the sense of power that came from careful sightings through his telescopic sight at unsuspecting targets seven or eight hundred yards away. Clean kills without warning from a safe distance were his specialty.

He rode to his secret little valley. Taking no chances on this job, he would leave the horse and mule in the valley and do the job on foot. Snag had none of the distaste for traveling on foot shared by most western men. With his big pockets full of dried venison, he could go for days without a fire and without having to worry about the obvious trail that a horse always leaves. His soft moccasins were difficult to track, and he always carried four pairs. They wore out quickly in the rocky, mountainous country when a man moved as fast as Snag. His body was as hard and lean as whipcord. He could move on foot faster than a man on horseback in these rough mountains.

As he rode down the narrow trail into the valley, he felt a sense of satisfaction. Little hideouts like this one were part of his special advantage. Living away from other people, living a wandering life, he came to know the country better than any ordinary man ever could. He walked confidently into the cave and suddenly dropped to the rock floor. Once inside, his first glance told him that some of his wood had been burned. His carefully collected dry grass and kindling were gone. Newer kindling was present, but it was not stacked like he would have done it. His keen sense of smell told him that the fire was old.

Snag could feel a strange tightness inside him as he came back to his feet and looked around the cave. Fear and anger touched him at the same time. He loved his hideouts; it was obscene that someone had discovered one. He felt soiled; the cleanliness of a place was ruined if other people found it and used it. The thought that someone had dared to intrude into his privacy brought tremors of rage across his face. At the same time, his sick mind reeled with the superstitious thought that this omen spelled trouble for him with this job. He found himself sweating. Now he didn't dare leave his stock here. He would have to change his plan. He recalled the intuitive malaise he had experienced earlier, and now this intrusion into one of his best hideouts had to be a definite bad luck sign.

It took him three hours to search the valley. He found horse sign, but it was so old and blurred he couldn't read how many animals had been here. Indecision raced through his mind. Would he have to change his plan? Maybe some traveler had stopped here and moved on, never to return. But who could that be? This was out of the way for travelers. He considered forgetting the job for now. Maybe he ought to wait here and kill the intruders if they returned to his valley. No, nobody but he would come to such a place in the winter. They wouldn't be back. Could he be sure? No. He would ride to the M Bar M north pasture. He knew no other place he could leave his animals close enough to the job but still have them safe from discovery.

Suddenly, the single narrow trail out of the valley had a malignant significance. He had to get out. He moved with uncharacteristic speed up the trail, fighting the rise of panic. He drew a quick deep breath of relief when he crested the ridge past the bottleneck at the valley's entrance. His fingers were stiff from gripping the Sharps rifle too tightly. Relief gave way to irritation as he thought about having to worry about his stock while stalking two men. Unless he could catch them separately, this job might be risky. The Sharps was not a weapon that could be reloaded at great speed.

He was doing too much thinking for a simple little job. The thing to do was to get on with it. Worrying about bad luck omens was tiring him; it was time for action, to get it done. He rode with impatience straight toward the place where the cabin was located according to the map.

He rode through a grove of trees and reined up in surprise. That stupid big man had put the cabin several miles out of its proper place on the map. Snag knew he had been in plain sight from the cabin for a full half minute before he could wheel his horse and mule back out of sight in the trees. Another slip. Another bad sign? He focused his attention on the cabin as he slid from the saddle with the Sharps in hand. Maybe this could be finished right now.

"Hold it right there!"

A shrill scream of surprise burst from Snag as he dropped to the ground, twisted, and fired the Sharps, all with the quickness of a startled animal. His shot was a reflex action, and he caught only a glimpse of a crouched man as he dropped, rolling into the brush. Snag spun to his feet and ran erratically through the trees making uncontrollable yelps of panic as he heard shots and the hum of a bullet past his ear. Something struck his left arm and tugged at the right side of his sheepskin coat. Dodging trees in terror, Snag ran for his life, high-pitched screams coming from him with every breath he took. Something hit his leg, knocking him off stride, and he smashed at full speed into a small fir tree. Spinning out of control, he fell into a shallow gully, but he landed on his feet and kept running. The shooting stopped, but Snag ran on, his screams now reduced to hysterical sobs and moans as he ran into the safety of thick, trackless woods.

XII

As soon as he saw Joe's horse standing about a hundred yards ahead with an empty saddle, Dan slid to the ground, pulling his Winchester as he dismounted, and dropped to one knee. He was following the routine Joe preferred. During their patrols of the north pasture, Joe rode with great caution, checking and observing with endless patience. Often he dismounted to reconnoiter on foot before he rode into an area that might present danger of an ambush. Dan's role was to follow at a distance of one or two hundred yards, watching Joe's back trail, ready to cover him if there was trouble.

Joe was out of sight, but that old man could hide behind a pine needle. They were almost home. He was probably taking a good look at the cabin before riding on in. The boom of a heavy rifle so startled Dan that the muzzle of his Winchester rose with a jerk. The lighter pop of a handgun came so quickly after the boom of the rifle that it was almost the same sound. A series of bloodcurdling screams caused a tingle to race up his back as four more shots echoed through the woods in front of him.

Dan could see nothing, but he heard a crashing and rolling in the brush while those terrible screams continued. The sounds were like those of a wounded bear tearing through a thicket, but no bear ever made an eerie, high-pitched howl like that. Something was terrified and hurt and running away. Dan had never heard such a sound from man nor beast.

His throat was suddenly so dry that he heard a distinct sound when he tried to swallow. The crashing in the brush stopped, but the screams tapered off into whimpers and moans before ending. When silence fell, it was complete. All the small creatures that create the routine little noises in every woodland were frozen into stillness. Dan could feel his heart beating so heavily that he was sure the pounding could be heard all around him.

A gust of wind created a nerve-racking sigh through the firs, and the other trees, now leafless, waved with a deafening rattle of branches. Every little scrape and rub of branches seemed ominous and threatening, as if some kind of unknown and horrible creatures were stalking him from every direction.

The late afternoon sun was already half-hidden behind the mountains. Dan rose from his kneeling position beside a tree, moving with agonizing caution. Nothing will attract a hostile eye more surely than a quick movement. If some kind of awful creature came after him, by God, it would find him on his feet.

He heard a soft shuffle of movement, and Dan felt his muscles tense up another notch, tighter than a banjo string. If something unknown was coming, he was eager to face it now while there was still good light for shooting. Whatever it was, the real thing couldn't be worse than standing here with his imagination running wild.

A horse came into view followed by a pack mule. The mule's reins were tied to the empty saddle on the horse. Dan saw a tiny flicker of movement. The muzzle of his Winchester was moving to cover that area when he saw a sliver of Joe's face peering around a tree trunk. Dan opened and closed his left fist. The movement was sufficient to draw Joe's eye. Joe's face came into full view and his meager nod signaled his recognition.

Joe selected his path to Dan and approached with the now familiar agility and silence that was the perfect opposite to his usual stiff, limping gait. When he came near, he pulled Dan's head close and whispered, "Dry-gulcher . . . got his horse and mule . . . uses a Sharps with a telescope . . . got lead in him . . . didn't git him down . . . he's still around . . . goin' for my horse . . . wait here . . . guard horses."

Dan waited in the failing light for the hour it took Joe to cover the hundred yards to his horse and return with it. When Joe was close, Dan whispered, "Bring the horses. I'll scout ahead till we get home." Their progress was so slow and careful that it was fully dark by the time they got to the cabin.

As soon as they were satisfied that the cabin was empty, Joe drew Dan outside and spoke quietly. "We got a new game here, Dan."

"What happened? I never heard a man make noises like that. I just stopped and shook all over, started hearing spooks behind every bush."

"I got a good look at him. Threw down on him and told him to hold still. Quicker'n a blink, he wheeled around and fired that big rifle before

I could get my trigger pulled. Missed me by maybe an inch. Then he started that horrible yellin' and ran off. I milked a handgun till it was dry at him, but he kept goin'. Ain't no way I could've missed every shot. He's carryin' lead souvenirs."

Joe paused and ran his fingers along the butt of his holstered handgun. It was an unconscious gesture. Dan had often seen men who lived with guns caress their weapons in this fashion. It was like a city man would touch his wallet when he saw a waiter coming with the meal check. Joe and the city man were both reassuring themselves that they had what they needed.

Joe spoke again. "I've heard rumors about a man like that for years, but I never pay much attention to loose talk. That feller's lost half his face or something. The story is that he roams the mountains killin' people with that big old Sharps rifle of his. Nobody knows where he holes up. I thought it was all bunk until today."

Dan found it hard to believe. "You mean we have a crazy man up here, a man who just wanders around killing people?"

"Damn sure sounded crazy, didn't he? But he don't just wander around. The talk is that he hires out. Kills for money. If that's straight talk, then somebody has put him on us, and if he's on us, we're in trouble. This ain't fun no more. That man looked wilder'n any catamount I ever seen."

Joe put his hand on Dan's shoulder. "Dan, be ready for it. He ain't human lookin'. When I looked at his face, it shook me. It made me slow. If I hadn't been on his right side with him holdin' the rifle in his right hand, he'd of killed me even though I had him dead to rights. I was just lucky enough to be on his awkward side when he turned to shoot. He's quicker'n greased lightnin', fearful quick."

Dan sat quietly while they both spent a few minutes listening and scanning the darkness before he spoke. "If he uses one of those Sharps rifles with a telescope sight, we can't wait for him. We got to go after him. The only way we have a chance is to get close. Otherwise, he'll pick us off at long range, and we can't even shoot back."

"That's good thinkin', Dan. We got his horse and mule, and I'm sure I got lead in him. He might be layin' out there dead or dyin' right now, or maybe hurt bad enough for us to run him down pretty easy." Joe paused and then said reluctantly, "I'll tell you the truth, Dan. It gives me the creeps to try to trail a man like that. Close or far, wounded or not, that's one bad man."

Dan walked out cautiously into the predawn darkness. He had two extra pairs of moccasins sewn into the inside of his sheepskin coat. He was proud of them. Buckskin outer layers with rabbit inner layers would make warm footgear in the deepening cold. The rabbit-skin inner liners still had their soft fur, and it was turned inward to the foot. It was amazing how much a man could remember from his childhood when the need came on him. He had never made moccasins before, but he remembered how his mother had made him sit and watch while the squaws made them.

His plan was simple. He would go to the place where Joe had shot at the man, wait for dawn, and then track him down if he could. Joe was positive that he had wounded this crazed killer. If so, he wouldn't travel fast or far. The problem was to track him without falling into a trap. It was bitter cold at this hour. Dan had to move with extreme care. Even soft grass made noise when it was frozen stiff, and he didn't like leaving an obvious trail in the frost that would lead right to him when light came.

Dawn came quietly under a lead-colored sky. Dan felt the touch of sleet on his cheek when he knelt to read sign. His man was wearing moccasins. Dan found where he had rolled and charged through a thicket to get away from Joe. Black spots of dried blood verified Joe's certainty that he had wounded the man. Dan knew that his advance was so slow that his quarry could simply walk away from him, but there was no choice. He had to consider the danger from a close ambush as well as the chance that his man might shoot him from a great distance. He dared not step out into the open.

Tracking wasn't a challenge for the first five hundred yards. Dan squatted down at one place for ten minutes looking at the spots of dried blood. Smears on the grass on one side and drops on the other side of the trail puzzled him. Was the man wounded on two sides? The smears could be from blood running down into the man's moccasins. The drops could be from another wound, probably an arm wound, bleeding down off the fingers. Every sign along the trail added to Dan's conviction that his man was hurt too badly to travel far. His progress slowed as his caution increased.

It was about noon when he found the spot where his quarry spent the night. There had been no fire. All he found was a small round spot of flattened grass. It looked exactly like a place where a deer had bedded down. The man hadn't even gathered branches to keep himself off the coldness of the ground. Dan wondered if he was hurt so badly that he could do no better for himself or if he was so tough that he wasn't bothered by the cold. He decided that nobody was *that* tough.

There was no more blood.

The trail vanished. Dan spent three hours casting around for some kind of sign. Finally, in a rocky little draw beside a stream, he found traces of sand on top of some smooth rocks. His man had walked on top of the rocks with sand on his moccasins. He was heading upstream so Dan moved in that direction about a hundred yards. He dared not step out into the open streambed, but he could see no tracks from the wood line. He stopped to consider. Was the man still simply trying to get away, to get distance, or was he heading somewhere?

He was circling back, was climbing and looping back toward the cabin!

The boom of the heavy rifle caused Dan to jerk with surprise in the stillness. There was no crack of a bullet passing nearby. Dan wasn't the target. He abandoned the trail and started toward the sound. He had to cross the open draw, and he did so with a quick rush. He heard the rifle fire again, and continued his advance toward the sound. He was close!

Climbing through the thick woods as fast as he dared, he realized that he was skirting around the curve of a steep slope. Caution stopped him when he came to a rock slide. A full fifty feet of unstable shale faced him before he could reach the concealment of the woods on the other side. Crossing rock slides was tricky under the best of conditions, and doing it quietly was impossible. As Dan searched for a way to skirt around the slide, he realized that the cabin was in full view. It seemed amazingly close. It was always a surprise in rough mountainous terrain; a man can walk his feet off climbing up and down but cover very little distance when measured as the crow flies. The cabin was only about fifteen hundred yards away.

Two horses were down in the little corral beside the cabin. Dan stared in horror. One of the animals was still kicking. That sorry bastard had shot two horses. What possible good had that done him? Dan had to climb about two hundred feet to get above the slide. Impatience tugged at him every step of the way, but it would be foolhardy to try to save time and get killed for it. Dan stopped every ten or twelve feet to search the ground on the other side of the slide. He was sure that his man was very close. The sun was dropping fast.

At first, Dan thought it was a bear. Then he caught his breath sharply when he realized that he had his man in sight. He was climbing through the trees, moving with painful difficulty. Dan tracked him with the sights of the Winchester, waiting for a clear shot through the trees, but the man vanished behind an outcrop of rocks. Dan waited patiently for him to reappear. Minutes passed. Dan cursed under his breath. He was running out of time for good shooting light. Either the man had stopped to rest at that spot, or he had changed direction to keep the rocks between him and Dan. He was only a little over a hundred yards away when he vanished.

The area above the rock slide where Dan planned to cross had only a few stunted trees. A bare space stretched out for about forty feet to the edge of healthy trees on the other side. It looked like a half mile to Dan. If he got caught out there, he was in serious trouble. If that fellow was on the other side of those rocks watching his back trail, crossing that open space would be suicidal.

Dan was tempted to try it anyway. His breath came faster at the thought of the risk. His neck was growing stiff and his legs were trying to cramp. Holding still can be desperately hard work. He decided to be patient. The painful movements of the hunted man gave Dan confidence that time was on his side. That fellow wasn't going to outrun anybody when it was that hard for him to walk.

Dan eased himself into a more comfortable position. He would wait until dark, cross to the trees on the far side of the open space, and then move to that cluster of rocks. The man might have settled in there for the night. If so, Dan would end this hunt very soon.

He gave serious thought to trying to capture the man, just so he could put his feet in a fire before he killed him. Anybody who would shoot horses was so mean he deserved more than killing; he deserved something special. Dan enjoyed the thought for a while until he realized that he couldn't torture anyone. He had never had reason to think about it before. He was a little disappointed with himself. Sometimes he wasn't as much of an Indian as he would like to be, or maybe not enough of a white man. Both races had plenty of meanness. He wondered which he needed more of to be able to enjoy torturing a man.

Time crawled by, and imperceptibly the light started to fade. Dan's field of vision began to diminish. The outcrop of rocks where the horse killer had disappeared blended into the darkening woods. The cloudy skies seemed to come closer to the ground, and the patter of falling sleet grew louder. The wind picked up, filling the woods with noise.

Dan felt a rising sense of satisfaction. The hunted man was wounded and had spent a miserable night on the ground without even a blanket to ward off the cold. Dan had found no trace along the trail to indicate that the man had eaten anything. His wounds would hurt him severely with every move he made. A night as dark as the bottom of a well; clouds blocking out the starlight; a brisk wind to give a covering blanket of noise in the woods—all of these favored Dan's ability to approach his man without being detected. The hunted man had to be tired, and his wounds might be causing fever by now.

Dan began to move when he could barely see the movement of his hand when held at arm's length. This situation was one of the few times Dan sincerely regretted being tall. Even with the cloud cover, the sky was lighter than the ground; he must stay low or the hunted man might see his outline. Careful not to make the slightest noise, Dan flexed his fingers and stretched to work out the kinks in his body from the long, motionless wait.

He crossed the open patch above the landfall quickly. There had been time to plan every step while there was light. Then he worked his way down the slope about fifty feet and maneuvered into a rough loop toward the outcrop of rocks. He wanted to approach the rocks from downhill, hoping to outline his quarry against the sky. Several times Dan closed his eyes and inhaled deeply through his nose, concentrating all his attention on trying to smell any trace of smoke. He could detect nothing.

This wild man must be incredibly tough. Dan was convinced that he was very close. He shuddered at the thought of how the cold would eat into a tired, hungry, wounded man without a fire or blankets. In spite of all the care he had taken, Dan was convinced that his pursuit had been detected. If the hunted man thought that he and Joe were both still in the cabin, he would surely have felt safe enough to build a fire. Dan's lips tightened at the thought of the traps that might be set for him if he was expected tonight.

When he worked his way to within about thirty feet of the outcrop, he could see the rounded tops of the rocks outlined against the sky. Dan dropped from his crouch to his left knee and carefully adjusted the legging on his right leg. It would not do for that legging containing his knife to have slipped, even slightly, around his leg. The cold was beginning to make his ears numb, but he dared not cover them. He decided to stay in his present position for a few minutes to listen. All he needed was for his man to take a good deep, unguarded breath. That would be all that was needed to locate him.

As he knelt, turning his head slowly back and forth, listening, Dan remembered his mother's teasing laughter while she watched him. She made him practice the motion of drawing the knife from the legging on the calf of his right leg. She demanded that he raise his right knee and drop his right shoulder at the same time to draw the knife with his eyes straight to the front. "You must always be looking at your enemies, not admiring your own pretty leg or your own knife," she had giggled. Dan remembered how his face had burned with a growing boy's sensitive pride and hatred for his own awkwardness. It had been like rehearsing a difficult dance step over and over while the sweat ran off him in rivers. He had carried the same knife since she had given it to him with great ceremony when he was six.

There! He felt his heart quicken. Just a little groan, a tiny sigh like a man in restless sleep. Dan felt like leaping to his feet and giving an exultant war cry. He waited until the slight trembling of anticipation ceased and the quickening of his heart had passed. When he felt perfectly calm again, he loosened his gloves, one cautious finger at a time, and removed them. With exquisite caution that was almost painful, he rolled the gloves and slipped them inside his coat. Now, feeling the ground ahead with his bare hands, he started forward.

XIII

Dan moved to the rocks on his hands and knees, feeling ahead and moving leaves and twigs away from the spots where his knees would touch the ground. The top of the outcrop was rounded and smoothed by the weather, but the fallen rocks around the perimeter were like huge, irregular pieces of broken dinner plates, some lying flat while others were at all angles. It was a shambles with dozens of nooks and crannies large enough to hide a man.

A series of plans flashed through Dan's mind. It might have been better if he had gone to ground a little distance away to await the man's showing himself in the morning. Had he known about this rock shambles, that's what Dan would have done, but he hadn't been able to see this from his vantage point. Now he was committed. Unless he withdrew, which he didn't want to risk now, he had no choice but to try to find his man among all the shards of rock.

A whisper of leather on rock warned Dan, and he dropped flat just as the deafening roar of the Sharps filled the night. The muzzle flash illuminated the area like a flash of lightning. Dan fired three shots as fast as he could work the Winchester's action, and again heard that hysterical, blood-freezing, inhuman scream. He couldn't see a thing. He was blinded by the muzzle flash of the Sharps and by those of his own Winchester.

He heard something fall or jump into the gravel and broken rock that trailed down the steep slope below the outcrop. It sounded like a man tumbling and sliding out of control. Whatever it was stopped rolling, but little rocks and pebbles continued to dribble down the hill. Firing at the sound with his blinded eyes closed this time against his own muzzle flashes, Dan fired three more fast rounds. Quickly ducking behind a slanted chunk of rock, he groped silently along, feeling his way for four or five steps from the place where he had fired.

Dan knew that blinking wouldn't help his flash-blinded eyes, but he found himself doing it anyway. His eyes would recover in a few minutes, and nothing he could do would hurry the process.

He found his left hand cupped at his ear and his head swinging back and forth as he tried desperately to pick up the slightest sound. He could hear stealthy movement in the loose rocks and gravel, followed by a series of almost inaudible but hair-raising growls and moans.

Dan, eyes closed again, emptied the Winchester at the noises, aiming low. He changed position to get away from his own muzzle flashes while his lead was still whining through the air, buzzing and singing through the night after ricochetting off the rocks. That awful inhuman shriek echoed through the hills along with the wind song of distorted, tumbling lead. Dan was growing used to the cries now, and it sounded like they were growing weaker.

Squatting in a crack between two slabs of rock barely wider and longer than his body with the empty Winchester lying beside him, Dan decided that he would wait for light before moving around anymore. Fatigue was adding weight to his arms and legs, but no thought of sleep was possible. Frequently, afraid that his ears would freeze, he would pull a hand out from under his coat to cover one. He was afraid to risk the noise it would make to reload the Winchester.

About once an hour a muffled moan or a coughing whine would come from the gravel slide, and pebbles would rattle and roll briefly. Dan's eyes felt like they were sinking back into his head. He could no longer prevent himself from shaking as the cold seemed to penetrate him. He flexed his fingers under his coat in an effort to keep them warm, but his arms became heavy. Years seemed to pass, and Dan found himself wondering if his hair was turning white in a night that would never end.

He knew that his vigilance never diminished, yet it was like awakening from a daze when he suddenly realized that he could see the rocks around him quite clearly. Then Dan saw his man. He was lying face down on the rock slide below the outcrop, wedged below a bush. He had been only fifty feet away all night. The Sharps rifle was ten feet farther down the slope; it looked like it had fallen from the man's hand and slid on down the slope until coming to rest against a dwarfed little sapling.

The pain when he came to his feet was so intense he feared that his first few steps might rupture muscles or break bones. Whatever the price, he had to move. He had to get out of these rocks and into the concealment of the woods. He was going to find a nice dense thicket, build a fire, and drink some hot water. He cursed himself for not bringing a handful of coffee beans.

Dan took several breaths and found that his hands worked smoothly when he jammed shells into his Winchester.

He moved closer and studied the figure. When the man fell, it looked as if he had slid on his stomach, head first, down the gravel slope, forcing the brim of his hat down under his face. There was a smeared black streak of blood clearly visible on the pale rocks leading to the body. The icy breeze moved the gray hair on the back of his head. His left arm was flung up, and his right was trapped under his body. The left hand, gloveless, was black with dried blood, and the lower right trouser leg was soaked.

Dan watched for a full fifteen minutes for any sign of breathing or other movement. He could see part of the face, and the exposed skin had the bluish gray look of death. Dan considered shooting into the body a couple of times to be sure and decided that it wasn't necessary.

He stood over the body for a moment, thinking how much smaller he looked now than he had yesterday afternoon. Big then, he looked small and shrunken now, rail thin. Wondering about the face that had so shaken Joe Ballas, Dan grasped the shoulder of the man's coat and started to roll him over. With blinding speed, the man grasped Dan's sleeve with his left hand and his right appeared from under his body holding a six-inch skinning knife.

Pulling Dan to him he struck four times before his grip on Dan's sleeve could be broken. The Winchester went clattering and sliding down the slope. Dan drew and shot him three times in the chest. Stepping back on wobbling legs, Dan stared in horror at the destroyed face, listening to the weak hiss of hate, watching the evil light die out of the eyes as blood and saliva drooled out of the shattered mouth and down the bloody chest.

Hunched over with deadening weakness and shocked by the pain, Dan was holding both hands to his wounded left side. He looked down and realized that his gun was still in his right hand. A drop of bright red blood was slipping down the barrel. He fired the last two rounds into the dead man before holstering the weapon. Stupid thing to do, but it made him feel better.

Dan could feel blood running down his leg, but habit was so strong that he pulled his pistol back out of its holster and reloaded before opening his coat to examine his wounds. Blood was pouring from two stab wounds in the left thigh and two in his lower belly. His head was spinning, and he thought he was going to pass out. His legs buckled under him. He dropped and rolled to his left side, holding his middle with both hands, sick with pain, curled up with his knees under his chin. He couldn't seem to get enough air; he was breathing like a steam engine.

He was stabbed in the guts by a dying man because he was stupidly careless. He was dying alone on a cold mountain because he was too thickheaded to mind his own business and keep riding. The thought of Alice calmed him, and his breathless panic began to subside. A glimmer of sad humor came to him when he voiced the thought aloud. "I suppose Alice is a pretty nice thing to get mixed up with if a man can't mind his own business." His head began to clear, although he was still trembling like a sick dog.

He sat up and instantly had a sensation like his head was full of rolling stones. The ground rocked and pitched under him. Not knowing what else to do, he sat quietly until the dizziness passed. He needed to put something on his wounds to stop the bleeding. He pulled his knife and cut a pair of his spare moccasins free from the inside of his coat. One moccasin would cover both of the wounds on his thigh, and the other would cover the ones in his lower body. Cynically, he spoke aloud to himself again. "That's nice to only need two of them. I'd hate to ruin both pairs of those new moccasins."

He made every move slowly and carefully, trying to avoid increasing the bleeding and pain. He pulled the rawhide laces from his leggings and tied the moccasins as snugly against the wounds as he could. As if it had been waiting for the excitement to be over, the cold dug into him again with icy fingers. His hands started shaking from the frigid temperature, completely out of control. "Don't make a damn now!" Dan boasted to the freezing wind. He laughed. "You're too late! Don't make any difference how much I shake. I already got myself tied back together."

He tried desperately to avoid putting weight on his left leg when he attempted to get to his feet. It didn't work. He was too weak to get up without using both legs. Once on his feet, he stood swaying and looking down at his Winchester. There was no way around it; he had to go pick it up. No warrior left his weapons on the field unless he was carried away dead. He walked very cautiously in the slippery gravel. He circled to approach the Winchester from the downhill side; if it started sliding again, he didn't want to chase it down the hill. He managed to bend down to reach it without falling.

It was fantastic how much better he felt when he straightened up and cradled the rifle in his arms. If this was to be the last of him, he would die with honor, his weapons beside him. The gentle Indian voice came to him again: *Always be a man. Your pride is priceless. Now is the time to watch your father so you can learn the way. No son ever had a better guide.* Funny how a man's mind wandered at a time like this. Dan wondered, as he had often done before, if his mother simply forgot that his dad wasn't an Indian.

He looked around. Feeling stronger, steadier on his feet, he started thinking how close he was to the cabin if he took a direct route. With no need to take special care, all he had to do was cover the distance. He was about to start the journey when he saw the Sharps. It was too heavy for him to carry now. Maybe Joe would come up later and get it for him.

The wild man might have something on him. Maybe a letter or something would tell who had hired him. As the shock wore off, Dan was in great pain, but he realized that some of his strength was flowing back in spite of the loss of blood. He looked down at himself. At least he didn't seem to be bleeding on the outside. If he was bleeding inside, then it was up to the inside to look after itself.

He went back to the body and knelt awkwardly on his right knee, trying to bend his wounded left leg as little as possible. That didn't work either. He set his jaw and did what was necessary. He got down over that dead old crazy man and searched him. Now what would a raggedy old ridge runner need with four money belts? Dan unbuckled them, jerked them from around the body, rebuckled them, and slung them around his neck. There would be time to look at them later. There wasn't a scrap of paper on the man. Dan looked at the bloody knife beside the dead hand. He didn't hesitate. He had earned that knife; it was going with him. He slid it under his gun belt by his left hip.

At last, Dan started down the hill. He could make it to the house before noon if he had to do it on his hands and knees. After all, it was just a matter of putting one foot in front of the other.

Dan was coming out of the woods near the cabin before the humor of it came to him. He was laughing about it as he staggered along with Joe, who'd appeared beside him somewhere along the way. "Putting one foot in front of the other can be hard as hell, Joe, when one foot is hung on a bad leg and stuck in a moccasin full of blood."

"You look like a side of beef hung up to age. Did you get that Sharps shooter?"

"We got each other, but I walked away if you can call this walking. Nothing on him to tell us anything unless it's in these belts around my neck. Looked like you hit him twice, Joe. Then I got him twice more last night, but it wasn't good enough. I thought he was dead this morning, but he wasn't. He got me with a knife when I came up to him."

"Bad?"

"Yeah. Got me twice in the leg and twice in the belly."

Joe made no response. He was walking beside Dan but making no offer to support him. When Dan wobbled at last into the cabin, Joe threw wood into the fireplace, filled the kettle with water, and hung it over the fire. Dan stripped off the money belts and threw them on the table. When he unbuckled his gun belt, which he had lengthened to strap on outside his coat, he noticed two knife punctures for the first time. "Look here, Joe, that old man stabbed me right through my gun belt."

Joe looked at the gun belt. Cautiously, he examined the punctures in Dan's coat, pulled the coat open, and looked at the inside. "Damn, son, that knife went through your gun belt, your coat, and a pair of moccasins under there. That's six or eight layers of leather. Those wounds in your belly can't be very deep. This his knife?" he asked, pointing to the bloody knife that had fallen to the floor when Dan had removed his gun belt.

Dan nodded.

"Well, that's no skinny stabbing knife like yours. Let's look at those wounds. We're goin' to have to wait a minute or two for the water to heat good. We'll soak off those moccasins you used for bandages real gentle so we don't start the blood runnin' again."

When he had finally soaked off the moccasins and Dan's pants, which were equally difficult, Joe pronounced the belly wounds to be shallow.

Looking at the wounds again wasn't making Dan feel better. "Joe, I know you're having fun, but I'm about to keel over."

"You go ahead," Joe said sympathetically. "You ain't got far to fall." He jerked open Dan's pack and pulled out his fancy white shirt. He produced a knife and, before Dan realized his intentions, slit it up the back.

"Ow! Hey, Joe, not that one. Aw! You know how much that thing cost?"

"You ain't got no business wearin' such a thing. Looks like some woman's unmentionables. Many cowpunchers ask you to dance when you wear this?"

"You mean old coot. That was an expensive shirt, and it was brand-new!"

With obvious satisfaction, Joe continued tearing the garment into strips. "Just what we need. With all these little frilly-dillys on it, it'll make good bandages."

Joe surprised Dan by folding the cloth meticulously into thick pads and doing a neat job of gently but firmly tying them over the wounds. The next surprise was when he produced a bottle of fine bourbon and thoroughly soaked the bandages and the areas around the wounds. Dan groaned through gritted teeth. "Why didn't you just heat a branding iron? Ugh! That hurts worse than getting stuck did."

"Good, shows it's workin'. Now put on some clean pants while I saddle the horses."

"Saddle the horses? What the hell for? I'm not going anywhere except to my bunk. I feel terrible, weak as a kitten. I need some rest."

"Take a drink of that bourbon. You'll feel better right off."

Dan shook his head. "You know what liquor does to Indians. I've never taken a drink in my life, don't dare touch the stuff."

"You can now. It's good for what ails you, kills the pain. You got a long ride ahead." Joe handed him the bottle. "About an inch, that'll get you started," he said, pointing to the lowered level of liquid desired in the bottle. "Make the first one a good 'un. That makes the next one go down easier."

"Long ride? Like hell. I'm not going anywhere! What are you talking—"

"Drink."

"No fooling, Joe. I don't drink . . ."

"You got to. If you got a gut punctured, that bourbon might keep it from gettin' infected. Now drink, and don't take no prissy little sip."

The old man was obviously serious, knew what he was talking about. Dan picked up the bottle and took three lusty swallows. He sat, speechless, while fire started at the back of his throat and went straight down to the bottom of his stomach. He watched through eyes blurred with tears while Joe examined the bottle, nodded, and said, "That's a start. Now put on some clean britches while I git the horses ready."

He walked out before Dan could regain his ability to speak. He sat, making no move to get up, and found after a couple of minutes that he felt a lot better. He eyed the bottle with interest. He poured another swallow down his throat. The burning was almost pleasant this time. He came very cautiously to his feet, walked the two steps necessary to get his canteen, and took a sip of water. The knife wounds weren't hurting nearly as bad now. He carried his canteen over to the table and placed it next to the bottle. He eased himself down on the box and took another drink.

Joe walked back in, looked pointedly at the bottle, nodded, and then jerked a clean pair of pants out of Dan's pack. "Want mama to put these on you, or are you goin' to try to be a big boy?"

"I don't need pants. I'm not going anywhere."

"You're ridin' down to the ranch. Right now. With or without pants, it don't make no difference to me."

"Why? I've already lost enough blood to fill a bucket."

" 'Cause I ain't no servant. I ain't runnin' and fetching for you. I ain't standing guard over you neither, freezin' my butt off while you sleep warm. You're goin' to the ranch. They can look after you. I got work to do." He threw the trousers across Dan's lap and grabbed the bottle off the table. "The horses is ready."

Once Dan got past the painful process of mounting, he found that riding hardly hurt at all. Joe set an easy pace, slowing frequently to let Dan ride beside him while he passed over the bottle. It was getting dark when Dan finished the first one and saw Joe pull a full one out of his saddlebag. Dan was feeling much, much better.

When they rode into sight of the M Bar M, the lights were shining through the windows of the bunkhouse and the foreman's cabin. Joe rode up to the front porch and hollered, "Cougan, hey, Cougan!"

Red Cougan stepped out on the front porch, lifting a lantern high to see the two mounted men. "Knew your voice, Joe. Why didn't you come on up and knock without all the yellin'?"

"Got a wounded man here, Red. I need help to get him off his horse and in the house."

Dan laughed and gave Joe a surprised look. "I'm not hurt bad, Red. I can sack out in the bunkhouse, and I don't need any help." Annie Cougan and Alice Martin walked out on the porch, looking anxiously at Dan. Dan swept off his hat and bowed in the saddle, almost screaming at the pain that struck him. He nearly fell off Big Red onto his face. He recovered his balance and tried to cover up the effort it cost him. "You ever learn to watch out for big bad Indians, Alice?" he asked with a big smile. She stepped to the edge of the porch, looking at him with open curiosity.

Joe said flatly, "Open up the big house, Alice. We can put him down in front of that wide fireplace. We got to keep him warm for a few days. There ain't much blood left in him."

Everybody started for the Martin family home, and Big Red followed along. Dan had lost the reins somehow and was fumbling around the big horse's neck feeling for them. He was strangely awkward and found that he had to strain to focus his eyes. They all stopped at the front porch and Dan heard Joe say, "Help me get him down, Red. He's a big devil, and he's drunk as last Saturday night."

Dan felt embarrassed. "Not correct. It's true that I'm not accustomed to hard spirits, but I assure you, one and all, that I am not drunk. I have never been drunk in my life."

Joe's voice seemed to come from far away when he said, "I fed him a bottle and a half of my bourbon over the last six hours. He's right; he ain't used to it. He's quite a feller to stay in the saddle with the skinful he's got, but he would have been hurtin' something fierce without it." Joe and Red reached up for Dan, and Alice came running to help. Dan tried to dismount without assistance, but they put him off balance grabbing at him. He ended up falling into the waiting hands of all three of them.

Dan could feel the surprisingly strong grip of Joe Ballas on his leg to keep it from being jarred by his fall. Red Cougan caught him around the chest, and Alice had her arms around his neck. Their faces were inches apart. He kissed her on the cheek and roared with laughter. "Hey, Joe, I just kissed the prettiest girl I ever saw. See there, Alice, Indians are all quick and treacherous." Dan thought all this was hilarious. He couldn't stop laughing.

Joe said quietly, "Never mind, Alice, he won't remember any of this in the morning."

Stung, Dan said in a hurt voice as they carried him into the house, "Why, I will too remember, Joe Ballas. Man don't forget important things like that. That was a most unkind thing to say. Most unkind, indeed. Man ought to kiss the prettiest woman he knows before he dies. That ain't a thing to forget about."

They eased him gently into a chair while Alice ran off somewhere. Joe put a match to a generous pile of kindling in the huge fireplace. Warmth began to flow into the room. "Now look what you did, Joe Ballas. You hurt her feelings and she ran away." Dan was having to concentrate very hard to speak clearly. He rubbed his hand across his mouth and commented very carefully, "Must have gotten pretty cold riding down here. Didn't notice before, but my lips feel numb." Red and Annie Cougan were trading amused looks. Curious, Dan asked, "Did I miss a joke?"

Alice came back into the room and threw a straw mattress on the floor in front of the fireplace. Then she started unfolding blankets from a stack she had dropped to the floor beside the mattress. Without looking at him, she asked, "You think you need to be quick and treacherous to get a kiss, Walking Hawk?"

The warmth from the fire seemed to be draining all the strength out of Dan. He had slept around three hours out of the last fifty-six. His eyes kept creeping shut. He struggled to figure out what to say. His chin was dropping toward his chest when he said, "Just saying goodbye. Can't look at you. Too hard for me. Can't stay here. Can't go back. Had to do it. Mark didn't even have a gun. Had to help. Got to keep riding. No place to stay . . ."

Dimly, he thought he heard Annie Cougan say softly, "He's trying to explain something. 'Can't stay here and can't go back.' What a sad thing to hear."

It sounded like Joe's hard voice that said, "All the best ones is sad. This here ain't no fair world. Help me lay him down out of that chair."

XIV

Dan woke suddenly, alarmed to find himself in an unfamiliar room. He felt a sense of rising panic when he realized that he was naked under the blankets and his weapons were not at hand. Cautiously scanning the room before making any moves, he found Alice seated in a large chair, covered with a blanket, watching him.

"You look young when you're asleep, like a little boy."

He didn't answer at first, looking around the room for his guns and clothes. There was no sign of them. "Where's my stuff?"

"Out on the back porch soaking. You got blood all over everything, even your guns. I was surprised at you. I thought you took care of your guns, at least. Pretty sloppy, it seemed to me, so I went ahead and cleaned them so they wouldn't rust."

He gave her a long, steady look. He thought she might be teasing him, but there wasn't a trace of humor in her expression. She sat returning his gaze. "I need my stuff. I need some privacy to get dressed. I got things to do that I always do first thing in the morning."

She called, "Red."

Cougan came in from what must be the kitchen. Dan could smell biscuits baking and bacon frying when Cougan opened the door and walked in talking. "Woke up did you, finally? I hope we ain't makin' too much noise cookin' breakfast and disturbin' your rest, sir."

"Get me my britches. I got to go outside for a minute. Where are my guns?"

Red walked to a heavy wooden table and picked up Dan's gun belt. "Alice cleaned 'em for you. Said you were careful about that. Said you'd appreciate it." He dropped the gun belt on the blanket beside Dan. "Your Winchester is leaning against the wall over yonder. Alice cleaned it, too, and she rubbed out some scratches on the stock."

Dan was concerned. He didn't like the idea of anyone handling his guns. He didn't like it one bit. He carefully worked himself up on an elbow, pulled the pistol from the holster, tested the action, and examined the loads.

"Satisfactory, I hope." Her voice was sarcastic, and when he looked up, her mouth was fixed in a sour expression.

"Thanks, Alice. I appreciate it. It's just that I'm used to doing certain things myself."

"No doubt." Her expression didn't soften.

"Well, she had her fun, Dan. I think she enjoyed helpin' me and Joe shuck you out of your clothes last night."

Alice sprang to her feet with her face flaming and shot a furious look at Red. "I did not, Red. What an awful thing to say."

"Never knew she was so interested in drunk, wounded men before. Wanted to see ever'thing, yes, sir."

"Red, you stop teasing her this minute. She was out with me in the kitchen when all that was going on." Annie stood in the kitchen doorway glowering at Red. "You look after Dan while Alice and me finish cooking breakfast. Dan, we're going to feed you right where you are. You ought to stay right on that bed for a couple of days except for trips to the outhouse. Those cuts won't take much to open up again, so you be real careful every move you make."

"I'm so thirsty, I think I could drink a river," Dan said. His throat was so dry it hurt.

"Yeah," said Red. "That's how it is with drunks. They always wake up the next morning as dry as a desert."

Dan felt warmth rising to his face. "I'm sorry about that. I don't drink, but Joe insisted that I take a little of his whiskey. He said that it would be good for me."

"A little!" Alice laughed. "A bottle and a half? Now you're ruined forever. You've touched hard whiskey. Now you're doomed to be just another drunk Indian lying around in the street in front of some saloon." Alice said it with a straight face, but Dan could see a glint of humor in her eyes.

"I suppose so," Dan replied. He worked himself painfully to a sitting position, letting the blanket drop. "I guess I've got to get used to doing without any privacy."

Alice made a little startled noise and rushed through the door into the kitchen. Annie followed and shut the door. Red brought a robe and helped Dan out the back door. As soon as he returned from a visit to the outhouse, Dan found himself breathing heavily and sweating from the pain of moving around on his wounded leg. Red produced a nightshirt and, by the time Dan slipped into it, he was glad to lie down again.

Annie came from the kitchen carrying a tray with a glass of water and a bowl of thin soup. Alice appeared carrying two large pillows, which she tucked behind him. Dan looked at the tray and threw a questioning look at the two women. "What's this? I thought I smelled bacon and biscuits. Is this all I get to eat?"

Annie said, "Joe didn't think the wounds in your stomach are serious, but he wasn't sure. He said to give you chicken soup for a couple of days, at least till we could tell if you're hurt inside."

"Yes, ma'am, but where's the chicken? This soup is so thin I can see the bottom of the bowl."

Alice said in a smug tone, "That's all you get, just the broth. Besides, I always heard that drunks have sensitive stomachs."

Wiping the thin film of perspiration from his brow, Dan said to Annie in a tired voice, "Why do spinsters hate drunks so much? Do you suppose they just hate seeing men have so much fun?"

Alice gave him a furious look and walked back to the kitchen. Annie smiled at Dan and said in a whisper, "Young fellow, she needs to have somebody talk back. All the single men around here are afraid of her. Now you eat that broth, and then rave about how good it is. She went out in the dark, got a chicken from the coop, cleaned it, and cooked that broth for you. It took her half the night. You pretend it's good even if you choke."

Dan nodded and slowly spooned the broth in circles in the bowl till it cooled enough to eat. Alice appeared in the doorway again before he put the spoon in his mouth. He put on a startled and enthusiastic expression, turned to Annie, and said, "My goodness, ma'am, what a surprise. I've eaten in some of the finest restaurants from New Orleans to New York, and I've never tasted anything so good. You make the finest chicken broth in the world. No question about it."

"Oh no," Annie said innocently. "Alice made that all by herself. I didn't do any part of it."

"Alice made this?" He sounded astonished and pretended he didn't see her standing in the doorway. Alice came into the room and drew a chair close to the straw mattress. She sat down and leaned forward with her elbows on her knees, looking from Dan to Annie and back again. "Alice, I must compliment you on this superb chicken broth. I had no idea you could prepare something so delicious. You must be an accomplished cook."

Smiling proudly, she said in a pleased, sweet voice, "Yes, you lying horse thief. I happen to love cooking, but I made that broth like Joe told me it had to be made. No pepper or anything to make it good. It's horrible. Anybody who'd like that broth would enjoy boiled chicken droppings."

The smile on Red's face froze and there was a quick, shocked intake of breath from Annie followed by a lengthy silence while Dan sat with his eyes locked with Alice's. He stuck out his hand and said, "No more lying."

Alice broke off the challenging stare to look down at his hand. She seemed undecided, but finally gripped it with her own. "No more lying? None at all?"

"Nope. I'm a reformed man. The broth is really bad, but I can't tell you how much I appreciate you making it for me. It was very sweet and considerate."

She sat with her eyes boring into him. "If you're going to be honest with us, do it about more important things than a bad bowl of soup. Who are you, Dan? What are you doing here?"

Red cleared his throat and shifted his feet restlessly. "You want me and Annie to leave, Alice?"

"You and Annie have to know everything about this ranch, just like I do, Red. I'd like you to stay."

Red's eyes darted to Dan briefly before he said, "I don't think it's right to dig into a man, Alice. Dan just hired on here; he ain't obliged to tell his life history."

"He's not just a hired hand. He's killed men to save my life. He's killed to protect my property. He's given me a modest fortune in cash money. And most important, he's making me fall in love with him, and he knows it. I think we have a right to know who he is and why he's doing these things."

The clock on the wall seemed to boom as it ticked in the motionless silence. Dan realized that he was actually holding his breath in shock. His gaze dropped from Alice's to the tray on his lap. "Would you bring me some more water, Annie?" He needed a minute to think. The words "kid honesty" came to him, and he remembered the tears in her eyes back in the cave when she called him a half-breed. She was so damned honest that things got out of control around her. She had him badly off balance again.

Annie rushed to the kitchen to get water for Dan. Red dropped into a chair, looking down at Dan with his elbows on his knees, matching Alice's posture. Dan, striving for time to decide how to handle the situation, asked, "Red, could you get me a pair of pants. Could I sit in a chair? I feel like a bug on the floor, and everybody is about to step on me." Red's eyes swung to Alice.

"Oh, get him some pants." Alice came to her feet. "Call Annie and me when he's dressed." She stalked into the kitchen.

Red walked across the room and dug out one of Dan's new shirts and a pair of trousers from a pack in the corner. When Dan gave him a questioning look, he said, "Joe brought some of your gear down with him. Guess you were in no shape to notice." He helped Dan slip his wounded leg into the trousers and steadied him with a strong hand as he eased into a chair. Dan slipped on his shirt without making any effort to tuck it in.

Red stood thoughtfully in front of Dan for a moment before he said, "I've known her since she was born. Her mama and daddy are my best friends, and they ain't here. I guess I kinda feel like her daddy right now. But, Dan, you ain't obliged to say nothing."

He looked away and rubbed his face for a moment, looking uncomfortable. "You got the right to keep your mouth shut and to tell her to go to hell and no hard feelings." He stood rubbing his hands awkwardly on his back pockets. "If you decide to say anything, tell the truth. I can't have no young man lying to my little girl. I ain't no gunman, but I'd have to call you out if you done a thing like that."

Suddenly, Dan felt a rush of relief. Doing was never the hard part of anything. Deciding, that was always where the problems lay, and he had made his decision.

Red raised his voice. "Annie, you and Alice come on in here. Dan's got his clothes on and is ready to talk." The door swung open immediately and Annie came walking through with Alice. In an irritated voice, Red said, "Just trot yourself right back in that kitchen, woman, and don't come back in here unless you're carryin' the coffeepot and some cups."

Annie reversed direction, heading back into the kitchen. Over her shoulder she spoke sternly to Dan. "Don't you say nothin' till I get back."

Glowering at the kitchen door, Red commented to Dan, "They're fearful hardheaded. Trainin' one of 'em takes all the patience a man has."

"What?" came the query from the kitchen.

"Never mind, Annie," Alice said in a loud voice, "Red was just telling us whose side he's on."

Red looked at Alice for a moment before he glanced at Dan and shrugged. He sat back in his chair, looking off into space as if he wished he were elsewhere. Annie bustled in with the pot and cups. "I guess you can have coffee, Dan. Joe didn't say anything about coffee before he rode out this morning."

"Joe rode out?" They all turned to Dan when he spoke. He had unconsciously dropped his left hand onto the wounded thigh. When Red nodded, Dan asked, "He went back up to the north pasture by himself?" Red nodded again. Dan could hear his own heavy breathing.

"I asked him not to go alone, to take one or two of the other men with him. He said, 'You don't take puppies with you when you're huntin' wolves.' Joe ain't like other men, Dan." Red's voice was tense. Dan found himself looking at his gun belt lying on the rumpled blankets on the floor. Red said grudgingly, "He said for you to come along if you get well. Said he didn't mind havin' you around."

Dan forced himself to relax. There was nothing he could do now. The memory of the struggle to get into his pants and up into this chair was too fresh in his mind. He wasn't fit to help anyone when sitting in a chair was tiring him so badly that he already wanted to lie down again.

Alice said quietly, "Dan, you look very pale. Wouldn't you rather lie down and rest a few minutes? I'm not feeling too good about jumping on you when you're so weak." Her face was flushed and her eyes showed concern.

Dan took a couple of deep breaths. "A couple of men went after my stepbrother with pistols because of a misunderstanding. I couldn't stand there and watch them kill him, so I shot them both. My father is a proud man of strong passions. He is very fond of me. No telling what he would do to keep me from hanging or being sent to jail. He would ruin himself and my whole family if necessary. The only solution was for me to run. I thought I could hide here for the winter, out of sight up on your north pasture. In the spring, I thought I might get to Canada."

Alice asked, "What's your real name?"

"I gave you my correct name, Alice. That's my name to live with and to die with. Even a fugitive from justice has to keep something of his pride."

Red rumbled, "That don't seem smart. Way out here you could change your name and the law wouldn't find you in a hundred years."

"You talk like an educated man. When we first met, you spoke like an illiterate cowhand." Alice's statement was really a question.

"I figured my normal speech would attract attention out here. I was trying to cover up, but it didn't work very well. I finally quit trying because I kept forgetting and making slips. That attracted more attention than ever. When you spend a lot of effort to learn to speak correctly, it becomes a hard habit to break. I'm not a good actor."

"Your family must be very rich for you to give away thousands of dollars so casually." Alice put another question in the form of a statement.

"All of my family are successful people financially. My dad, my stepmother, my brothers—that is, my stepbrothers—are all clever people in business. I had some little talent along those lines before I had to leave."

"Do you know what was in those money belts you took from that man up in the mountains?" Alice asked.

"No, I never got around to looking at them." Dan shifted uncomfortably in his chair. He really didn't care about that right now. He was beginning to feel sick.

"Dan, each of them had more than a thousand dollars in it. I counted it last night. You have a little over five thousand dollars there," Alice said.

Dan shrugged indifferently, then stiffened when the gesture cost him a stab of pain. His irritation came out with a sarcastic, "That's nice. If I can kill enough men around here, I'll get rich. All these crooks seem to be getting humps on their backs carrying money around with them." Dan couldn't help looking wistfully at the bedding on the floor.

Alice's voice didn't have its usual firm confidence when she asked, "What about that other thing I mentioned earlier? Let's get everything out in the open."

Dan was feeling sicker by the minute. He had to end this in a hurry. He had to lie down. "Yeah, I been looking at you. I'm guilty of that. That's the only shameful thing I've done, and I'm sorry about it. I guess it's natural to want something you know you can't have. There's no sense in my getting interested in you, but it's like catching cold: It just happens when you're unlucky."

"Thank you very much, Mr. Walker. You really have a gift for saying the nicest things!" Dan looked up to find Alice on her feet, hands on her hips, anger written all over her.

Dan ran out of both strength and patience at the same time. He cursed himself for asking to sit in a chair; it was killing him. The room was getting unbearably hot. "I don't mean to be rude, Alice, but I just have to lie down. I don't feel well at all."

He felt Red grab his arm and give him a powerful lift. Red guided him to the bedding on the floor and eased him down. His voice was sympathetic when he said, "Talkin' can wear a man down. It truly can." Dan went to sleep as soon as his head hit the pillow.

When he woke again, he couldn't tell how much time had passed. His throat was dry again and his pants were binding his wounded leg in a painful way. His shirt had slipped around somehow and bunched up on him. Alice was asleep in her big chair with a blanket wrapped around her.

Dan looked longingly at the soft flannel nightshirt lying beside the bed. This business about clothes was irritating. He didn't belong here. The all-male bunkhouse was beginning to seem like a paradise. At least there the men would ignore him naked or dressed. Being ignored was almost as nice as real privacy.

His leg was swelling, no doubt about it. Dan struggled out of his pants under the blankets. The effort left him bathed in sweat, but it was worth it. He lay back, blowing like he'd run a mile while the pain died out of his leg. He finally got the shirt off too. It had bunched up in a tight band under his armpits. He shrugged himself into the nightshirt. Finally, he lay still, breathing heavily and feeling sweat run off him. He looked at Alice again and found her smiling at him.

"I've never seen a man go through such a struggle rather than ask for a little help. It was entertaining."

Dan was not amused. "Alice, would you get me a real big drink of water, please? I'm terribly thirsty."

"Of course." She went toward the kitchen so fast she was almost running. She came back almost immediately and knelt beside him. As he struggled to sit up, she slid her arm around him to help. When he took the glass of water, she quickly tucked the pillows behind him. He drank the water and relaxed against the pillows with a groan of relief. He sat for a moment with his eyes closed, listening to his own ragged breathing.

"Weak as a cat," he said sadly. "Can't seem to move without getting out of breath."

She gently swabbed his face with a cool, damp towel. Her voice was very quiet and soothing. "Don't worry about it. You've lost a lost of blood. You just need a little rest and time to heal." She rose and vanished into the kitchen again, returning quickly with a bowl in her hands. She dropped down beside him and offered a spoonful of broth. When he reached for the spoon, she drew away and said sharply, "Stop that! You just be still!"

"I can feed myself, Alice. It's embarrassing to sit here and be fed like a baby."

She set the bowl of broth aside and leaned across his chest with her face very close to his. She sat looking into his eyes for a long moment before she leaned forward and kissed him. It was a slow, lingering caress, her lips soft and sweet. Dan was afraid to raise a hand, afraid to move for fear she would draw away. She pulled back and slowly opened her eyes, looking into his for another long moment.

Her voice was so low it was almost a whisper. "I have decided that I belong to you." Dan thought that she was the most beautiful thing he had ever seen. He sat staring at her, still afraid to move for fear she would draw away from him. He hoped she would stay close, just stay close for a little while longer.

"I love you." He had never said those words to a woman, but it wasn't awkward. It was as natural as breathing.

Her eyes were smiling into his when she turned away and picked up the bowl of broth. She extended the spoon toward him, and he pulled back again in protest. He heard a quiet almost-whisper, "I love you, Dan." Her smile widened when he leaned forward and accepted a spoonful of broth.

XV

Dan did nothing but eat chicken broth and sleep for the remainder of that day and night. Alice stayed beside him the whole time, either sitting beside his straw bed in front of the fireplace or sleeping in her chair nearby. Red and Annie had moved into one of the upstairs bedrooms of the Martins' house to help look after Dan. The following morning Dan and Alice were already drinking coffee together at the breakfast table in the kitchen when Annie came down to light the cooking fire.

"My, isn't it nice to walk into a kitchen in the morning and find the fire lighted and everything already warm. Good to see you up and around, Dan. It looks like you two are getting along a lot better nowadays. Did you declare a truce?" Annie asked.

"Annie, I told Alice yesterday that I love her. She said she didn't mind."

"Oh Dan, for heaven's sake! I said no such thing! Annie, we love each other. It's not such a sudden thing, really, but we just got around to telling each other. He's a little uncomfortable with what it's going to mean. Dan's still very worried about his past interfering with any plans we might try to make."

"Red likes you, Dan. He predicted that you two were going to get together after the first night you had supper with us." She smiled at Alice. "He said it was nice to see you get interested in someone at last." Glancing at Dan she added, "You sure don't fit the picture of a fast-gun killer outlaw. You've done nothing but good things around here."

"Thank you, Annie. I grew up half Indian warrior, half white businessman. The outlaw part is the result of bad luck. Maybe in Canada all that can be forgotten."

Annie turned to Alice quickly. "You've decided to go to Canada with Dan? I hate to think of you leaving the M Bar M!"

Alice's expression was half-smiling, half-challenging when she looked at Dan. "He hasn't asked me about it, Annie. I'm just finding out how arrogant he really is."

Annie raised her eyes to the ceiling. "Another one. Maybe that's why Red Cougan and Joe Ballas like him so much. Two more hardheaded men never existed. Now they have another one to keep them company."

"Alice, I told you yesterday that I thought it necessary to go to Canada," Dan said in an accusing voice. "You can't say you didn't know about that."

"Sure, but you didn't ask me what I thought about it," she responded primly.

"Arguing again? It got quiet for a spell yesterday. I was hoping you two were getting tired of fightin' all the time," Red said from the kitchen doorway.

"We weren't arguing, just getting the record straight. Dan was saying that we were going to Canada, and I was saying that he didn't ask me about it," Alice said with a smile.

"I'm just not used to thinking in terms of two rather than one yet," Dan said defensively.

"Since when do you think you need to do the thinking for both of us?" Alice asked quietly.

"I didn't say that. Now be fair, Alice, and stop picking a fight. I said . . . now I've forgotten what I said. Maybe I ought to go lie down somewhere where it's quiet. I'm getting bites all over from White Fang Alice the Terrible." Dan pretended to start getting up from the table.

"Oh, sit still. I was just teasing," Alice said. She laughed and put a restraining hand on his arm.

Red stood watching them till they looked up at him. He nodded judiciously and said, "I figured this was goin' to happen. It sounds like you two have decided to start a partnership. When did all this happen?"

Alice responded, "We told each other we were in love along about the middle of the afternoon yesterday, Red. But with Dan doing nothing but sleep all the time it was hard to get excited about telling anyone. It was terribly romantic. I told Dan that I loved him, and he went right to sleep."

Red looked accusingly at Dan. "He didn't say nothin'?"

Alice looked down at the table in a pretense of sadness. "He said he didn't mind."

Red said in a disappointed tone, "Aw, Dan, you didn't say that, did you?"

Annie interrupted from in front of the stove, "Don't pay her no mind. They're both happy and actin' silly."

"Yeah, I liked her better when she was a boy. She didn't act up like she does now," Dan said, frowning.

"Little boys always get spoiled from the attention they get when they're sick," Alice said ominously. "It's always necessary to get them straightened out again as soon as they get well."

"Ouch," Red said and turned to Dan. "Sounds like a tough future for you, Dan." His expression became concerned. "What's wrong?"

Dan sat slumped over, holding his arm with a pained expression on his face. He looked up at Alice and said with a strained voice, "This is terrible! Look here, Alice, look at this!"

Her smile instantly replaced with a look of fear, Alice jumped up and came around the table to him quickly. "What is it, Dan? What's wrong?"

Gasping painfully, Dan rubbed his arm and said, "Look! Feathers! I . . . I think I'm growing feathers. I got to have something besides chicken broth to eat, quick!"

While Annie and Red doubled over laughing, Alice slumped weakly back into her chair and said, "That wasn't one bit funny. Don't you ever do anything like that to me again."

With a fierce frown, Dan said in a threatening voice, "Fetch my breakfast, woman, or I'll get a stick. My patience is stretching thin."

Annie said sympathetically, "If he's like this when he's sick, you better start worrying what that little boy's gonna be like when he's well. He needs trainin' bad, Alice."

"I dunno. He talks like a man with some good ideas, seems to me," Red put in, winning a warning glance from Annie.

Alice came slowly to her feet and walked to Annie's side. "What shall we burn for them this morning, Annie?" she asked sweetly.

"Speakin' of sticks," Red said. "I found a neat straight one with a fork in it. I got the fork all padded and fixed. All I need is to see if a little needs to be cut off to fit your height. I think it'll work good as a crutch while that leg heals, Dan."

"It's decent of you to be doing all this for me, Red. I'll not forget it.

I'm a big burden to everybody, but I think I'm getting better fast. In fact, I think it'll be best for me to get out of Alice's house so you and Annie can go back home. It's too much to ask you to move out of your home to come here and chaperone Alice because I'm here. I think I need to move back into the bunkhouse today."

Alice spoke from the stove where she was frying bacon. "The bunkhouse is for hired hands of the M Bar M. You aren't a hired hand anymore. You're fired. I'll figure your wages after breakfast. Now you're a guest, and guests stay here." She didn't bother to turn her head to see the response to her comment.

There was a brief pause, then Alice turned to Annie. "You and Red don't mind staying here with Dan and me for a while do you, Annie?"

"Nope," Annie said quickly.

"See, Dan," Red said in a lecturing tone. "That's the way women like to talk things over after they get you married. Did you hear the way she asked my opinion as the head of the house?"

Alice turned from the stove and asked seriously, "Do you mind, Red? Really?"

Red leaned back in his chair. "It's terrible inconvenient, ma'am. Takin' on all this, seems to me, is a lot of extra to my job. Seems to me I should get a raise." He waggled his empty cup. "Man can't do good work when coffee's so short neither, and he has to wait till near noon to get some breakfast."

"What would you think about your boss pouring your coffee for you?" Alice asked, filling his cup.

"I'd say she was softening me up to either take a cut in wages or be told to shut up. I better shut up while I'm still ahead. Besides, I don't mind campin' out in the boss's big fancy house for a while. I'm used to hardship."

Alice leaned over and kissed him on the cheek. "Thanks, Red."

As color rose in his face, he turned to Dan and said, "You watch me, son. It's a thing you got to learn. They ain't hard on you at all if you know how to handle 'em. I bet there ain't another foreman in Montana who gets his boss to kiss him before breakfast."

Annie spoke sharply as she put a plate in front of him. "Red, behave yourself."

"It's hell to have two bosses, Dan. One of 'em all teeth and claws and the other'n . . ."

"Hush! Eat your breakfast or I'll throw it out," Annie said.

Watching Dan fill his plate, Alice said timidly, "Dan, don't you think you'd better be a little careful? You don't want to make yourself sick."

He hesitated, fork in midair, watching Red smirk derisively. "I'll try to act like a big boy," he said gently. Alice looked disgusted, so he touched the back of her hand and added, "It's a nice feeling to have someone care. I'll be careful." He received a nice smile, so he ate as much as he wanted, feeling smug and clever.

"Dan, when I visited with my mother and dad before coming home to the ranch, dad was looking strong and well. He said that he expected the doctors to let him come home and go back to work. I got a letter last week from him. Dad said he had hoped to be home in the spring, but the doctors have let him come earlier. They should be coming home today or tomorrow." Alice was smiling, her happiness obvious. "Red and Annie know about it, of course, but I haven't thought to tell you because of all the excitement."

"Today or tomorrow? Alice, I must make some other arrangement. It would ruin your mother and dad's homecoming to have me all over the parlor floor. I can't be guilty of such an intrusion."

"That's easy to solve," Alice responded. "You're getting better faster than we thought you would. If you feel strong enough to get up and down the stairs, you could have the guest room. We can keep the fire going at night. It's warm up there when the fire's going good down here."

Dan looked doubtfully at the stairs. "Really, it might be easier for everybody for me to be out in the bunkhouse."

Alice said firmly, "You don't belong in the bunkhouse. I don't want you out there."

Red asked, "Why can't you come to our house, Dan? We got an extra room you can get to without climbing stairs. We'd be glad to have you."

Alice was beginning to color up again. "None of you are paying attention. I have never had a . . . an interest in anyone before. I want Dan close to me." She looked embarrassed. "I don't think he's all that well yet." She stopped awkwardly, then blurted, "I want to look after him myself."

Dan wished fervently that he could get around without every move hurting him. All he could manage to do was to lay his hand, palm up, on the kitchen table. When she accepted the invitation and laid her hand shyly in his, he said quietly, "Thank you, Alice. When a beautiful

woman says something like that, a man would have to be made of stone
not to feel proud as a king."

Red cleared his throat and said, "We got a high class of women
around this here place. That's a fact."

Annie laughed and said, "Well, would you listen to that? Dan, you're a
good influence. You must be holdin' a gun on him under the table.
When Red starts sayin' nice things, something strange is happening."
She pretended to test Red for fever by feeling his forehead.

Dan was secretly glad that Ben and Nell Martin didn't arrive until the
following afternoon. It seemed almost impossible for him to move
without his leg hurting. Yet, he did feel a little stronger. The weakness
from losing so much blood was passing.

When Alice spotted the buggy coming up the trail to the ranch, he
went to stand with her on the front porch to greet her parents. Red was
off riding the range, but Annie joined them. Ben Martin, a man of
medium height with silver white hair, his face ruddy from the cold ride,
dismounted and walked around the horses to assist his wife down from
the buggy.

Ben and Nell both greeted Annie eagerly and hugged Alice. Dan felt
awkward and strange, leaning on his crutch. It was obvious that they
were wondering why the devil this wobbly stranger was standing on their
front porch. Alice turned quickly, still embracing Ben, and said,
"Mother and Dad, I'd like to introduce Dan Walker." Ben Martin,
although he was painfully thin, moved and spoke like a healthy man.
Dan thought that his recovery must be complete.

Dan stepped forward awkwardly, and Ben removed his arm from
around Alice to shake hands briefly, his eyes the same frigid blue as the
winter sky behind him. Nell came forward to greet Dan, neatly
preventing him from having to step toward her. Her face showed open
curiosity. Nell Martin was about what Dan expected from Alice's
description, a doll-like woman, dressed fashionably, who seemed timid
when introduced. Alice spoke in a nervous rush, "Let's go inside out of
the cold. Dan's still not strong. He really should have stayed inside. Oh,
we have so much to tell you."

Ben Martin's tone was stiff when he responded, "Yes, maybe it's time
we heard about what's going on."

They were no sooner seated in the parlor when Dan noticed a flicker
of irritation cross Ben's face. From habit, Dan had moved to a large chair

close to the fireplace. Instantly, Dan struggled back to his feet and said, "Perhaps you'd prefer to sit here, sir?" His intuition told him that he had unwittingly taken Ben Martin's favorite chair.

Martin answered in a cool, formal tone, "By all means, make yourself at home."

Dan stood, clumsily fooling with the crutch, feeling the tension crackling in the air. Spoken in that tone of voice, the man might as well have said, "Why don't you get the hell out of here? You aren't welcome."

He could feel his face flushing. There was a short but deadly silence. "I think you might like to talk a while, just your family and old friends." He shot a quick glance at Annie, whose return glance was sympathetic, then at Alice, whose expression was unreadable. "If I may be excused, I'll just go upstairs for a while."

Martin's voice was ominous. "Upstairs?" He shot a questioning look at Alice.

She sat leaning forward slightly with her eyes narrowed. Her voice was sharp but controlled when she said, "Please sit down, Dan. My mother and dad need to be brought up to date on everything, and you are the only one who can provide some of the details." She turned to her father and the effort to restrain her anger became more obvious. "Dan Walker is my guest. Your manner indicates you are looking for the right moment to insult a man who has done more for you and this ranch than you have any idea. I suggest that you listen closely for a while before you do or say something you will deeply regret."

Martin's eyes widened in shock, then narrowed in fury. "I don't think I need instructions from you about my conduct in my own home, young lady."

Alice met his hot look without blinking and responded, "I should hope not. It seems to me that you are forming some wrong opinions before you know enough to make any decisions." Father and daughter were staring each other down.

Nell Martin said in a cutting voice, "I would like to freshen up after a long trip. A cup of coffee would be nice, too. Can this fatiguing battle between you two be postponed long enough for me to be comfortable while I watch it?" She rose and turned a smiling face to Dan. "You look dreadfully tired, young man. Please sit down and try to relax. These fights sometimes last a long time. It's difficult to enjoy them if you aren't comfortable."

Dan, still standing in front of the inviting chair, thought, Oops! Another country heard from! His estimate of Nell Martin suddenly jumped. It was now obvious that there were not just two strong personalities in the Martin family. The edge of command in her voice was there for anyone to hear. She calmly expected to be obeyed. He sat down.

A thunderous knock at the door startled them all. It continued until Annie threw open the door. Red rushed in and yelled at Martin, "Ben! You're home! You look great! Nell! Welcome back. You look great, too." He shook Ben's hand and put his arm around Nell at the same time when they rose and went to meet him. "Thought I'd be back before you all got home, but I got held up. Met Dan yet? Sure, there he is. How's the leg, Dan? How'd you all like that crutch I made for him? Ain't that fancy?" Red stood grinning and rubbing his cold hands together. "Where's the coffee?"

Nell turned to Alice and said, "You and Annie make some coffee, will you, please? Your father and I will go upstairs and freshen up a bit. Will you keep Mr. Walker company, Red? Ben and I will be back down in a few minutes. We'll all sit down together over coffee and have a good fight." She walked to the foot of the stairs and waited pointedly for her husband. Ben Martin joined her, the muscles working along his jaw while he stalked across the room.

Annie took Alice by the arm, motioned to the kitchen, and said, "Let's get the coffee made." They walked into the kitchen.

Red looked at Dan and asked quietly, "What's going on? Ben looked like he was mad enough to chew barbed wire."

Dan replied, "I don't know, Red. I think it's a case of instant dislike. He took one look at me, and that was enough."

"Damn! That's bad luck. That ain't like Ben, neither. He ain't hard to get along with ordinarily." Red's voice was puzzled.

Dan changed his seat. His mind was racing. He hadn't been prepared for such an unfriendly greeting. If Ben Martin was so upset over him sitting in the wrong chair, the man's mental competence was suspect. A chilling idea came to him. He had never considered the possibility that Alice's father's illness was mental. Dan whispered, "Red, what kind of sickness has Mr. Martin had?"

Red caught on instantly, gave Dan a hard look, and answered, "Consumption. He was always coughing up blood. He didn't have no appetite, just kept fadin' away, gettin' thinner and weaker. But there ain't nothin' crazy about Ben Martin, Dan."

Dan sat quietly while Alice returned with a tray of cups. She put them on the heavy wooden table, turned to Red, and said, "Help me move chairs. We'll have this conference around the table." By the time Red had the chairs arranged, Annie brought a huge coffeepot from the kitchen. Alice hurried to the fireplace and used a poker to arrange the coals upon which Annie put the pot.

Red said, "Looks like you're settin' up for a good old slam-bang M Bar M family conference. Expectin' it to last awhile?"

"As long as necessary," Alice said with a determined voice. "You sit right here, Dan. You there, Red, and, Annie, I want you right here." She had arranged it so that she and Dan would be directly across the table from her parents while Red and Annie were at the ends.

Dan remained on his feet, and Alice looked a question at him. "When your mother comes in, I'd rather be on my feet. It hurts too much to be getting up over and over again."

She said harshly, "Sit. I'll make your apologies if any are needed." But that wasn't necessary. Ben and Nell Martin came down the stairs at that moment. When they took their seats, Dan had a feeling that they were all at home with this, that this must be a custom, a way they worked out disagreements. He decided to keep his mouth shut.

Nobody said a word until Annie poured the cups of coffee, replaced the pot in the fireplace, and was in her seat. Then Ben Martin asked, looking at Dan, "Who are you, sir? What are you doing here?"

Before Dan could respond, Alice spoke. "He is my guest. He saved my life when I was attacked by renegade Indians. When he brought me home safely, Red hired him to help Joe watch the north pasture. He was hurt doing that job, and Joe brought him here to recover. I have since fired him, paid his wages, and asked him to stay here as my guest." Her next comment convinced Dan that he had guessed correctly. He was present at a formal gathering, a procedure by which these people settled family and ranch problems. "Now it's my turn to ask a question. Why have you acted so curtly toward my guest, a man you have never seen before?"

"Can't this man speak for himself?"

"It isn't your turn. Answer my question first. Why have you acted like you have?"

Ben Martin's voice was restrained, but both his hands were in tight, angry fists on the table in front of him. "When I came through Buckhorn, I talked to Ira Rice. He told me how concerned he is about things on the M Bar M. He said that his manager had been attacked and beaten by a stranger. He said that his man was badly injured and driven off the place. Rice said that he feared you might be acting like a love-struck girl and responding to a bad influence." He turned to Dan but was obviously still speaking to Alice when he continued, "He said that the man is a half-breed gunman who rode in from nowhere. Does that answer your question?"

"Yes, thank you. In answer to your other question, Dan Walker needs no one to speak for him. He speaks beautifully, thank you. Now about him being a bad influence. The only influence on the operation of this ranch he has had so far is to give me over twenty-four hundred dollars when Rice suddenly threatened to cancel our loan. He and Joe took the money off the bodies of men who tried to kill them and me. He and Joe guessed that the money came from the rustling of our cattle. He has also been wounded trying to defend our stock up on the north pasture. He has participated in no business decisions."

For the first time a look of surprise broke through Martin's rigid expression. "You been working with Joe Ballas, riding with him?"

Red cleared his throat and leaned forward. "I'm responsible, Ben. I hired him. Our hands ain't fightin' men, except for Joe. Joe said he would watch the north pasture if I would hire Dan to go up there with him. If hirin' him was a mistake, I'm the one what done it."

Dan watched the fists on the table relax. Martin sipped his coffee and sat back in his chair. "You're sitting there looking cool as can be, young man. Let's hear your voice. Do you get along with Joe Ballas?"

A devil took control of Dan in that instant. He responded quietly, "Yes, sir. He's such a gentle, kindly old man I couldn't help but like him."

Ben Martin's piercing eyes were fixed on him over the rim of his coffee cup. Evidently Dan's remark caught him just as he was taking a swallow. It went down badly. Coffee sloshed over into the saucer when he hurriedly replaced the cup. He whipped out his handkerchief and covered his mouth. Dan couldn't tell if the man was coughing, strangling, or laughing until he looked up. Smiling, he said, "Well, you may be a half-breed gunman from nowhere, but you damn sure have a sense of humor."

XVI

Martin recovered quickly, took another sip of coffee as if to prove he could do so gracefully, and continued, "As I understand the situation, Red hired this young man, and you fired him?"

Alice nodded. "Yes, Daddy, that's right."

He rubbed his mouth with his hand. "You fired him and then asked him to come here as a guest? I don't understand. The two actions seem to contradict one another. Why did you fire him if he has been so helpful?"

The feeling of anger and tension was gone. Dan could feel himself relaxing as if a knot inside him was being loosened. Then Alice jerked the knot tight again when she said simply, "Because I'm in love with him."

Martin sat there with a stunned expression, but his wife turned glowing eyes toward Alice. Martin recovered quickly and asked, "Isn't this happening a bit quickly? Seems to me that you've only been home a few weeks."

"It might seem so to you, Daddy, but you get to know a man pretty fast living in a cave." Alice's face was guileless.

He stared at her for three or four seconds in silence. Finally, he said, "I guess you were right when you said I shouldn't make any decisions until I knew more. What does that remark about living in a cave mean?" Smiling, Alice told the story of the fight with the Indians, the flight to the cave, and how Dan brought her back to the ranch. She included Dan's comment about expecting her father to pour him a drink and get out his best cigars. Martin came to his feet at once.

"Mr. Walker, I no longer smoke tobacco. My illness put a stop to that, but there used to be some nice bourbon around here somewhere."

Dan started to struggle to his feet also, but Martin's upraised hand stopped him. Dan said, "Don't trouble yourself, sir. I don't indulge in hard spirits." He looked around at the smirks on the faces of Red, Annie, and Alice before he added grudgingly, "Except for medicinal purposes."

Red commented dryly, "But since you're already up, Ben, there's others present."

Ben Martin laughed and said, "Some things never change," and walked away from the table. He crossed the room to an ornate cabinet, drew out two bottles, and returned. "Bourbon for those who prefer it, wine for the others." Alice ran out to the kitchen and came back with a tray on which delicate, long-stemmed crystal shared space with stubby, plain shot glasses.

When everyone was seated again, Martin asked Dan frankly, "It's unusual to meet a man who doesn't drink. Mind if I ask why?"

Dan said, "My Iroquois mother said that it makes most whites and all Indians act foolish. My father says that it's fine to drink in moderation at home, but never before or during important discussions. However, since my mother felt strongly about it, I was forbidden to touch it. Both the affection and the discipline in my family was quite strong."

"You still follow your father's rules at your age?"

"Well, not exactly, sir. I try to act prudently. My father's way of life has been very successful. Successful methods should be respected. I see no reason to make mistakes he has already warned me about. Irrational conduct is usually costly in business. I was trained to be businesslike."

Ben Martin's expression was that of a man who could hardly believe his ears. He looked to Red, but Cougan was wearing the blank expression of a man listening to someone recite Greek poetry. "What's this about you turning over a huge sum of money to Alice? Was that businesslike?"

Bluntly, Dan sketched the story of how the money was obtained. Then he added, "It seemed the only honest thing to do, sir. Under the circumstances, it seemed clear that it was money obtained from theft and illegal sale of ranch assets. It was hardly a huge sum."

"When I was in Buckhorn I heard about those two dead men being found in the stable. So, since you've been here, you've killed six men, Joe's killed one, and the two of you ran one out of the country."

"Yes, sir, and there's another who hasn't been mentioned. The man who cut me up. He died up on the mountain."

"Ah, yes. Would you tell about that, please?"

Dan told the story.

"I've heard rumors about such a man for years. Never put much stock in those tales, but I suppose they were true. It seems that it's dangerous business to attack you, Mr. Walker. During all this conversation you have not explained where you are from and why you just happened to be passing when my daughter needed help."

Dan explained why he had left home.

"I believe that now adds up to nine men you have killed in less than a year. Is that the lot?" When Dan nodded, Martin went on, "A while back my daughter said flatly that she was in love with you. You have said nothing. What are your feelings and intentions, sir?"

"I'm in love with Alice, Mr. Martin, but I'm afraid you've caught me short on intentions. She and I haven't had time to make plans. I've been so sick with my wounds that there hasn't been much opportunity for serious conversation. There's another thing, sir. I think that fellow Channing is still around somewhere. I think he hired those men to try to kill Joe, Alice, and me. I don't understand it, but I'm still worried about it. Maybe he hired that crazy man up on the mountain, too. I have no way of proving what we suspect."

While Ben Martin sat looking at him speculatively, Dan asked, "Why would that banker, Ira Rice, hire such a man as Channing to work out here? Why did he make it his business to say all those bad things to you in town? Why did he pick such a bad time to come out here and demand money? He knew, or thought he knew, that Alice wouldn't have any money till after the next roundup and sale of M Bar M cattle. He's bound to have known that she would have no way to pay him. Seems to me you have an unfriendly banker, Mr. Martin."

"More unfriendly than you know, Mr. Walker. When I came through Buckhorn, I tried to borrow three thousand dollars. That's what I need to pay off the doctors. He said no."

"A trifling sum, sir. I've had occasion to estimate the present and potential value of your property here. Before I left home, the prevailing opinion was that Montana would be accepted as a state in the Union at any moment. Statehood will provide the settled conditions conducive to profitable commerce." Dan tried to get up. He couldn't make it. He was stiff and worn out from the long conversation. It seemed the most natural thing for him to look at Alice. She said, "Of course, I'll get it for you," as if Dan had spoken aloud. She left the room.

Ben Martin leaned forward curiously. "How did she know what you want?"

Dan was feeling smug. "Your daughter is just very clever, Mr. Martin."

Red, with exaggerated courtesy, said, "Mr. Martin or Mr. Walker, would one of you pass the bottle? I remember the time when I called one of you Ben and the other'n Dan, but I guess them days is past."

Martin looked at Dan and said, "Ben is fine for me. How about Dan for you?"

Dan nodded just as Alice dropped the four money belts on the table in front of him. He fumbled awkwardly with them for a moment before raising his eyes to Alice. She reached forward and helped open the pockets in the belts, dumping money on the table in a disorderly pile. Dan said quietly, "This money came off the body of that old crazy man who tried to kill me. Now, I guess it belongs to Alice and me. If it's all right with her, you take what you need."

Dan sat through a long silence while everyone stared at the pile of money, some of it stiff and stuck together with dried blood. Martin looked at his daughter. The silence stretched out while the father and the daughter sat staring at each other. Alice sat leaning forward with her elbows on the table, her chin cupped in her hands. It was a contest of wills. Alice lost. She sat back and laughed. "I should make you ask, 'What do you think?' shouldn't I? I'm sorry, Daddy. Dan was joking about me having a vote. He calls the turn. There's blood on that money, a dead man's and Dan's. He's the boss. Take what you need. If I need anything, I'll turn to him, not you, Daddy. It's a whole new world to me." She laughed nervously. "Dan thinks it's a trifling sum anyway."

Dan was sick of it. His head was churning with anger. All he wanted to do was sit here and make a nice impression on Alice's family. She had been so excited, so thrilled that her parents were coming home that he had jumped out of bed to share the joy with her. Now he was exhausted. He was fed up with being tired out by just sitting in a chair.

He said irritably, "I'm just not up to anything anymore. Just can't seem to get well. I must ask to be excused. I'm so tired I'm not sure I can get up out of this chair by myself. I'm terribly sorry, but I don't think I can climb those stairs to make it to bed, either."

Alice said, "Oh Dan, you haven't eaten any supper yet. I'll bring you something on a tray."

With Red under one arm and Ben under the other, Dan said on the way to the stairs, "Don't bother, Alice, I'm too tired to be hungry." But he knew she would bring it, and he knew she would make him eat it. She was going to look after him even if it killed him. He thought about it all the way up those dreadful stairs. By God, he declared, he liked her looking after him so much, he was going to let her do it even if it did kill him.

The silence stretched and stretched. All of them sat waiting for someone else to say something. Finally, Ben said, "Joe Ballas. That was Joe Ballas. Did you hear him? That was Joe, with six inches more height, and fifty pounds more weight, and thirty years less age, and a lot more education. But that was Joe."

Red said, "Joe sure took to him, right from the start."

"That isn't it, Red. We must be careful here. We have been fed a clever story. There's too much likeness. This man, Walker, he's too pat, too perfect. Joe's whippin' one on us! Me and him came here a long time ago." Ben Martin poured himself another drink. "That old man hasn't always been old. When me and him came to this country, we was young. These dumb bastards nowadays don't know how things were." He turned to Nell. "We've talked about this before, honey. Don't draw back. This is too serious."

Nell Martin said quietly, "Truth is truth. Our daughter is involved. This is not the time to be silly. Let's talk about life as we know it, not something out of a book."

Annie burst out, "I don't care. I know what I see. Those two deserve their chance. First time I've seen her care about a man. Look how she wants to look after him. Cleans his guns, washes his clothes, washes his face. And listen to him! Kills a man, and comes home soaked in blood, and says, "This come off the body. This belongs to me and her." She turned to Red and said, "Darlin', we got to have respect for what that means."

"That ain't what Ben is sayin'." Red sat looking Ben Martin in the eye. "You think that is Joe Ballas' son, don't you, Ben?"

Ben Martin said flatly. "Damn right! He's half Indian, and Joe Ballas never looked serious at a white woman in his whole life. He was the picture of Joe when he sat there in front of all of us, counting how many men he had killed on his fingers. It was like you and me would count how many pairs of socks we own, tryin' to remember 'cause it isn't very important. That young man talks like a Philadelphia lawyer, but he still sounds like Joe. By God, me and Joe go back a long way. When he comes home, I'll ask him straight out. He won't lie to me."

"Ask!" They all sat still in their chairs. It was as if they had called him out of the dark, windswept mountains. Cold air penetrated the room from the open door, causing flutter and flicker of the lantern light, but he stood now in plain sight. Joe Ballas stood before them with frost on his furs and fire in his eyes.

Ben didn't flinch. "Joe, is Dan Walker your son?"

"No, but only because his daddy is a better man." Joe kicked the door shut, swept off his fur coat, and dropped it to the floor. "Where's Alice?"

"She made up something for Dan to eat. She's upstairs feeding him," Ben answered.

Joe stood by the fire. "I heard Annie say she was washin' his clothes, cleanin' his guns, washin' his face?"

Annie nodded. "She won't let me help. Won't let me touch nothin' of his."

Joe asked Ben, "She say anythin' to you?"

"Says she loves him."

"He make an offer?"

"What do you mean, Joe?" Ben's voice was puzzled.

"Since this love announcement, he offer somethin'?"

"Well, I mentioned needing some money to pay the doctors, and he poured out a huge pile of money on our table. Said it was his and Alice's and to take what was needed if she agreed."

Joe crouched with his back to the fire. "Good. Real good. That money's a better trophy than a scalp or a stolen horse. It's all workin' out. It's gonna be all right."

Ben went to the fireside and put his hand on Joe's shoulder. "Joe, how much did you hear?"

"I heard you say you thought that Dan Walker is really Dan Ballas, and you're nearly right. He would be if I'd had any real say about it. I stole horses all over the country to buy his mother. I come ridin' in with a whole herd, by God. There stood Big Dan Walker with a cheap tradin' knife and a pair of blankets. She come runnin' out and fell at his feet. Her daddy looked at me and those horses and just shrugged like as to say 'What can you do with women?' and gave her to Walker. I ain't never got over it to this day."

They waited in silence. Alice came into the room drying her hands. She froze when she saw Joe by the fire. He signaled with a flip of his hand, and she ran to him. He tucked her into his side and sat on the hearth with his arm around her, a fistful of her hair in his hand. His voice was wooden when he continued, "I decided to kill Big Dan

Walker, the best friend any man ever had in this world. Gray Bird was big with young Dan, and I couldn't stand it. I had to have her, and I had to have the baby she was gonna bear. I come on him in the night from behind. He sunk a knife in me in midair when I jumped for his back. Then he said, 'Aw, Joe, don't you die,' and carried me back to his hogan."

There was a spellbound quiet, with only the sound of Joe's heavy breathing in the big room. Joe's hand was twisting and stroking Alice's hair. Finally, he went on, "He carried me back and made Gray Bird nurse me to keep me from dyin'. She hated it. She would have cried and laughed and danced at my grave if I'd a died, but she hated me for livin'. I had just proved I wasn't up to it, and Iroquois women don't have no sympathy for men who ain't up to the mark. So, I got this limp from his daddy cuttin' me."

He shuddered. "My guts went into a knot when I saw that knife young Dan carries. My insides remember that blade real good." His voice was unsteady when he continued, "They all had such contempt for me that they didn't even drag me outta the hogan when young Dan was born. I saw him come into the world, me and the other . . . women."

The room was filled with the smell of wood smoke and Joe's wet leather. His face was twisted with shame, and his eyes were brimming with tears. Ben turned down the lanterns until the room was filled with the dancing shadows of the fire. Then he handed Joe the bottle of bourbon, and Joe held it up while they watched bubbles rise by the light of the fire behind him. When the bottle came down at last, Joe offered it to Alice. She shook her head and handed it to Red. He drank and passed it to Ben. From Ben it went to Nell and from her to Annie and back to Alice. Nell and Annie drank from the bottle as casually as the men. Alice did the same when it came back to her.

Joe went on, "So that's my son, at least, to my mind he is. I couldn't stay around, since his mama couldn't stand the smell of me, so I came here and helped out while Ben started this here ranch. I saw little Alice come into the world, and I felt good. I looked and looked around these parts for a proper stud, and there weren't any. I thought she was gonna be barren. Then my boy came here, and she took to him. This ain't such a bad world after all." He drank deeply from the bottle again.

Nell Martin's voice was clear and strong in the quiet room. "You're a fine man, Joe Ballas. I wish you hadn't used the word 'stud,' but this is a country where men love horses. No mother could ask for a more loving and devoted friend."

"Joe, this young man is wanted by the law. I'm worried about that," Ben said reluctantly.

"If the law comes here after my boy, I'll kill the law," Joe said without hesitation. "And you get between my boy and his woman here, I'll kill you too, Ben. Gray Bird's daddy gave her away cheap, and maybe it was best, 'cause she sure enough loved Big Dan Walker. I ain't never seen a happier woman than she was. Alice is goin' to have her chance, too. She's goin' to my boy, and I'll kill anybody what gets in the way. I've seen the look on him. If he can't have her, he won't take nothin'. It would pain me to kill you, Ben, but without Alice, my boy don't have no future. He'll turn into a bitter old man like me. There ain't gonna be no mistakes this time."

He raised the bottle to the light. It was empty. Ben moved to the cabinet quickly and brought another. Joe tilted the bottle over his cupped hand, then flipped the liquid into the fire. In the explosive flash of blue flame a wide smile was revealed, softening the hard lines of his face, and the biting sweet smell of burning bourbon filled the room. He raised the bottle to his lips briefly, then passed it to Alice, and she started it around the group again. Joe started laughing, and they all froze, watching him.

He turned to Ben and said, "Pile of money, eh? You said he laid a pile of money on your table?"

Ben nodded, "A hell of a pile."

With another peal of laughter, Joe slapped his knee and hugged Alice to him. "By God, he ain't as tight as that big Scot daddy of his. A cheap little knife and two blankets was all his mama brought." Suddenly the whole room was rocking with laughter, and Alice hid her face with the flap of Joe's buckskin vest.

XVII

It seemed to Dan that he came around a corner that night. When he woke the next morning, he had lost the feeling of being a helpless, wounded animal. He rose and felt only a mild warning twinge from the leg when he pulled on his trousers. The heat was gone from his face, and the leg seemed to be coming down from its puffy, swollen tenderness to a nearly normal shape. Joe had been right about the wounds in his lower belly. They must have been only a little more than skin deep. They were hardly sore to the touch now. He had only minor pain when he bent to tighten his leggings and pull on his moccasins. He was tempted to try the stairs without the crutch, but he finally decided to use it.

Moving very quietly in the early morning darkness, Dan slipped down the stairs and into the kitchen. He hesitated when a gust of warm air flowed over him as he opened the kitchen door. The smell of fresh coffee was strong in the dark room. Joe's voice came from the shadows, "Come on in and light the lantern."

Dan pulled the lantern down from the hook in the ceiling, lighted it, adjusted the wick, and replaced it. Then he poured a cup of coffee from the pot on the stove and sat beside Joe at the breakfast table.

"Leg healin'?"

"Slow."

"Well, you lost a lot of blood. You should be gettin' over that by now. If you don't get no fever, you should be able to ride in another week or so. But you'll have to ride like you was settin' on eggs. It might be a month before you feel right. Don't worry about it. You ain't gonna limp around like me the rest of your days."

"I limp when I feel like it, and I don't when I don't," Dan said sarcastically.

They were laughing quietly together when Alice came into the room. "Damn poorly trained squaws around here, sleepin' all day, making the men wait for a bite to eat," Joe said in an irritated voice. "Some fool scrubbed the coffeepot. Can't make no good coffee in a clean pot."

Alice filled her cup and sat down before she answered, "It isn't even light outside yet. One more cute remark like that and I'll go right back to bed."

Dan said sadly, "Grumpy in the morning. She was right pleasant when she was a boy."

She kissed her finger and stuck it on his cheek. "Good morning, invalid." She did the same to Joe, saying, "Good morning, mean old man."

"Your daddy looks good, Alice, like the old days," Joe said.

"He does look better, but he's still too thin, seems to me."

"Naw, he was always skinny. You take after him thataway."

"Joe, this is your last chance. If you say one more mean thing to me, I'm going back upstairs."

"Now, now, that weren't mean, honey. That were the simple, gospel truth. Right, Dan?"

Dan scanned her up and down thoroughly with a thoughtful look. "She obviously suffers from an enormously pulchritudinous magnitude of femininity."

Joe snickered. "You talk to her like that, she'll go tell her mama."

Alice nodded to Dan and said, "Thank you, sir. I recognize a compliment even if it is hidden under a pile of linguistic pomposity."

Joe asked, "A pile of what?"

"Never mind. What were you two talking about when I came in?"

Joe answered, "We was figuring how soon Dan would be ready to hit the saddle again. We got work to do."

"What work?" she asked.

"We've got to find a snake and stomp it, a snake named Dutch MacRae or Alan Channing or whatever he's callin' hisself now." Joe's voice was casual. "Don't make sense to sit up on the north pasture waitin' for him to send more men after us. Soon's Dan is ready, we need to go lookin'."

"Don't make any plans till you talk to my dad. Now that he's back home, he may have some ideas."

"Why?" asked Dan. "I don't work here. I'm just a guest."

"Oh Dan, please don't be difficult. After all, this is Dad's ranch. When I show him the books, I think he'll want to string Alan Channing to the nearest tree."

"Bad?" asked Dan.

"Unbelievable. I've warned him, but he's still in for a terrible shock. Rice wrote to him over and over again saying that everything was going fine. Then, he put pressure on me and, as soon as Daddy and Mom came home, he turned down their request for a loan." She turned to Dan. "Maybe you've made me suspicious, but I don't understand all this. It doesn't make sense. He acts like he's trying to ruin us. It's amazing to me that a banker would get involved in something like this and act like a common criminal."

Dan lifted his head to listen and saw Joe cock his head at the same time. "Sounds like your mother and dad are on the way down."

When Ben and Nell walked into the kitchen, Ben's first comment was, "Dan, I'm sorry about yesterday. I had so much to catch up on that I forgot you're still recovering." At Dan's shrug, he continued, "Nell and me decided that it's all right with us for you to court Alice, but we'd like a little time before things go past that stage."

"Please, Ben, can't we eat breakfast first?" Nell laughed.

"Yeah, sure. Just seemed to me that it's better to let the man know. He and Alice damned sure didn't wait for nothin'. Met me on the front porch before I could even thaw out." Ben sat down, leaned over, and stared suggestively at the bottom of the cup in front of him until Nell brought the pot and poured his coffee.

"You're going to have breakfast with us aren't you, Joe?" asked Nell.

"Naw, Nell, I ain't got time. I got to meet the territorial governor and three bank presidents out in the barn in five minutes."

Nell responded, "Alice, will you tell the butler to inform those gentlemen that Mr. Ballas will be delayed for a few minutes? Tell them that Mr. Ballas' cook was slow this morning."

"Yes'um, I would, but the butler ain't up yet." Alice drawled. "Want me to help with breakfast?"

"You sit still beside your young giant there. I've been dreaming of getting back into my own kitchen for a long time. I'll take care of everything."

The conversation during breakfast was merely pleasant small talk, but as soon as Nell started removing the plates, Joe said, "When Dan's ready, seems to me that we ought to go after that feller Channing. It's plain that he's the one causin' trouble."

Ben answered, "It may be too late to go after anybody. Ira Rice did more than refuse me an additional loan when I talked to him. He told me that he was so distressed with the way things were going that he wants his money. That cursed loan paper I signed says that we must pay in full within thirty days of demand. I thought that was just small-print stuff when we took the loan. I never thought that he would do this to me. We can't pay it all in one year even if he waited till after our next market drive." Ben's shoulders drooped with discouragement.

He turned to Alice. "Honey, you told me that the ranch books are in bad shape. Well, before I even look at them I can tell you, it doesn't look like it makes any difference. Our account at the bank will just carry us till spring. Even if we used all of it right now to try to pay up, it wouldn't be near enough."

"But, Daddy, you've always said that you could do so much better with the railroad and all, being able to get to the eastern market without a long drive. Even without that, we've always done good just selling to the mining camps."

"I've been gambling, Alice. I've been taking all the land I could get my hands on. With the railroad finished now and the chance for Montana to become a state getting better every day, I can see all kinds of people coming out here looking for a place. The M Bar M is located where we get enough rain to farm without irrigating, mostly. The rest can be irrigated with our own streams from the mountains. I figure land values will go sky-high in a few years." He shook his head sadly. "Your mother and I thought we might not live to see it, but you'd be rich."

Dan asked bluntly, "May I ask how much money is involved here?"

Without hesitation, Ben turned to him and replied, "Fourteen thousand dollars. It was fifteen thousand, but Alice paid off two years of interest and a thousand of the principal with the money you gave her. This debt isn't all the result of my illness, Dan. I borrowed a lot of it to buy land. I can't see Rice taking this attitude. The loan is current, with the interest paid up to date, but he wants all his money back right now. I could pay him with the normal profits here in three or four years without any strain."

When Dan turned his eyes to her, Alice shrugged and shook her head. "Daddy's right for normal years, but now it's impossible to say. It depends on how many of our cows have been stolen. A ranch without cows isn't going to pay any debts. Our other ranges pay expenses plus some, but the big profit has always come from the north pasture. If we have to restock up there, it might be two or three years before we make a good profit again. Every few years we have a real hard winter and lose a lot of cows and calves. The markets go to pieces sometimes, too." She shrugged again and gave him a weak smile. "The ranching business can be tough."

"What it comes down to then, is that you need another ten thousand dollars?"

Ben answered, "I don't see how it's right for me to take that money you put on the table last night, young fellow. It turns out that a lot more would be needed to get me out of this hole. You might just lose your money. What I really need is for somebody to buy the loan who is willing to give me a little time. The trouble is that all these bankers stick together. Rice will probably warn them off. Banks don't like to make loans to outfits outside of their local area anyhow."

Dan sat thoughtfully staring off into space. He was desperately trying to figure out how to get in touch with Big Dan without exposing himself. He had ridden halfway across the country to avoid the law, and he knew that he would not allow himself to be taken. He had decided long ago that he would not kill a lawman. That meant he had to run or make the law kill him if he was caught; he would not be taken to jail. He knew that he could ride to the nearest telegraph office and solve Ben Martin's problem, but he would have to identify himself to pick up the money no matter how Big Dan arranged to get it to him.

Joe Ballas' voice was amused. "Big Dan Walker got rich, didn't he?"

"How did you know my father is called Big Dan?"

"Man who listens as much as I do learns a lot. You think he might have that much and be willin' to put it up?"

"Yes. Actually, I could provide it from my own resources. It only amounts to, let's see, fourteen thousand for the note on the ranch plus three thousand for the doctors. If we add three thousand dollars running money in case the north pasture needs to be restocked, that's only twenty thousand dollars. I just need a safe way to let him know I need it."

"Hear that, Alice? You got yourself quite a boyfriend. He says, 'That's only twenty thousand dollars.' Ain't you glad it ain't no big problem?" He turned to Dan. "Why don't I send a wire to him for you?" The amused tone in Joe's voice was puzzling.

"I'd still have to identify myself to get the money, Joe."

"Not if he sent it to me."

"Dad's a suspicious man. I don't think he'd respond to a wire supposedly from me instructing him to turn this much money over to a stranger."

"There don't need to be no instructions from you. I'd send the wire. I'd ask for him to send the money to me, Joe Ballas. I'd just tell him I need it, and thank you very much."

Dan stared at him, wondering if the old man was getting simple. "Dad doesn't send money to everybody who asks for it, Joe." He looked around uncomprehendingly at Alice's smiling face and Ben's suddenly hopeful one.

Alice said quickly, "Joe told us last night after you went to bed. He told us that he knew your father before you were born. He said that he and your father were friends."

Dan sat back in astonishment. "Why didn't you ever mention it to me?"

"If I told you everything I know, then you'd know more'n me, wouldn't you? Why don't I just send him a wire sayin' that a bird told me to ask him to send the money? The law know your Indian name?"

"I don't think so."

"Don't make no difference. When I get the money, you can be miles away. If the law finds out about it and figures everything out, what good does it do 'em?"

"Oh Joe, that would work. Of course it would," Alice said enthusiastically.

"You got to learn the outlaw way of thinkin', Alice. You bein' romantically tangled up with one," Joe said with a sneer.

"Right," Dan added with an evil smile. "And if this works out, I'll force your daddy to make you be nice to me else I'll foreclose on the ranch."

"I reckon I need to get along. By the time I ride a hundred miles to a telegraph office, set around waiting for an answer, go to some bank to get the money, and then get back here, it might take some time. There ain't no tellin' what kind of weather might come along this time of year." Joe's eyes were boring into Dan. "You think this is goin' to work, outlaw?"

Dan nodded. "Yes, but it's dangerous. Rice might not accept a bank draft. It's madness for one man to carry so much cash on the trail alone. We've got to send some men with you. Isn't there anyone around here you'd be willing to trust?"

Joe sat deep in thought for a moment before he replied, "Middle of winter and all, not much business for him, Tom Tolar might go. He's trailwise and almighty fast with a gun."

Dan couldn't help sounding surprised. "Tolar? A gunhand?"

Joe smirked. "You ain't the only man come driftin' in here with trouble behind him. Tolar was the second fastest man in these parts till you come. That boy's been up the crick and across the mountain. His woman's been keepin' him too close. She don't even like for him to wear a gun around town. I bet he'd like a sniff of fresh air."

"Second fastest?"

His smirk still in place, Joe said, "I ain't slowed down a bit, son, not a bit. The older the fiddler, the sweeter the music." He came to his feet and looked at Ben. "I'm headin' for town. I'll get grub for me and Tolar, put it on your tab with Robers at the store, and head out. How much you want me to pay Tom for makin' the trip?"

Ben said, "It's gun wages, Joe. Offer him a hundred dollars. It's too important to take a chance on him turning you down."

Joe gave a satisfied nod, then asked, "What about the north pasture?"

"It'll just have to keep," Ben said flatly.

Rice admitted him as soon as he had gone through his cautious procedure to identify him. Channing's face, windburned a deep red from his ride in a biting cold night, carried a set, angry expression. "Whatever you got to talk about better be good. It's gonna be hell ridin' back tonight in this weather."

"I thought you left here saying you were going to get rid of Walker and Ballas. Then you were going to clean out the M Bar M. Did you change your mind?"

"Hell no. Them two are probably dead meat by now. I'm getting men together now to start moving cows."

"That's interesting news. It's too bad you weren't here four days ago. You could have seen Ballas right here in Buckhorn buying supplies over at Robers' store. I sent for you that very day. What took you so long to get here?"

"I can't just sit around waitin' for the men I need to come drifting by. I got to go find 'em. I didn't get your message till yesterday. I rode my ass off gettin' here. What's this about Ballas bein' here in town? I hired the best man in the business to get rid of him and Walker. He may not be the fastest, but he ain't never failed. Ballas should be dead by now."

"He was as alive as I ever saw him when he rode out," Rice responded flatly.

"What do you suppose he's up to, ridin' off in this weather?"

"I don't know, but I have a guess. That's why I sent for you. We may have a chance to solve both your problem and mine if I'm right."

"You're just guessing?"

"That's right, but I think it's a smart guess." Rice could hear the smugness in his own voice and didn't give a damn.

Channing shook off his parka and stood rubbing his chapped hands together. "You must smell money in it or you'd not be botherin' me. Let's hear this guess of yours."

"You remember I told you I put pressure on Martin's daughter, and she suddenly came up with money? I thought Walker gave it to her. Now I'm not so sure. Martin may have found a backer, maybe one of the big miners or maybe even another bank. I called in my loan to him. He's got thirty days to pay up. Now that he's back on the M Bar M, he'll start making money again. If I'm going to get that ranch, I must do it now before he can recover. I think Ballas may have gone after more money to bail him out. If I'm right, it will be big money, several thousand dollars."

The heated room was making Channing's nose run. He dragged his arm across it while his gaze never wavered from Rice's face. "You think that damn Ballas has gone after enough money to pay the whole loan off?"

"That's what I suspect. I'm not certain about any of this, but you want to get rid of him anyway. Watch the roads and trails, ambush him, get rid of him. If he's carrying money, you get a big bonus. If he isn't, you've still got him out of your way."

"How much money we talkin' about?" Channing asked while a vicious smile of greed and anticipation spread across his face.

"The loan is for fourteen thousand dollars."

Channing's eyes widened and he sucked in a quick breath. "You think that old man might be comin' back here with that kind of money? All by himself except for that dumb Tolar? What good would a big dumb bareknuckle fighter do him?"

"I can't answer that. I've told you it's all a guess, but if it's true, it's a tremendous opportunity for you to make a big profit and for me to get a ranch. Martin just might come up with this kind of money once, but he could never do it twice."

"What happened to your fancy rules, like no killin'? What happened to that?"

Rice spread his hands and shrugged. "Things change. Each opportunity of this kind must be weighed on its own merit. The situation is different. As long as this activity takes place away from town and I am not directly involved, you can get what you want, and so can I. You get Ballas. Your hired killer gets Walker. You ride away rich with a free run at making more from rustling those cows, and I get the land I want. If I'm right, this may be the chance of a lifetime for us both. It's not a time to be too cautious. Sometimes a big risk must be taken to earn a big profit."

XVIII

Dan rode beside Ben Martin, enjoying the sight of the M Bar M as they rode down from the hills. He was looking forward to the end of the long ride. It was almost three weeks since Joe had left, and the tension was stretching everybody's nerves. Ben had been unable to sit still any longer, so he had decided to ride to the north pasture. Dan and Sam Dalton, a longtime M Bar M hired hand, went along. They had taken three days to look around and check the cattle. It was a relief to them all to find nothing disturbed and the cows taking the cold weather in stride. Now the ranch was in sight, and Dan was so hungry his stomach thought his throat was cut. Unfortunately, the ride had done nothing to relieve the tension about Joe's long absence.

"Ben, tomorrow morning I'm going to go looking for Joe. He should have been back by now. We're running out of time."

"I'm sure glad you decided to do it. Keeps me from having to ask you. I ought to do it, but that kind of trip in this weather would probably mess up all the doctors have done for me. Joe travels slow and cautious, but it's been too long now. There must have been some kind of trouble. You sure you're up to a long ride like that?"

"I'm as good as ever. I don't even think about my leg anymore. I might get a little sore if I had to walk all day or something like that, but it doesn't bother me in the saddle."

Ben took a quick look back. Dalton was riding far enough behind them that there was no chance for him to overhear. "Maybe we ought to have a little talk away from the women."

"Now is as good a time as we'll get, Ben. What's on your mind?"

The older man removed his hat to smooth the wool scarf he had pulled across the top of his head and tied under his chin to cover his ears. His face showed tension. "The first Texas cattle drive came to Montana in 1869. I got some of those cows. Seemed to me I could make more money selling food to the miners than I could mining. Besides, I like this kind of work better. Anyway, I thought Nell and I would have about ten kids with eight or nine of 'em being sons. We wanted enough land for all of 'em. We waited for what seemed like forever, and finally Alice came along. I thought she would be the first of a string, but Nell just never had no more."

Dan rode with his gaze roving the sides of the trail, making no comment out of respect for the clear sound of sadness in Ben's voice. After a few moments he glanced at Ben out of the corners of his eyes and found the silver-haired man wearing a devilish grin. "It isn't that I didn't try, Dan. I kept at it night and day, but it just turned out that Alice was all we got for all that work. I wouldn't have you think we just gave up and quit."

The horses shied nervously when both men burst out laughing. Both glanced back at Sam at the same instant to be sure he hadn't heard. With an openly curious grin, he was spurring his horse to catch up. Ben waved him back, and his mount slowed again. Dan felt a warm glow deep inside. The signal was clear. The trial period, the time of testing and watching and weighing, was over. Ben's remarks were so personal, so frank and open, that his actual words weren't the real message he was sending. What he was really saying was, "I accept you as part of my family. I trust you. We can talk together as kinsmen." The thought affected Dan so deeply that he rode with a tight throat for several moments.

Ben continued, "Anyhow, Nell and I kept building and adding to this place. Somehow we never seriously considered that Alice would leave here. It was all going to belong to her someday. We wanted her to know the land and how to get a living from it, and she learned well, by golly.

But now, with your trouble, you two will probably have to leave the country. Otherwise, the law might come up on you all of a sudden and ruin everything. We're kind of left out. It don't look like we have anything to work for when Alice leaves. We're kind of at a loss right now. Sure wish there was some way you could stay here."

Dan's saddle squeaked as he shifted his weight uncomfortably. "I don't think that's in the cards. By myself, I can jump up and run with no problem, but Alice needs a home. If they caught me, they would never take me to jail. I won't let it happen. My dad would go to war. He'd fight the whole government with guns if he had to. Think what would happen to Alice. I can't stay in this country, Ben. If a lawman came riding in tomorrow, I'd be in the saddle and gone. I'd take Alice, if she'd go, but I'd be gone as fast as this red horse can travel." He paused a moment, than he added, "Of course, if she didn't go with me, I'd just have to come back for her later. I didn't mean for anything like this to happen, but it did. I don't feel right anymore when she's not around."

"Are you sure there's no chance to make peace with the law? If you'd have to spend some time in the penitentiary, Alice would wait. She's makin' out to be a real steady woman, Dan."

"They want me for murder, two of 'em, in fact. It might mean jail, but they'd probably hang me."

"For killing two men coming at your brother with guns? No jury out here would have trouble with that. What do they expect a man to do? Run off and cry? I tell you, Dan, you're better off leaving a place where folks think like that. That's no place to live."

They rode in silence for a while before Ben said reluctantly, "Well, maybe it won't be too bad for us the way it has to be. If you two settle close to the border, maybe we could get up there for visits in the summers. This is mighty sightly country to ride through when the weather's nice. My Nellie's a pretty thing in the saddle, too. You haven't seen her ride yet. It's a real nice thing to watch. Alice rides good, too, but she rides like a cowhand; it's all business to her, fastest way to get from here to yonder. Nellie rides like a lady, just for pure pleasure. Yeah, it's a thing to see."

Dan's attention suddenly focused on the grounds around the ranch buildings, and he drew rein. "Got visitors!" The dark marks of several horses leading to the ranch buildings was plain in the light snow.

"Could be anybody. Folks drop by to visit." Ben was leaning forward in the saddle, peering at the tracks through narrowed eyes.

"I don't like the look of it." He could feel Big Red fidgeting restlessly beneath him. With the ranch buildings in sight, the big horse was eager to feel the warmth of a stall and to start working his way through a bucket of grain.

"They plan to stay awhile. They got the horses put away in the barn." Ben's face was rigid. "You think it might be the law?"

"No way to tell. Do you suppose that damn Channing would dare try to get me at the main ranch? He's done some wild things, but I never even considered that he might hit here." He pulled Big Red into a clump of trees. Ben Martin followed, dismounted with Dan, and moved forward in the concealment of the trees to observe the house. Dalton joined them.

Dalton, obviously startled, asked, "What's wrong, boss?"

"Maybe nothing, Sam. We got a bunch of visitors down there. May be just neighbors, but it looks like five or six horses rode in. We weren't expecting anyone, but that don't mean a thing. Seems like it might be smart to stop and think it over before we ride in. Sam, if it's the law, you don't remember nobody named Dan Walker. Got that?" Ben's voice was bleak.

Dalton gave Dan an appraising look and seemed to be thinking it over. "No good, boss. Everybody around these parts will remember him bein' at the Stenholm dance. I remember him good, but he rode out of here a long time ago, headin' south. Said men had to be crazy to put up with this here cold weather. Big man, that Walker, ugly as sin he was, mean-lookin'."

Ben turned to Dan with a grim smile and said, "I don't hire fools. I've got the best crew of men in Montana."

Dalton winked at Dan and added, "I sure wouldn't like to ride into that open ground in front of the house if somebody unfriendly was in there. What do we do?"

Dan went to Big Red and took a heavy leather case from the saddle. "I forgot this thing. Joe took it from that old man up on the mountain when he first met up with him. He gave it to me, saying it was too awkward to be any use. I been meaning to use it, but I kept forgetting I brought it along." He removed the telescope from the case, steadied it against a tree, and began the unfamiliar procedure of bringing it into focus on the ranch.

Slowly Dan moved the instrument to scan across the front of the house and around the yard. He could see clearly where the horses had been tethered at the front porch before being taken to the barn. He could count six trails in the cleaner snow farther from the house. "There are six of them," he muttered to Ben and Sam. "Maybe you better keep watch for a while, Ben. If anyone shows himself, you would know who they are better than I would."

Ben took the telescope awkwardly and began his own careful inspection of the ranch. Dan could see no movement, but he knew that this meant nothing. Nobody walked around outside in the bitter cold without good reason. This was a good time of year to find lots of things to do inside, near the fire. Even putting the horses into the barn was not suspicious. It would be cruel to leave the animals standing in the cold wind, even during a short visit.

"Takes a little patience to use this thing, but it works good once you get the hang of it." Ben wiped at his eye. "You want to take a look, Sam?"

"Yeah, I ain't never used one of them. Show me how it works," Sam answered eagerly.

An hour passed, with the telescope passing from one to the other of them. The sun was dropping fast, and the cold was beginning to get to them. One would watch while the other two would walk deeper into the trees to stamp feet and swing arms. Suddenly, Ben, who was watching, said, "There! Somebody came out of the house. He's walking to the woodpile. I don't know him. I never saw him before." He watched silently for a moment, then said, "He went back inside with the wood." He lowered the telescope for a moment to wipe his eye again. When he resumed his observation, he said harshly to Dan, "I don't know whether it's law or outlaw, but I got strangers in my house, and there's nobody there but Nell and Alice. I got four men in the bunkhouse, and Red should be around there somewhere, but I don't see no sign of them."

"Watch close. It's nearly time to eat. We'll see who goes to the cookshack and how they act," Dan said, trying to keep his voice calm. His stomach was in a knot. He felt a burning, wild rage at the thought that Alice might be in danger. He wanted desperately to leap into the saddle and ride down there. He kept trying to slow his breathing, kept telling himself to think and not to be a fool.

Ben's body was rigid and his voice shaking when he said, "You called it, Dan. Here they come."

Dan saw the cook step out and start whanging the triangle of metal in front of the cookshack. Because of the distance, the tinny noise came to them dimly and out of sequence with the movements of the cook. He could see men come out of the Martin home and the bunkhouse, but he couldn't identify them. They seemed to be acting normally. "What can you see, Ben?"

"Nobody is holding a gun on my men, I can tell you that. They're standing around shaking hands now. Looks like they're tradin' names. Looks friendly. Only three came out of the house, so there's three still in there, if we got 'em tallied right." He watched in silence until the men disappeared into the cookshack. When he turned to Dan, his voice was calm. "I don't know those men, Dan, but they and my men acted just as sweet as pie. Do you suppose we might be counting packhorses? Maybe there are just three of them."

"Maybe so. Your men would have acted differently if those strangers were outlaws. There wouldn't have been any handshaking. But if it's the law, there'd be no reason for them to act unfriendly. I'm beginning to think you have a posse at your house, Ben. Nell might have a federal marshal and a couple of deputies eating at the house while the rest of the posse eats with your men. Or, there may be only three of them, if each of those men has a packhorse."

"Well, we're both pretty dumb, standing here grinning like fools at each other. I'm relieved that my ranch hasn't been raided, but we're both forgetting what this means to you, Dan. It means you can't come home."

Dan squatted on his heels, breathing deeply. He had been wound up so tight that the sudden release of tension left him feeling shaky. He looked up at Ben with a weak grin and said, "Right now, I'm so relieved that Alice and Nell are safe it's going to take me a minute to feel bad about anything else. I was scared shitless for a while there."

All three of them burst out laughing. The scare had been so bad that they all acted a little giddy. Dalton said, "Ain't it funny how somethin' awful can seem to be pretty good if you was expectin' something worse?"

Ben agreed. "Damn truth, Sam. That's the way of it."

Dan, still sitting on his heels, suddenly felt the impact of what he faced. He said, "I feel like a lost kid all of a sudden. I hadn't realized how much I was looking forward to riding in. I was already thinking about having Alice come running out looking glad to see me." He felt like a cold knife was being twisted inside him. "You said it right, Ben. This place has become home to me, and now I can't ever go back."

"Now wait a minute, Dan. Don't jump the gun. That posse can't camp at my place for very long. They have to ride on. We need to make a plan. First of all, we don't know much about what's happening yet. How about you keeping your eyes open while Sam and I ride on down to the ranch? We can plan a signal. If it's the law, Sam can clown around in the yard, holding his hands up like he was turning himself in. If it's just some friendly strangers, I'll drop my hat on the ground. If we're wrong, and we got some outlaws or something down there, we won't make any signal at all. We might not be able to make a signal anyway, if that's the case."

Dan glanced at Sam Dalton and said, "Your boss would have made a good outlaw."

Without a blink of hesitation, Dalton responded, "I don't work for no fool. I got the best boss in Montana."

"I'm mighty near broke, Dalton. You ain't up for a raise anyhow," Ben said defensively.

Dalton looked at Dan and shrugged. "Man has to keep tryin'."

"If we have outlaws down there, we'll still have you loose out here to do something for us. If it's just friendly folks, you can ride on in. If it's the law, ride back up to the north pasture and keep your eyes open and wait. From what Joe says, nobody can find you in that kind of country unless you want to be found." Ben looked from Dan to Sam and back again. "We got everything covered?"

Dan nodded. "Sounds good to me. I'll be here watching."

Dalton pulled off his glove and extended his hand. "Good luck, whatever way it goes, Walker." His grip was firm.

Ben shook hands also before he walked to his horse. Mounted, he turned again to Dan. "Be careful, Walker. If anything happens to you, Alice will blame me for it just as sure as shit stinks. I have enough trouble without that." He put his horse down the slope without looking back.

Dan sat watching them make their way to the ranch. He estimated the distance to be about five hundred yards. If men swarmed out of the ranch after him, he was unconcerned. On Big Red in this kind of country, he wouldn't have been more relaxed if his lead was ten miles. He picked up the telescope and focused it on the front porch. He could feel the involuntary tightening of his muscles as the two horsemen neared the buildings. They stopped in front of the porch and dismounted.

Dan watched the front door open and Alice came running out. She threw her arms around Ben and clung to him. His eyes started watering, and he cursed as he frantically wiped them with his gloved hand. When he got the telescope in position again, the first thing he saw was a limping man come out the front door. Joe Ballas! There could be no mistake. He would know that faked semi-invalid way of movement anywhere.

Ben rushed to the doorway and shook hands with someone half-concealed by one of the porch columns. What was all this? Alice was dancing up and down and clapping her hands. Ben, in a kind of awkward dance step, minced across the porch and down the steps. Standing on the frozen ground in front of the house, he removed his hat with a flourish and sailed it across the yard. Now he was running after it. Dan could see Alice and Joe clapping their hands as if applauding. He could hardly believe his eyes, but there it was. Ben Martin was dancing on his hat!

Now they were all looking up at the mountain where Dan was crouched behind a tree. Everyone was waving for him to come. Well, Ben had certainly given the dropped-hat signal that the strangers were friendly. He had done it with a flair that Dan didn't know was in the old man. From the saddle as Big Red headed down the slope, he could see him still stomping his hat into a shapeless mess. Even at this distance, the sound of laughing and cheering carried plainly through the cold mountain air. Big Red came to a gallop.

When he reached the flat about a hundred yards from the house, Alice came running to meet him. She wasn't even wearing a coat. She met him thirty yards from the house, and he had a tough job getting Big Red stopped. Dan slid from the saddle, pulling off his coat. Her face was one big smile of joy. He wrapped the coat around her and she blurted, "He's come. He's come. It's your brother, Dan. Mark came back with Joe. They brought the money. They brought the news. Oh, it's wonderful!"

The sound of running footsteps brought his eyes up from Alice's radiant face to see Mark sliding to a stop, wearing a big grin. He stuck out his hand and said, "Hello, big brother, I see you found Matt and me a little sister."

Unable to speak, Dan ignored the extended hand. With one arm around Alice, he flung the other around Mark and stood holding them both close to him. His throat was working with the effort to talk, but he couldn't get a word out. He felt tears gathering in his eyes and didn't care who saw it. Dan had just gone through the worst moments of his life, scared almost into a boneless, quaking jelly. Crushed against him, Alice looked up with enormous eyes, and said softly, "I love you." She reached up and flicked the tears off his face with quick, gentle fingers.

Mark said proudly, "I like your girl, Dan."

Dan's throat finally came unlocked, but his voice was hoarse and unsteady when he said, "Yeah, Mark, she's nice, but I liked her better when she was a boy."

Mark said blankly, "Beg pardon? What did you say?"

XIX

"Oh, never mind, Mark. It's a little joke between Alice and me. We'll tell you about it later." The three of them started walking slowly toward the big ranch house, Alice in the middle with an arm around each of them. Dan could see the massive Tom Tolar now, standing on the front porch with a broad smile showing through his beard. Ben was standing beside him with his wrecked hat pulled down over his ears and an arm around Nell, who had her arms wrapped around herself against the cold wind. Joe stood leaning against one of the porch columns, acting as if his poor old body needed the support. The other men had retreated to the warmth of the cookshack.

Everyone was eager to get back into the warm house as soon as Mark, Alice, and Dan came to the porch. Dan hadn't had time to remove his hat before Joe's hard voice challenged him. "Fake," he said harshly. "You ain't no real outlaw. Your rich daddy done fixed everything for you."

"What? What are you talking about, Joe?" Dan asked.

"You can go home any time, according to Mark," Joe said accusingly. "They done called what you done to those poor little city boys 'justifiable homicide.' You ain't no outlaw. You been runnin' from nothin'."

Alice was snuggled under Dan's arm. Mark stood on the other side of him with his hand on Dan's shoulder. He nodded and said, "It's the truth, Dan. We've been looking everywhere for you. Big Dan figured you would run to some far place, and you certainly did what he expected. We figured you'd be somewhere in the northwest part of the country if you weren't in Canada already, so I came up here and started looking for you. Big Dan sent me a wire when he received the request for money from Joe Ballas. He told me to go to Joe and to refuse to give him the money till he led me to you." He turned to Ballas and pointed to a pair of saddlebags thrown carelessly into the corner. "There's the money, Joe."

Joe walked across the room, picked up the bags, and dropped them onto the heavy oak table. "Open it up, Mark. Let's see what all that cash looks like in one place."

Mark did so, with everyone gathered around watching. When he started pulling out the contents, a stunned silence fell. The saddlebags contained only books, neatly wrapped in waxed paper.

Joe said sadly, "Mark, you're a nice feller, but you ain't a patch on your big brother. The money's in my bags over yonder. I figured I'd better look after it for you. You sleep too sound, youngster. Me and Dan need to give you some trainin'."

Mark looked as if he couldn't decide whether to be angry, embarrassed, or relieved. "I have, indeed, been sleeping with that money! How did you . . . ?"

"Ain't no trick for an old horse thief, son. Ain't no trick at all. I just wanted to be sure it got here safe. It was safest with me, and that's a fact."

"We offered a reward to anyone who told Dan that he could come home, that the trouble was past. Big Dan will want to talk to you about that, Joe. You were the first man to tell him," Mark said.

"Is that what took you so long, Joe? You had to wait for Mark to arrive before you could get the money?" Dan asked.

"That's right. Big Dan sent me a wire sayin' to sit tight and wait for that boy. Weren't nothin' I could do but sit on my thumbs and let my feet hang down till he come along. Then, when he did come, he had those three hardcases with him you seen out in the yard when you and Ben was watchin' from up on the hill. That's the hardest waitin' I ever done."

"Dan, we need to talk about what's going on here," Mark said with a concerned look. "Some men tried to ambush us on the way here. Joe and Tom Tolar killed two of them on the trail."

"It's your old friend, that Channing feller," Joe said. After a pause, he added, "One of them fellers lived long enough to tell Tom who done it. Channing was with 'em, but he run off like a yeller dog. I couldn't foller him 'cause I needed to bring that money home."

Dan was puzzled. "How did Channing know you were going to be on that trail? Do you think he knew about the money?"

Tom Tolar said, "They was sure set up to bushwack us, Dan. Joe was scoutin' ahead. He give me the high sign, so I stopped Mark and his men and went huntin'. Joe got one, and I got one. The one I got took a little while to die. I tried to make him as comfortable as I could. He said I treated him white, so he talked."

"What exactly did he say?" Dan asked.

"He said that Dutch MacRae told him that there would be a big payday if they could gun down two men carrying a mother lode of cash. MacRae told him there would be a thousand dollars in it for him, but the men carrying the money had to die. Joe says that Channing calls himself MacRae sometimes."

"But how do you suppose Channing knew about you going after money?" Dan asked.

Joe's voice was sarcastic. "Let's see now. Nobody but me has left this here ranch. That means that somebody in town saw me buying supplies and leavin' with Tom. That somebody would have to figure I was ridin' after the money and tell Channing. Who in town knows that M Bar M needs big money fast? Who in town brought that feller Channing into the game in the first place? Who in town stands to get a ranch for about a quarter of what it's worth if the loan against it ain't paid?"

"You think Rice, the banker, is behind all this trouble, Joe?" Tom asked in a shocked voice.

Joe glanced at Dan, flipped a thumb at Tom, and said sourly, "I just said he was passable fast with a gun. I didn't say nothin' about him being quick no other way, but maybe there's some hope for him. Sometimes livin' with a smart woman helps. Old Tom here acts like he's startin' to think now and again, in spite of how bad it must hurt his head."

Tom laughed, glanced at Dan, and replied, "That's Joe. He don't say nothin' unless he can say somethin' nice, does he?"

Ben, who had been standing quietly all the while, finally spoke. "There isn't any proof, but it makes sense. Rice was mighty eager to lend money to M Bar M, but he insisted on having Channing out here. Red told me Channing messed up everything on this ranch. I couldn't believe any kind of decent manager could do such a bad job. Then, when we're in a real bind, and before we can get things set right, Rice demands his money."

Dan responded, "We have nothing on Rice unless we can catch Channing and make him talk. Seems to me that the best order of business is to get out from under that loan first. Then, if they are in this together, we might catch Channing by watching Rice. If we could catch them together, we might get something out of one of them."

"In the meantime," Ben said, "I have good neighbors all over the place who might like to know how Rice dealt with the M Bar M. I think we might have room for a new bank around here pretty soon."

"First things first," Dan insisted. "I suggest that we ride to town first thing tomorrow and redeem that loan. Then we've got to find a way to catch Channing. He's always around causing trouble. Seems as if Joe and I are kept busy all the time trying to keep from getting killed by men he hires."

The jovial Tom Tolar spoke quietly. "Channing won't leave alive if he comes to Buckhorn again. I'm wearin' a gun till he's six feet under. This here is tiresome, havin' men hired to dry-gulch me. I'm gonna spread the word that I'm interested in Channing. If he comes to town, I'm likely to hear about it real quick."

"Do you think you can spread the word like that without Rice hearing about it?" asked Dan.

"I do," Tom replied simply.

Nell spoke firmly. "I think you men have gone as far with this as you can go right now. The rest of this day is going to be spent celebrating Mark's arrival with the money we needed so badly. Let's show him how much we appreciate his being such a good messenger. I think we can be forgiven if we celebrate at the same time about Dan's not being a fugitive any longer."

Joe Ballas was ranging far ahead with Dan following a couple of hundred yards behind, their habitual procedure from the north pasture now honed to wordless teamwork. Farther back, Mark rode with Ben and Tom. Two of Mark's men rode as flankers, with the third riding farther back as a rear guard. Any further attempt to try to take the money could not achieve surprise and would be a costly enterprise against seven armed and alert men.

Ben had instructed Red to stay behind and to be sure the hands were armed and alert at the ranch. Two of the men had been sent to the north pasture with instructions to avoid a fight but to bring warning if there was any trouble. There was to be no more chance for Channing to catch the M Bar M by surprise, no matter what he tried.

They rode into Buckhorn at mid-afternoon. Ben went straight into the bank, followed by Mark and Dan. Tolar went home, Joe vanished into the saloon, and the rest of the men posted themselves along the main street. As they walked in, the wind blew a powdery cloud of snow through the open door.

The lone teller in the lobby had hardly glanced up from his ledgers before Rice came out of his office. He went to Ben at once, saying, "Good to see you, Martin. What can I do for you?"

"I'm here to pay my loan in full, Rice. It'll be the last business we do with this bank. I'll be needing to empty my account here, too."

"Why, you sound angry, Mr. Martin. I hope you haven't taken offense. I've only done what I have seen as necessary to protect the bank."

Ben turned to the teller and spoke harshly. "Total my account here and give me the cash." He pulled a package from his coat and threw it on a table in the lobby. "That's to cover the loan. Count it and let's get this finished."

"Please, please, gentlemen, can't we step into my office? Anyone could walk in here at any moment. We would have proper privacy in my office and avoid interruption," Rice said in a voice that betrayed his nervousness.

"The more people who know about this, the better, as far as I'm concerned, Rice," Ben countered. "In fact, I'm going to make a special effort to spread the word around about how this loan has been handled. I think my neighbors will want to know how helpful you've been."

When Rice tried to protest further, Ben flatly ordered him to get on with the business at hand. The clerk dropped his pretense of working on the ledgers and sat watching closely. The transaction was quickly completed. Ben crushed the copy of the loan when it was handed to him, jammed the crumpled paper contemptuously into his coat pocket, and walked to the teller's cage to pick up the money from his account. As soon as he counted the money, he stalked out of the bank without another word.

As they walked toward the saloon, Mark said quietly, "Dan, we can have a good man here in a couple of weeks. This town needs a bank. The one it has now looks shaky to me. What do you think?"

"We'll look into it. There's tremendous potential for growth here, but we'll need to have a telegraph line brought into Buckhorn. It's hard to predict how things will go in the future, but new mines are opening up every day. I think there's a bigger fortune to be made in copper than in gold and silver. We'll discuss it with Big Dan. He'll probably recommend to the other stockholders that we establish a branch here from our bank in Butte. I think he'll like the idea of our Butte facility broadening its base into both the cattle and the sheep industry here in Montana."

Dan turned to Ben. "In any event, I propose to freeze Rice right out of Buckhorn, and I don't think it'll take long if your neighbors listen to you."

Ben gave a short laugh. "They'll listen."

The atmosphere in the hotel dining room was festive. Word had spread around that M Bar M was celebrating, and the whole town came to congratulate Ben on his return to good health. Robers closed his store early. He and his wife were eager to join the celebration. Tom and Katherine came in with their two little boys, and Dan was delighted to observe the warm welcome they received from everyone.

The room was full of laughter, the clatter of eating utensils, and the smell of food being served when the muffled sound of two closely spaced shots sounded clearly above the din. Silence fell at once, as everyone froze into a shocked, alert stillness. The sudden quiet made the sound of a lone third shot seem louder than the first two.

The men in the room came to their feet and moved toward the door when the sound of the hoofs of a galloping horse came plainly into the quiet room. Dan saw Tom Tolar throw open the door just as the sound of three more shots echoed through the room. Both panes of the window on the street side of the hotel shattered, and Tom staggered back away from the door.

Bedlam broke out in the crowded dining room as people dove for the floor. Screams and the sound of breaking dishes followed Dan as he darted through the open door and dodged quickly into the darkness away from the lighted doorway. He could still hear the hoofbeats of the racing horse, but he could see nothing with eyes still dazzled by the bright lights in the hotel dining room. From the darkness on the other side of the door came Joe's unruffled voice. "The bank door's hangin' open. Let's go see if that's where them first shots came from."

The frigid wind was biting cold as Dan walked cautiously up one side of the street, his eyes gradually adjusting to the darkness until he could see Joe's limping, shadowy figure on the other side. He approached the half-open bank door cautiously and called, "Rice?" When there was no answer, he called again, "Anybody in the bank?" The only sound was the rattling of Robers' store sign down the street swinging in the wind on rusty chains.

Dan gave a quick look at Joe and received a nod. He stepped through the door and to one side, gun drawn. Joe was an instant behind him and moved to the other side. The dimly lit bank lobby was empty. The door to Rice's office was open. Dan slipped forward quietly and glanced into the small room. A double door behind Rice's desk was open, revealing the bank vault, which was also standing open. Rice was lying on his face behind his desk.

"What's happening in there?" It was Robers' voice from the street in front of the bank.

"Come in and shut the damn door," Joe called. Robers, carrying a double-barreled shotgun, stepped inside and kicked the door closed. He joined Joe in the doorway leading into Rice's office, watching while Dan gently rolled the small man over. His face was bright with blood from his nose and mouth.

Rice looked up into Dan's face and asked, "How bad am I hurt?"

Before Dan could answer, Joe said, "You're lung shut, Rice. I can tell from here. That means you may have a few minutes, but it won't be long. You're a goner." When Dan gave him a look, Joe's hard voice continued, "Ain't no sense lyin' to the dyin', Dan, no sense at all."

Dan turned back to Rice and asked, "What happened here? Who did this?"

Rice's voice was surprisingly strong and calm when he responded, "Channing shot me and robbed the bank. He thought I tried to get him killed when I sent him after Ballas. I only saw Ballas and Tom Tolar leave here, but he said he ran into six men. He thought I crossed him, and he knew I just received all that money from Martin, so he came for it tonight. I never thought he'd turn on me like that."

"Was he alone?" Dan asked, but Rice's gaze drifted from Dan's face as if he were idly scanning the room. Then he simply stopped breathing.

Joe said flatly, "It's sad to see a little poison snake like him die so easy. Don't seem right."

Dan rose from his kneeling position beside Rice and turned to Robers. "Anybody hurt back at the hotel?"

Robers growled, "Yeah, Tom was creased along the inside of his leg. He ain't hurt bad, although he was bleeding right smart."

"I think I'll go check on him. Will you open your store for Joe and me? We'll be going after Channing this time. We didn't bring enough stuff to town with us to start trailing a man in this weather." When Robers nodded, Dan looked at Joe. "Get a lantern and take a look at the tracks. I'll meet you over at the store."

Dan trotted back to the hotel to get out of the biting wind as quickly as he could. His coat and hat were still hanging in the dining room. The first thing he saw when he entered was Tom Tolar sitting in a chair while Katherine put the finishing touches on a bandaged upper thigh. Everyone was gathered around to watch. "How bad is it, Tom?"

Tolar, his face pale, spoke through gritted teeth while Katherine pulled the bandage tighter. "Just took some meat out of the inside of my thigh, Dan. Ain't no bad hit, but it hurts like the very devil!" He grabbed a bottle from the table beside him, took a swig, and extended it to Dan. When Dan shook his head, Tom drank again, shrugged off Katherine's warning look, and said, "Don't worry about me. You got your own job to do."

XX

Dan rode behind Joe through a world of white glare. The snow was not deep, but it painfully reflected the brilliant sunlight into the eyes. They were, for the moment at least, blessed with good fortune. The bright sky offered no threat to drop new snow on Channing's trail, and the wind had conveniently died. The tracks, obscured by neither fallen nor blown snow, could be followed by a drunken sailor.

While Joe scouted ahead, Dan led the two spare horses and a pack mule loaned to them by townsmen of Buckhorn. If Channing had ridden all night, both he and his mount would be tired. However, that would put them at least eight hours behind him. The tracks plainly indicated he was setting a pace that would soon use up his horse. He would need a fresh one soon. The absence of a pack animal probably indicated that he had no plans to camp out and was heading for some kind of shelter. Joe kept the pace at a mile-eating trot, obviously feeling that an ambush was unlikely this close to Buckhorn.

Joe stopped at about noon and had the saddle stripped off his steaming mount by the time Dan joined him. While he was throwing his gear onto one of the spare horses, he said, "We come near twenty mile already, through rough country. His horse is about to fall out from under him. He's got a hideout close, I betcha. Maybe he's headin' for an old tradin' post that used to be up here. He's got a fresh bronc stashed somewhere close."

He swung up and put his horse to a trot, leaving Dan in the process of switching his own saddle to the other spare mount. Big Red showed no sign of fatigue, but this might be a long chase. Dan knelt for a moment to study the tracks. It was difficult to be sure, but it looked like they were fresher. They may have gained a little, even though Channing was about to kill his horse. The man rode like a damn fool; he seemed to have no interest in the routine ways to conserve the strength of his mount.

Dan stuffed a chunk of store-bought jerky into his cheek. It was good. His respect for Robers went up a notch. Some storekeepers sold jerky a dog wouldn't eat. He hit the saddle and was at a trot again in about two jumps.

Dan saw Joe look back and then put his horse to a lope. He looked like he was ignoring the trail now, riding to a definite location. Half an hour later he slowed, dropped off his horse, and walked into the woods atop a small knoll. Dan rode to join him. He was crouched at the edge of the trees, looking down a slope at an old log cabin with a barn beyond it.

Dan saw the problem instantly. They were in a narrow canyon with rock slopes rising steeply on both sides. The woods around the building had been cleared all the way to the slopes. Any rider trying to get past would have to ride about a hundred yards across open ground. If there was someone in that cabin, he would have an excellent short-range shot at anyone trying to pass. Smoke rose from the chimney.

"You figure we got trouble?" Dan asked quietly.

Joe answered, "If you got time, look in those woods on the far side over yonder. Ain't no sense stakin' horses out in the woods 'less you gonna use 'em. I see two. Way I figure it, there's two men in those woods wantin' us to think they's in that cabin. If a posse come here, they figure to get some free shots before they ride off. Then the posse is in trouble with wounded men to look after."

Dan added, "And they figure they can get clean away because they're on fresh horses and ours are tired already."

Joe chuckled. " 'Cept they're watchin' for riders. You suppose you could get across that open ground out there on foot 'thout them seein'?"

Several minutes of quiet followed while Dan looked for routes where he might cross without being seen. Although the area had been cleared, it was broken by gullies and littered with rocks and tree stumps. He saw two paths where it could possibly be done and said so, pointing them out.

"Let's see if we're right," Joe said, dropping to the ground and crawling forward.

Dan found it to be easier than he expected. Although he was exposed to one of the cabin windows, the route he selected allowed him to get across in less than thirty minutes. When he reached the woods, he kept going until he felt sure he was behind anyone covering the open area from the wood line. He began to stalk, searching and listening.

He found a man in ten minutes, although he almost walked right past him. The man was sitting with his back comfortably resting against a large tree. From Dan's viewpoint, approaching him from behind, the man was hidden by the trunk of the tree, but the rifle cradled in his lap was visible on both sides. He froze only six feet behind the man while he searched for the other. He was convinced that they would be close together.

Dan's heart nearly stopped when the man in front of him spoke. "Maybe there ain't nobody comin'."

The other man's voice sounded like he was about twenty feet to the left when he answered, "That's fine with me. Save us a bunch of trouble. We already got paid anyhow."

The man looked up and found himself staring into the bore of a Colt .44 when Dan leaned around the tree, dropping to one knee beside him. After a convulsive jerk of surprise, he sat as still as a stone while Dan lifted the rifle from across his lap and the six-gun from his holster. At

Dan's signal with the barrel of the Colt, he got to his feet, and Dan rose with him.

As soon as he was erect, Dan and the other outlaw spotted each other at the same time. When he tried to swing his rifle, Dan shot him. The force of the bullet drove the man onto his back, but he spun on the ground, still trying to bring his rifle into play. Dan shot him again. Other than flinching with the sound of each shot, Dan's prisoner made no move.

Dan's whistle brought Joe to his feet, still fifty feet away. When he drew near, Joe casually commented, "We was right about there only bein' two of 'em. Let's go to the cabin and talk to this little feller. I'll take these horses of theirs, go get ours, and meet you there." He looked at Dan's prisoner and made a motion toward the dying man. "You pick up your partner and carry him to the cabin with you." He went to the downed outlaw and began to go through his pockets. The man quit breathing before Joe was finished with the search. Joe waved a wad of bills in the air and smirked before he limped toward the outlaws' horses.

The interior of the cabin was hot. They had obviously fed the fire heavily to avoid having to return during their wait in ambush. The place was littered with garbage and rank with the smell of sweat and urine. Joe arrived with the horses, dismounted, and made a sour face when he smelled the inside of the cabin. He limped straight to the prisoner and asked, "You gonna talk?"

The man snarled, "I got nothin' to say. We ain't done nothin'. You two come ridin' in here and shot my partner. We didn't do nothin'."

"You got nothin' to say?" Joe asked quietly.

"I ain't sayin' nothin'."

Without another word, Joe drew and shot the man through the body three times. The bullets drove him back against the wall. He stood there for a second or two with his face blank with surprise and shock before he slid to the floor and rolled onto his face. Joe stooped over him, patted his pockets, removed another roll of bills, and started toward the fireplace. A shovel was leaning against the chimney. He used it to pile coals against the wall, and flames immediately started flickering upward. With a burning fagot in his hand, he started toward the door. His voice was perfectly normal when he said, "We lost some time. Soon as I set the barn on fire, we better get back to what we was doin' before we was rudely interrupted."

Joe studied the hoofprints of the two outlaw mounts, walked into the barn with Dan following, and looked at the prints in the stalls by the light of the flaming fagot. Satisfied, he threw the burning torch into a pile of hay. He opened the gate to one of the stalls and drove out a tired horse, whipping it with his hat. "Them coyotes was gonna leave that poor animal closed up in here to starve."

After a quick glance at the tracks left by the departing animal, he said, "That's the one we been following." He wore a disgusted expression. "We was gainin', but we lost about an hour killin' coyotes," he said with frustration plain in his voice. "We're still half a day behind. No help for it, I reckon. That damn Channing hired every two-bit back shooter in the country, seems like." He seemed to float into the saddle, a graceful effortless motion. "We're improving the quality of the neighbors around here." Five minutes later, he was already trotting alongside the trail left by Channing's new mount.

The two additional horses taken from the dead outlaws were enough to make the remuda unhandy for Dan. The following day, he and Joe rode those horses hard, then released them. By nightfall of the day after that, they agreed that they were only about two hours behind when darkness stopped them. Dan built a fire. By the time Joe had heated canned beans and thawed canned peaches for the meal, Dan had switched the saddles to fresh horses. "You figure to trail by moonlight?" Joe asked.

"I do," Dan responded. "I don't know where I am, so I can't figure out where Channing's headed. But he's been on the same horse for two days. I want to get him before he finds another fresh one if I can. I think we can come up on his camp by midnight. If he keeps riding tonight, his horse will be dead by morning. Looks to me like Channing's time is near."

"Been a long time since I been in these parts, if I ever was," Joe commented. "I been tryin' to figure where he's headin'. Only thing out here might be the railroad."

"How far is it from here, Joe?"

"I ain't sure, but your idea to push on tonight makes sense. He ain't runnin' like a smart man. He's just runnin'. Maybe he figures, if he can git to the rails, he can make it to a big town and disappear. He ain't no tenderfoot exactly, Dan, but he ain't all that good out here. If he stays away from the towns, he don't have a Chinaman's chance up agin' us."

Joe scraped the cans across the ground, filling them with snow to douse the tiny fire. Before he mounted, he hung the empty cans in the tangled branches of a nearby tree. "Many's the time somebody's left an old empty can near his fire, and it come in awful handy for me. Little things like that can be a big help to a man who's travelin' light."

Dan, already mounted, replied, "Yeah, my daddy told me that when I was three or four." He saw Joe's shadowy figure hesitate for a second before he mounted.

"Man gets old, he rambles on." The voice was sheepish.

"It's a wonder how a man's mouth keeps working when the rest of him is worn out." Dan turned Big Red to the trail, taking the lead for the first time.

Joe rode up beside him. The horses were at a walk. After a few seconds, he asked quietly, "You sore about somethin', Dan?"

Dan rode for fifty yards before replying, "Nope. I find myself getting fond of you, Joe. I never took a liking to a damn rattlesnake before. It makes me nervous." The trail led across the center of a moonlit clearing. Dan turned Big Red into the shadows along the edge of the opening in the woods. "I couldn't have shot that man back there like you did. I was standing there wondering what the hell to do with him. Didn't make sense to turn him loose. That bastard might be coming up behind us right now if we'd done that. It was a problem."

Joe responded promptly, "That's our advantage, partner. That wasn't no problem at all for me. It was in your face that you didn't know what to do. What one has trouble with, the other'n handles. That makes good partners. Watch yourself." He reined in to allow Dan to move into the lead, the extra horses and pack animal bunching behind him when he slowed.

An hour later, Dan saw the fire. It was shielded, but he could see the reflected, flickering glow. He stopped, waited for Joe to catch up, and said, "Trick. He figures for us to waste an hour or so stalking the fire while he rides on."

Joe said shortly, "Ride around it. I'll check and catch up with you later."

Dan rode a wide circle around the fire. The moon was so bright that he avoided looking at the open patches of snow. Every time he looked out over one of the brilliant moonlit clearings, the shadows turned into impenetrable black curtains to his dazzled eyes. He found the trail on his first cast across the country beyond the fire. Dan didn't think Channing's trick to delay them was particularly clever, but it did indicate that the man suspected they were on his trail and were drawing closer.

The snow had melted and packed somewhat in the sun. It was now crusted over. Big Red's hooves were incredibly noisy in the quiet of the windless, clear, cold night.

Uneasily, Dan shifted his weight in the saddle. His leg, while not a serious problem, was tender. It felt like it might be swelling again. Four hard days in the saddle was a severe test for wounds so newly healed. Also, his lips were beginning to crack from the harsh combination of mountain sun and cold. Nevertheless, he felt good. He figured that Channing was probably about as worn down as the horse he was riding. The man was failing in his effort to run away; he was going to have to turn and fight soon.

Dan's mind was racing. He couldn't figure how he could overtake Channing without giving warning with all this noise in the snow. All Channing had to do was pick a good place for an ambush and wait. He would hear Dan coming a hundred yards away. How would he do it? Probably, he would ride across one of those big clearings, then circle back. He would position himself well back in the woods, hoping to get a shot at a follower caught out in the light of the clearing. Even if the tracker was smart and followed the shadows of the wood line around the open place, he would still be outlined by the light in the clearing if he passed between it and the ambusher.

The country was smoothing out. There were more clearings. Dan decided to try to follow Channing's general direction, only cutting across the trail once in a while to ensure that the man didn't change direction. He rode a mile before he turned back toward where he thought the trail should be. When he found it, he crossed to the other side and rode another mile. He continued to use this procedure until he found no trail when he crossed back. When he looked in the direction from which Channing should be coming, he found a convenient low, wooded hill. He rode the short distance to it and dismounted. Either Channing had decided to change his direction or Dan was ahead of him.

Impatience rode him as he stood beside Big Red in the early morning. The moon was setting; there would be a couple of hours of thin starlight and bitter cold, then the dawn of a new day. If his guess was correct, he was ahead of Channing and on his line of march. He had a chance to turn the tables. This time it would be Dan lying in ambush. It was a gamble. If Channing had changed direction, Dan was losing time standing here like a fool, waiting to spring a trap on thin air. On the other hand, he had no intention of waiting long. If he was in front of his man, it wasn't by much. If he was coming this way, it would be soon.

Big Red's head came up, ears erect. Dan's gloved hand slid gently down the animal's nose. Dan stood scanning the open ground in the direction his horse's eyes were fixed. Then he heard the faint crunch and grind of footsteps in the crusty snow. He had to struggle to control his breath. He could feel his heart pounding.

Drawing cold air deep into his lungs a couple of times, he flexed his cold fingers, twisted his body to loosen his tight muscles, and pulled his Winchester from the saddle boot. Plain and clear, he could hear the sound of footsteps, of a man walking. Channing's horse must have died under him. He was coming on foot. Dan cursed silently to himself as the light continued to fade; the moon was slowly slipping behind the mountains.

A distant but increasing rumble, a faint vibration, began to intrude into the deathly stillness of the windless night. Then, plainly, the shrill whistle of a train. The heavy footsteps, cracking in the crusted snow, picked up a faster pace, almost running now. At last, Dan saw a vague, shadowy figure plunge out of the wood line into the clearing in front of him. Staggering and slipping, his heavy breathing and hoarse muttering came distinctly now over the crunch of unsteady footsteps.

Dan stepped forward and three or four steps to the side, away from Big Red. Channing didn't act like he heard the movement, probably deafened by his own din. "Channing!"

The figure wobbled unsteadily to a stop and turned. "What's that? Somebody there?" The voice was a harsh whisper.

Dan methodically emptied the Winchester, carefully pacing his shots to ensure a careful aim. His target was on the ground after the second round. Dan couldn't be sure in the weak light, but he thought he could see the body twitch with each shot.

He built a huge bonfire next to the body. An hour of dragging and hauling deadfall wood went into the building of that fire. When he looked across the roaring blaze another half an hour later and saw Joe ride into sight, he laughed at the expression on the old man's face when Dan stood and gave a full-throated victory cry, dancing with his rifle over his head. He wondered what his own face looked like when the grim old man slid off his horse, joined the dance, and gave the same cry of victory and joy.

A few minutes later, holding his hands to the warmth of the fire, Joe asked with a straight face, "You wanta set down here and eat what's left of that son of a bitch, or you wanta go home now?"

XXI

Dan was almost in shock. So many things had happened so quickly that he was halfway convinced that he was dreaming. When he and Joe rode into the ranch yard this afternoon, he had been eagerly looking forward to seeing Alice. Sure enough, she came running out in the snow and trotted alongside Big Red, holding the stirrup and smiling up at Dan. He stopped the horse, dismounted, and carried her to the porch, pretending to scold her about ruining her pretty shoes in the snow.

When he walked into the parlor, there sat Big Dan, Margaret, Matthew, Mark, Ben, Nell, Red, and Annie around the big oak table. They pretended to ignore him. There was a brief silence until Nell looked up and said calmly, "Dan, if you're going to be in and out all the time, please wipe your boots when you come in the house." Then, with a roar of voices and laughter, it seemed as if everyone pounced on him.

Then, as suddenly as it started, the babble stopped. Joe Ballas stood in the open doorway. He was staring at Big Dan, his body rigid and his face pale as death. Big Dan stood motionless in the stony silence for a full, deadly five seconds before he said in an ominous voice, "Don't step through that door, Joe Ballas, don't step into this room unless you're bringing in some of that good whiskey you always have hidden around someplace."

Joe's stance didn't change. His gaze darted around the room briefly, as if calculating the odds against him. Finally, with his face still as rigid as ever, he said, "I gotta go to the barn." The door crashed shut behind him. The babble and laughter started immediately as they all rushed like curious children to the windows to watch Joe limp like a pitiful old man to the barn. Moments later, he reappeared with his arms full of bottles.

When Alice opened the door for him, he walked past her saying bitterly, "I told you, Alice. I told you Dan's daddy was tight!"

Nell and Annie rushed out together, returning in seconds with trays of water glasses. Alice ushered the group into the area in front of the huge fireplace and Joe went around the room, followed by Nell and Annie with the glasses. He poured a water glass full of whiskey for each of them except himself. Pulling the cork from a full bottle, he raised it high over his head and announced, "A toast to the soon-to-be-wed. Long life, good health, and lots of sons." While everyone except them applauded and drank, Dan looked at Alice and found her looking at him.

Mark asked suddenly, "You have asked her, haven't you, Dan? We aren't drinking prematurely, are we?"

When Dan answered, he could hear the embarrassment in his own voice. "Well, I haven't exactly asked, that is, we, uh, we didn't do it that way, but . . ."

Matthew walked to Alice and dropped a pillow at her feet. He turned to Dan and said, "I hear you have a sore leg. Get down carefully. No need to hurt yourself."

Dan could feel his face heating. This was utterly ridiculous. He started to say something, but he couldn't figure what to say. He knew that he looked like a fool, with a red face and a mouth that opened a couple of times with no words coming out. Joe said gently, "Drink. And no prissy sip."

Dan took a sip, and everyone groaned in disappointment, so he took a couple of swallows. Annie handed him a glass of water, and he gave her a grateful look while he stood with a paralyzed throat. Mark pointed at the pillow lying at Alice's feet. Dan dropped to his knees, looking up at Alice in acute embarrassment. She seemed to be having a fine time. "Alice, will you marry me?"

She looked at him sympathetically, shook her head sadly, and said, "No."

Groans went up from the group. Matthew said quickly in a loud whisper, "Tell her you love her, Dan. That always gets 'em."

"Alice, I love you. Will you marry me?"

"No," Alice said again, and her eyes widened when she saw his altered expression.

Dan was not only feeling foolish now, acutely so, but he felt a flash of terrible anger. This might be a joke to them, but it was no longer funny to him. A proposal of marriage, even under these lighthearted conditions, was not a joking matter. His proposal was sincere, and Dan felt the sting of painful humiliation and horror that such a thing could become a subject for humor. He was deeply hurt; he had thought Alice was his, that she had told him so. Suddenly, the teasing, joking attitude in the room was grotesque and obscene.

He had just returned from personally killing two men and being involved in the death of a third, thinking he was making his own woman and her family safe. Exploding with rage, he came to his feet so quickly that he knew it caught the others by surprise. "I seem to have made a terrible mistake." He looked at the remains of the bourbon in his glass, turned and threw it, glass and all, into the fireplace. "I misjudged you," he said with such cold force that Alice drew back as if she thought he might strike her. "Find yourself another fool."

Everyone seemed shocked into immobility by the sudden violence of his reaction. He snagged his coat and hat in one move and was out the door. With his first step onto the porch, he almost screamed in frustration and shame; the first thing he saw was Big Red standing patiently, still saddled, in the cold. He had been so entranced with Alice and so delighted to see his family that he had forgotten the big horse. Dan heard a sudden chorus of calls, heard the words "just teasing" and "joking" when he found himself in the saddle. He didn't remember mounting; he must have been blind with anger, but he dimly recalled putting Big Red into a lope and rubbing him between the ears the way the patient, loyal animal liked.

He didn't know how long he rode. It was as if he had been asleep in the saddle and suddenly woke. The western sky was glowing with color as the sun dropped. The icy breath of a north wind was in his face, laden with the clean spice of fir and pine. The easy, familiar movement of the treasured horse under him and the pleasant sense of motion had a soothing, calming effect. So, he was running again. No, not running this time, just leaving. He wondered which departure made him sadder, the first or this one.

He realized that he was on the road to Buckhorn at the same instant that he remembered the money in his saddlebags. "No matter," he said aloud and watched Big Red's ears twitch. "The damn town's on the way to Canada, and I like riding into the wind. Besides, I need to buy another packhorse and some plunder for the road. Alice can keep my gray for a souvenir."

Dan didn't see a single light when he rode into Buckhorn. The front door to the hotel was locked, and no one answered his pounding. He rode to the livery stable, which was also deserted. He put Big Red into a stall, rubbed him down until he was arm weary, and fed him. Then Dan climbed to the loft with his blankets, burrowed into the hay, and slept.

He woke at first light and lay admiring the frost on the sill of the loft door for a few moments before he pulled himself out of the hay. He had Big Red saddled in ten minutes and rode to the hotel. It was still closed and locked. He rode to Tom's house and knocked. A blast of warm air laden with the smell of coffee and frying bacon washed over him when Tom opened the door. "Tom, I got the money from the bank. Will you look after it till the law, or whoever, does whatever they want to do with it?"

"Sure, I'll look after it. Come in out of the cold, Dan. Don't just stand there. Katherine, Dan's here!" he called. "He's gonna eat with us this morning."

"No, Tom. Don't put her to that trouble. I don't want to bust in. How's the leg?"

"Ain't no trouble. Leg's fine. Come on in the kitchen where it's warmer. Gimme that coat and hat. Katherine won't let you eat with your hat on anyway."

Dan felt the unceasing, wide-eyed stare of Tom's two little boys while Katherine bustled around the kitchen feeding them and putting breakfast for the adults on the table. Those boys watched him so closely that Dan began to wonder if they ever blinked. He asked, "I need a packhorse. You know of one for sale?"

"Not offhand. You and Joe took about all of the extra stuff in town when you went after Channing. I guess you got him, since you brought in the money."

Katherine asked, "What do you need to buy a packhorse for? The M Bar M has the best horses around here anyway. Why not use one of them?"

"I left kind of quickly, to tell the truth. I didn't do a lot of planning. No matter. I can get what I need here in town, but I'll need another horse to help carry it," Dan said. He could see the questioning looks on their faces, so he added, "I'm riding on, maybe to Canada. Hear it's pretty. Never been there."

Tom blurted, "But I thought you and Alice . . ."

Dan cut in, "Me too, Tom, but we were both wrong. I miscalculated there and made myself look pretty foolish. Those things happen, I guess."

Katherine gave Dan a wide-eyed look. "Miscalculated? How do you mean? What are you talking about? Is her family opposed?"

The feeling of humiliation was coming back to Dan. He said gently, "Please, Katherine, if you don't mind, I would rather talk about something else."

A dead silence fell, full of tension. Dan said, "I didn't mean to be rude. I beg your pardon, but I'm a little tender this morning. Yesterday I asked Alice to marry me, and she said no."

Katherine said flatly, "I don't believe it."

Tom said, "Me neither."

"That girl's been walking on air. There must be some terrible misunderstanding. You can't just ride away like this," she said sharply. Catching Dan's surprised expression, she added more softly, "Now I must beg *your* pardon, but I know her well and love her. You're going to hurt her terribly if you ride away. She loves you. It would be a cruel thing to do."

Tom said, "That's right."

The sound of horses stopping in front of the house caused Tom to exchange glances with Katherine. He leaned back and pulled the curtain away from the window. After a look outside, he said to Dan, "Somebody lookin' for you, I reckon."

Dan came to his feet and looked out the window to see his whole family, Alice and her family along with Red and Annie, and Joe Ballas in Tom's front yard. Alice, dressed in pants and a huge coat that came to her knees, had her arms around Big Red's neck. Dan's tall gray was there, carrying a pack. Joe Ballas tied the gray's reins to Big Red's saddle. Alice walked to the front door. Her hair was stuffed up under a hat that was jammed down over her ears. There was a timid knock.

Tom said, "There's the back door, Yellow Hawk. Looks like they got your horse, but you can run on foot."

Dan gave him a disgusted look and went to open the door. When Alice saw him, her eyes widened. Her face was pink from the cold. She looked at him pleadingly and said, "I'm looking for the man who saved my life. I fell in love with him when I was a woman, but I forgot how proud and sensitive he is and made him mad at me with a silly joke. He liked me better when I was a boy, so I changed back to a boy. I want him to take me wherever he goes."

Dan said coldly, "No."

She looked at him with tears in her eyes. "Please?"

He said, "I got no use for a no-account boy. I liked you better when you were a girl."

She tugged at the hat awkwardly; the sleeves of the coat were so long that she had to stop and pull them up. She finally got it off. Her blond hair fell around her shoulders. Her voice was serious. "Girl again. Whatever you want, that's what you get."

He stared at her. "No more damn fool jokes, making me look like an idiot."

She said, "No more damn fool jokes. I'm a reformed woman. It was your brothers who put me up to it. They're going to be rotten in-laws." She dropped to her knees. "Dan, I love you. Will you marry me?"

He picked her up and held her in his arms. "Why, hell yes. How about you? Will you marry me?"

She kissed him and said, "Why, hell yes."

Tom Tolar shouted to the silent group in front of his house, "Anybody want some breakfast?"

They answered together, *"Why, hell yes!"*

ABOUT THE AUTHOR

John S. McCord is a retired U.S. Army lieutenant colonel. He has published articles for such magazines as *Army, Frontier, Highlander,* and *Organic Gardening. Walking Hawk* is his first full-length novel.